M000074050

The Sweet Scent of Murder

The Sweet Scent of Murder

A Mavis Davis Mystery

Susan P. Baker

Five Star • Waterville, Maine

Set in 11 pt. Plantin.

LIBRARY OF CONGRESS CATALOGING-IN-PUBLICATION DATA

Baker, Susan P.
The sweet scent of murder : a Mavis Davis mystery / Susan P. Baker. — 1st ed.
p. cm.
ISBN-13: 978-1-59414-469-1 (hc : alk. paper)
1. Private investigators—Texas—Houston—Fiction. 2. Missing children—Fiction. 3. Houston (Tex.)—Fiction. I. Title.
PS3602.A588S94 2006
813'.54—dc22 2006008410

First Edition. First Printing: February 2007.

Published in 2007 in conjunction with Tekno Books and Ed Gorman.

Printed in the United States of America on permanent paper
10 9 8 7 6 5 4 3 2 1

For my sister, Bonnie, the educator in the family.

Acknowledgments

With great appreciation to Patricia Ledbetter Wright, Sandra Gardner, Catherine Robert, and Victoria Rust, as well as the Galveston Novel and Short Story Writers, for their assistance as readers and critics.

Chapter One

"No woman could shoot that well without a lot of practice."

Those words out of the mouth of my alleged boyfriend would have been enough to send me on a rampage when I was a lot younger, but in what I thought of as my dotage, I kept my cool. After all, as a private investigator, I had to be professional, act maturely, make insightful decisions. Oh, to hell with it. "You're full of shit, Ben Sorensen. You know how I used to feel about guns. I swear I've never shot one before."

"And I say nobody hits the target the first time, Mavis, not even you." Ben charged through the front door of my office, Mavis Davis Investigations. I originally named it Mavis Davis Productions because we also do copying, type documents for lawyers, serve legal papers, and whatever else the legal community demands. I changed the name, though, after I solved my first murder case, the murder of Doris Jones. Besides, we were getting calls from people who thought we made movies.

"Cross my heart and hope to die." I steadied the cowbell that hung over the door.

"You're lying again, Mavis."

"Them's fightin' words, Ben," I said, half ready to square off with him. He'd been carrying on about my shooting ability all the way back from the firing range. I had long grown tired of it, my anger causing my face to grow as red as my hair. Not seeing anyone in the reception area, I called, "Hi, Margaret, we're back." An echo answered my holler.

"Well, no man either, Mavis." He glowered down at me, his nose an inch from mine. I could smell that earthly scent that ordinarily attracted me to him, but just now I felt too defensive to allow it any appeal. "It takes practice. You know how many hours I had to spend at the firing range as a police cadet?"

Sergeant Ben Sorensen had been a cadet back in the dark ages. Now he was a narc with decades under his belt. "Yes, Ben dear," I said through clenched teeth. "You already told me a hundred million times, but I'm telling you that I have never fired a gun before. Read my lips. Never would I lie about a stupid thing like that. The only time I ever even held one was when I picked up Willard Thompson's in Fort Worth." I peeked into the kitchen in search of my staff. At least they hadn't burned the place down.

"Impossible." His six-foot-four frame blocked the hallway.

I squared off with him, but even on my tiptoes my five-foot-ten-inches didn't bring my eyes even with his. "What's the big deal? All you do is aim and pull the trigger. A monkey could do it." I shouldered my way past him. Where was everybody? "Candy. Margaret." Some wonderful support staff. They should work for a magician since they'd gotten so good at a disappearing act.

"All I'm saying," Ben continued, right behind me like a heeler, "is that shooting a gun is a learned skill. Some men never get good at it no matter how much they practice."

Sometimes Ben is so tiresome. I threw an exaggerated frown in his direction, hoping he'd get the hint. When he opened his mouth again, I said, "Ben. Table it, will you?

Can't you see that Margaret and Candy aren't here and that I'm worried? How about a little consideration?"

He backed away. "Sorry, Mavis. Give me your gun, and I'll put it in the safe, okay?"

"Are you still concerned about me carrying it? I told you. I'm not going to. It's just that ever since those guys shot at me in Fort Worth, I want a gun so I'll feel more secure. So I'll be able to breathe easier. I won't carry it otherwise." He stared at me, his hand out, so I reached into my purse for the flannel bag in which I keep my .38. I don't want it to get dirty or get bits of purse paraphernalia in the barrel. "Do you remember the combination?"

"Yes, Mavis." Ben grinned.

He had given me the safe for my birthday after purchasing it at an estate auction. It was a three-foot-tall iron jobbie and literally weighed about a ton. Four strong men had struggled to move it inside.

"Holler if Margaret and Candy are back there, will you? I'm worried." Margaret and Candy usually left a note if both of them had to go somewhere. Not only was there no note, but I'd found the front door unlocked. What was that about?

Someone could have come in and taken our computer. I hadn't even paid off my credit card for it yet. On Westheimer, anything was possible. Thieves came in all sizes, shapes, and colors. They were so accomplished, they could steal a television while you were watching it, and you wouldn't even know it. Not that we had a television in the office. Once someone stole the old sign off the front door, the one that said Mavis Davis Productions, Owned and Operated by Mavis Davis. I swear. We were a nameless entity for two weeks.

"Mavis," Ben yelled. "Come on back."

I jogged through our little house-office to the only private room, the place where I always take clients to interview them before I begin my detective work. Well—to be honest about it—that's only happened once, but I have high expectations. I interview people there sometimes when we do our home studies on adoptions and child custody cases, too.

Candy, our half-day high school helper, sat behind my desk like she owned the place. Candy's a sweetheart, but sometimes she's a bit too ambitious. Any day now I expect to be out of a job. Candy had sprayed her hair red that day. Not the natural red that God gave me but an obvious, man-made, glaring, bright, garish red, with glitter in it, no less. Her eyes flashed with excitement. Her face glowed like a full moon on a cloudless night. All five of her earrings dangled as she tossed her head. She wore a sequined, blue denim jacket over a black top. I couldn't see the rest of her, thank goodness.

Across from Candy sat her polar opposite, a boy about her age who wore a Polo shirt, neatly pressed slacks, and highly polished loafers. Candy would have termed him a "prep," no doubt. Shiny cheeks, clean-cut hair, and wonderful posture.

Ben towered over them and stared at Candy like he would a dog that had just crapped on the rug. Most of the time Ben and I get along well, but sometimes my relationship with him is a bit troublesome. He can be annoying when he tries to run my life, or Margaret's, or Candy's, or when he starts talking about settling down and me having babies.

I didn't see Margaret Applebaum, my assistant. I suspected that she'd made herself scarce on purpose; the reason would most likely become apparent momentarily.

"What's this all about?" I asked, my eyes darting from face to face.

"Candy's agreed to take a kidnapping case, Mavis," Ben said, pulling himself up to his full height, which could be intimidating when my energy level had ebbed.

"Like, I didn't say it was a kidnapping, Mavis," Candy

said with a sneer at Ben. "I said Tommy said it was probably a kidnapping, but his mom thinks she's like a runaway."

Assuming the prep was Tommy, I looked to him for an explanation. He stood—a real gentleman. "Thomas Lawson, Miss Davis," he said, extending his hand, "but you may call me Tommy."

We shook. He had a mature handshake, for a kid. "Nice to meet you, Tommy." My eyes cut back to Candy, and I arched an eyebrow at her. "You've agreed to take on this young man's case?"

"Well, like I think we can help him out, you know, Mavis? His sister's like missing."

I understood then why Margaret had absented herself. She knew better than to accept responsibility. We went back a long way.

"Up, Candy," I said as I approached my chair. She might be too young to understand territoriality, so I wasn't going to get bent out of shape about it, but I liked to decide which cases we took, and I liked to make those decisions from my chair. "Sit down, Ben. You may as well stay for a minute until we clear this up."

We all got situated, and then I turned to Tommy. "What's this about your sister?"

"She's missing, Mavis," Candy said. "Like I told you. Tommy clued me in at school, so I told him we could find her, like if we get started right away before the trail gets cold. You know what I mean?"

"Cool it, Candy. I want to hear Tommy's version."

"Candy's correct, Miss Davis. Jeanine is missing." Tommy sat on the edge of his chair and clutched at the rim of my desk. "She went to school on Tuesday and never came home. Mother thinks she ran away, but I think somebody kidnapped her."

"It's been two days," Ben said. "Have your parents received a ransom note?"

I glared at Ben. Was anyone going to let me do my job? Ben shrugged and slid back in his chair, crossing his legs. "Sorry, Mavis."

"Has there been a ransom note, Tommy?" I asked.

"No. Jeanine left a note in her room that said she was going to spend Tuesday night with Melanie, so Mother didn't get worried until yesterday when she didn't come home again."

"Melanie is—a friend?"

"Right," Tommy said. "Mother called Melanie's house and found out that Jeanine didn't spend Tuesday night there. She called a bunch of Jeanine's other friends, but no one knows anything."

"But your mom thinks Jeanine like ran away, right dude?" Candy asked.

He nodded. "Yeah." He turned to me. "See, Miss Davis, I heard Mother and Jeanine arguing the other night. Jeanine's like Mother. She's got a short fuse sometimes. At first, I figured she was trying to scare Mother by staying away for a few days. I thought she'd show up at school, though, but she didn't. And I asked some of the kids about her. Nobody knows where she is."

"Has your mother called the police?" I asked.

"Sure. She said it would serve Jeanine right if she had to come home in a police car. It would embarrass her. The police took a report. They said she was probably a runaway, but also suggested a possible kidnapping because of where we live and all."

"And where's that, pray tell?" I pulled a legal pad out of my desk and grabbed a pen.

"River Oaks," he said.

"River Oaks." I tried to hide my concern, it being *the* exclusive section of Houston, but didn't do very well. Nodding, I chewed on my lower lip and remained calm out of a desire to refrain from upsetting the boy, but under my desk, my knee bounced up and down like a jackhammer.

I wanted to hear more, but not necessarily with Ben there. "Ben, dear, I don't want to keep you. I think the fact that there's no ransom note is probably evidence that it's a runaway, don't you?" I hoped he'd get the hint and leave without my asking.

He did. With a sigh of resignation, he shook his head as he rose. "I'll just lock up your gun before I go. Call me later, okay? We can clean our weapons together." He winked.

I nodded and wondered if he meant what I hoped he meant. As for my business, sometimes he wasn't so understanding—but he was working on it.

I let Candy stay. After all, she was responsible for bringing Tommy to us for help. She moved over to a chair next to him. "See, dude. I told you she'd help you."

"I haven't said I would yet, Candy. I need to get more information first."

We all watched Ben go out the door, and when we heard the cowbell clang, Candy started in. "Mavis, Tommy's already written out a check for our retainer fee." She dropped a folded piece of paper in front of me.

"*Our* retainer fee?" My glance at Candy would have made Margaret cower. Candy's a lot more aggressive. She didn't even flinch. I unfolded the check. "Two thousand dollars?"

"Do you need more?" Tommy stood. "I can get it. I just have to transfer it from my savings account. That's all I had in my checking, but if you want more, I could write you another check if you'll give me a day to transfer the funds, or I could go to the bank and get you a cashier's check, Miss Davis."

I hoped the astonishment wasn't showing on my face. "No, Tommy. This is fine, but let's talk a little more before I accept it." I hesitated to take money from children and wanted to do the right thing. "Tell me about the argument that Jeanine had with your mother."

Tommy glanced at Candy and then sat back down. He was a nice-looking boy, not like some of the dark ones that dropped by to see Candy. Tommy had dishwater blond hair and washed-out blue eyes sheltered by long, black lashes. Thin, when he stood I could see that he was probably at least my height, around five-foot-ten. He spoke in a quiet way and had a gentle manner.

"I couldn't hear all of it, Miss Davis. They were in Mother's bedroom with the door closed. Jeanine said that Mother made her sick. She said she was ashamed to be her daughter." He stared into his lap, hands folded, thumbs twiddling. Then he looked up and said, "Mother said that Jeanine was too young to understand, that when she grew up, she'd have a different viewpoint."

"How old is Jeanine?" I asked.

"Sixteen—but she's really mature for her age."

"And you?"

"Eighteen."

"Do you know what they were talking about?"

"No. Jeanine's been acting kind of weird the past few days."

"Where do you think Jeanine has gone?"

"That's just it." He shook his head. "I don't know. I've asked a bunch of her girlfriends, like I said, but no one seems to know anything. It's not like Jeanine to do this. She loves school and wouldn't miss it for anything. She's into all that social stuff, you know? Never misses a party. Drives to school early to be with her friends before classes. I just can't see her doing this unless something really bad is going on."

I nodded. I knew girls like that when I was in high school. Social butterflies existed even in the dark ages. "You got a picture?"

"I gave it to Candy."

Candy handed it to me. "She's beautiful," I said after a quick glance. She had shiny black hair and cornflower blue eyes. Perfectly clear, peachy complexion. Perfect smile framing perfectly straight teeth. Little pug nose and rosebud lips. Didn't look a thing like her brother.

As if reading my mind, Tommy said, "We don't look a thing alike. You can't tell from that picture, but she's short, about five feet tall. There's a lot of energy packed in her, though, Miss Davis, and she's stubborn. When she makes up her mind that she's going to do something, she does it. If she did run away, she must be awfully angry at Mother."

"Are you close to her?"

"We were closer when we were younger, but I guess so, yeah. Not in the sense that I had to look after her or anything—she didn't really need looking after—except when she lost her temper. But even though I don't hang around with the same kids, we always find time to spend a few minutes together every day. Normally she would have called me by now."

"Tommy's right, Mavis," Candy said. "Like Jeanine is into cheerleading and all that shit—I mean junk—but she's got a reputation for getting mad and staying mad. You know?"

I nodded. I felt sympathy for the boy, but I wasn't sure I wanted to get into the business of searching for runaways. Why couldn't it have been a good, juicy murder? Still, that retainer tempted me. I could do a lot of things with twenty big ones. My Mustang needed extensive body work after someone tried to shoot it to death in Fort Worth. My credit card bill that carried the computer charge would be coming due. The option contract on our house-office loomed. And what if it wasn't a runaway? I didn't object to getting involved in kidnapping cases. Could I have tried harder to justify taking the case?

"What do you say, Mavis?" Candy asked. "Let's do it. You know if we don't find Jeanine soon, she'll flunk the whole semester. Not to mention the fact that the first of the month is coming up."

Candy had a way of looking at me that made me want to be more responsible. She's pragmatic. I like to set a good example for her. Right now I couldn't think of any reason for refusing Tommy. I had nothing better to do with my time, but I couldn't take the money. Not from a kid.

"I could take a couple of days to look for her, Tommy, since we don't have any major cases going, but I can't promise you anything," I said. "You've got to understand that I've never done a runaway before and if that's okay—"

"That means yes, Tommy," Candy said. "Mavis always talks around something instead of saying yes. See? I told you she'd help you. Like, she's really cool, huh? See what I mean?"

I covered my smile. Candy had me pegged.

Tommy expelled a deep breath, his expression grim. "Thanks, Miss Davis."

"So what are we waiting for, huh, Mavis? Ask Tommy all the names and addresses of Jeanine's friends. Then we can get started. Time is money."

"Right, Candy." Sarcasm was lost on her. "One thing, though. About the money, Tommy. I appreciate the offer, but I can't take it. I'll just do this as a favor to Candy."

"That's dead. Why, Mavis?" Candy asked.

"Step outside for a minute, Candy," I said. Then to Tommy, "Excuse us a minute."

Out in the hall, after I'd closed the door behind us, Candy said, "You have to take the money, Mavis. We need it. This is no time to be proud."

"Listen, Candy, I'm not taking money from a kid. I don't mind looking around for a few days since I'm not doing anything, but two thousand dollars? I can't believe you even asked him for it."

Candy stamped her foot. "He can afford it. They're rich."

"Doesn't matter. And you've got to let me call the shots. Don't forget that you're a kid, too, and I'm the boss here."

Candy huffed in apparent disgust, but after we exchanged a few more words, she got my message. Returning inside to Tommy, I said, "We're not going to take your money." I pushed the check back at him.

Tommy didn't pick it up. Glancing from me to Candy and back again, he said, "That's awfully nice of you, Miss Davis, but I don't want the money back. You take it and I expect you to earn it."

"Tommy," I said, picking up the check and holding it out to him, "you keep your money. I said I'll look around for your sister anyway."

Ignoring my outstretched hand, Tommy dug into his pocket and came up with his keys and a piece of paper. Throwing the piece of paper on my desk, he said, "I'm eighteen, an adult. If I can fight in a war, I can hire a PI. That's the list of people who might know something." He rounded my desk and headed out into the hall. "Thanks, Miss Davis. I'll expect daily reports."

"Come back here, kid," I called, pushing out my chair. "I'm not taking your money."

Tommy reached the front with me only a few steps behind, but he bolted outside without stopping, slamming the door in my face. By the time I got it open, he'd reached his car. "I'm not taking your money, kid," I hollered. "I'll hold the check in my safe for you."

He waved and pulled out, leaving me standing on my front stoop hollering like a lunatic. The nerve of kids nowadays. Where are their boundaries?

Chapter Two

"Tommy's kind of a nerd, Mavis," Candy said as we drove to River Oaks to see Melanie, Jeanine's best friend. "But he's nice."

"He didn't look like a nerd to me. I thought he was a prep."

"Nah, dude, he dresses like a prep 'cuz he's rich, but he's a nerd all right." She studied the piece of paper with Melanie's address on it and watched for the right house. "Wow. Do you see that place? Looks like Twelve Oaks." You couldn't tell from looking at her, but Candy was into old movies and memorabilia in the worst way.

"How can you tell the difference between nerds and preps?" The gap between our ages had just widened like a farm-to-market road turning into superhighway.

"Nerds are brains, Mavis."

"I thought geeks were brains."

"They're kind of the same thing." She gave me a look that I can only describe as derisive. "Like they all hang out together and bring their lunch to school and wear glasses. They just act different. They don't have girlfriends that are popular; if they have them at all, they're just other nerds. Look at that house. The grass looks a foot deep. And those flowers. Wow."

"Tommy didn't have glasses, Candy."

"Nah, but he used to. I bet Jeanine like made him get contacts so he wouldn't be such an embarrassment to her, you know what I mean? Look, Mavis. A Rolls Royce and a Mercedes-Benz. Wait," she said, glancing at the paper again, "this is it. Pull in, Mavis. This is Melanie's. No wonder she always looks like she's got on new clothes. I bet her closet's the size of my bedroom, dude."

I drove between trees that lined a circular driveway and parked my wounded Mustang behind the Mercedes. I told myself that anybody could have a Rolls Royce or a Mercedes, but my Mustang was a classic. A collector's item. There were only a few left in the world. Moneyed people didn't intimidate me.

"Okay, Candy," I said as we approached the front door, "you just let me do the talking. Try to restrain yourself and don't comment on their house. Wealthy people take all this for granted."

"Hey, like I'm cool, Mavis," Candy said as she tugged at her jean jacket. "Don't worry about me."

As we stepped onto the brick portico, I straightened my skirt seams and tucked in my blouse. I ran my fingers across my eyebrows, pushed my hair behind my ears, and, finally, punched the doorbell. By the time the butler—complete with livery—came to the door, I felt pretty confident.

Flashing my ID, I said, "My name's Mavis Davis. We're here to see Melanie, sir. Is she at home?"

He sniffed and flexed his nostrils as though we emitted an odor and, with a bored expression, opened the door wider. "You may wait in the resource room."

It seemed he meant the library. And what a library. I swear they had almost as many books as the Houston Public. I stared in awe. Candy wandered from shelf to shelf and read the bindings.

"Mavis," Candy whispered, "come look at some of these books."

"You don't have to whisper, Candy," I said in a normal tone. It somehow sounded unnatural as it echoed through the room. I wanted to tell her that we were just as good as the folks who owned that house, but it didn't seem quite the time or place to begin a new lecture series.

"Like there isn't one paperback in the whole place, Mavis. These books must have cost a fu—a ton. Look at the other side of the room," she said, pointing. "Like a whole section of DVDs."

"Don't get carried away."

"You think they'd let me borrow some? They've got all the classics, Mavis. Like I don't know where they got them. Some of these I've been looking to rent, but can't find 'em."

"No, I don't think they'd let you borrow them, Candy. It's not like you and Melanie are friends, right? Compose yourself."

"Miss Davis?"

A young sophisticate-type posed in the doorway. I hoped she hadn't overheard us. She had a flawless look—as though she just came from finishing school. Layered pastel clothing draped her body as though made to order. Blonde hair cut in the latest style framed a classic face with bloodshot hazel eyes ringed by smeared mascara.

"Hi," I said, "you must be Melanie." I extended my hand. She floated over and shook it. Other than Candy, who probably isn't representative of the norm, I'm not sure how teenage girls greet people, but that seemed to work all right.

"Hey, Melanie," Candy said almost shyly.

Melanie glanced at Candy who stood near the DVDs. For a moment I feared she wouldn't acknowledge Candy's greeting. A lump formed in my throat, but Melanie glanced at me, back to Candy, and said, "Hello, Candace."

I'd never thought of Candy as a Candace before.

"Would you care to sit down, Miss Davis?"

"We'll only be a minute, Melanie. I want to ask you a few questions about Jeanine Lawson." Her face showed no reaction. "Have you heard from her?"

Melanie sat in an antique armchair. "Please, sit a minute," she said. "You, too, Candace. Come sit down."

Candy shrugged, and we crossed to the sofa together as though joined at the hip.

"Tommy called and said you'd probably contact me, Miss Davis. I told him that I didn't know much." Melanie stared into her lap. "I want to help," she whispered with a glance at the doorway, "but I don't want to get Jeanine into trouble."

She sat with her knees together, her feet resting to one side, crossed at the ankles. She was as graceful as the models at the YWCA charm school classes my mother had forced me to attend at age thirteen. I wondered whether Melanie's type had to take classes or if they were born knowing how to stand, walk, and sit.

"Tommy's worried that she might already be in trouble," I said.

"I know." Her eyes flitted around the room like a butterfly and came to rest on mine. "Jeanine didn't spend the night here. She just asked me to tell her mother that she did, but her mother talked to my mother, so I didn't get a chance."

"Like do you know where she went?" Candy asked.

"I'm not sure. She was real confused about something."

"What?" I asked.

Melanie glanced at the doorway again and leaned toward us. "I don't know. Something to do with her mother."

Candy and I exchanged bewildered looks.

"Do you know what they had argued about?" I asked.

She shook her head. "No, but it must be real bad if I haven't heard from her." Her eyes darted from one of us to the other, and she chewed her lower lip.

"Melanie," Candy said, "like it's okay to tell us what you know. Everything you say will be kept in the strictest confidence."

I knew then that Candy had been reading detective novels again.

"Besides her mother, do you know of anything else that was bothering her?" I asked. "Anything that might make her want to leave home?"

Melanie stared at me for a moment, her forehead wrinkling. "She'd been having problems with her boyfriend."

"Oh yeah?" Candy asked. "Like what kind of problems?"

"He wants to get married."

"At sixteen?" I couldn't believe it. I didn't know boys ever wanted to get married, much less when they were still children. "Was he serious?"

"Oh yes, ma'am," Melanie said. "Jeanine actually considered it. They talked about getting an apartment of their own and everything, but she decided she didn't love him enough."

"Wow," Candy said. "Like that's heavy-duty."

Melanie nodded. "She figured her mother would cut off her allowance, too, and that wouldn't do."

With the size of Tommy's bankroll, I completely understood. I should have such problems. "Is that all settled then, Melanie? I mean, between her and her boyfriend?"

"Yes. She told him a couple of weeks ago."

"So that couldn't have been the reason she left then, right?" I asked.

"Yes, ma'am."

"Are you sure you don't know what happened between her

and her mother, Melanie?" Candy asked. "Like you know you can tell us."

Melanie shook her head. "She wouldn't tell me, and I can't think of anything else that was bugging her. She acted kind of funny, but if it didn't have to do with her mother, I don't know what it could be."

"So where do you think she went, Melanie?" I asked. "Does she have other friends she could be staying with?"

"She could be anywhere, Miss Davis. I'm sure she has enough money to get by for a few days, but I really think I would have heard. There's always someone in our group who's getting mad and going off, but everyone knows about it. Word gets out." She leaned toward me, her fingers fiddling with the piping on the arm of her chair. "Usually we hide each other from our parents, in the closet or something, but all our friends know where we are. I don't know where Jeanine is." She shook her head. "I really don't."

"She's not in your closet right now?" I asked.

"No. Really. And I called around to her boyfriend and some other kids. I would have told Tommy. Now I'm worried, too. Do you think she's run away for real?"

"I don't know, Melanie." I stood. It didn't seem likely that she really knew where Jeanine was, and if she knew something about Mrs. Lawson, she wasn't going to say. "Would you do me a favor?"

"Anything." She rose and came close to me. "Jeanine's my best friend."

I handed her a card. "Would you put the word out at school tomorrow that I'll be on campus and that if anyone knows anything, it's all right to talk to me? And call me if you hear anything?"

"Okay. Will you let me know if you find her? Tell her to call me on my cell." She wiped away a tear.

Even rich kids need hugs. I gave Melanie a little one.

Her mouth turned up in a funny smile. "I hope you find her."

"Thanks, Melanie. I'm sure she's just fine." I hated lying but thought reassuring the girl to be the better part of valor.

"I guess we'll jet out of here," Candy said.

"Yes, let's go, Candace."

After dropping Candy off, I hit every section of the Galleria shopping mall, which took until closing. No one recognized the girl in the photograph as anyone who had been in lately, though several people recognized her as a regular customer. I decided to get a good night's sleep and try at the school the next day.

Friday afternoon, I went to the Lamar High School campus. Although I got permission from the head of security to speak to Jeanine's counselor and vice principal, citing privacy laws, they couldn't or wouldn't tell me anything. And since security ushered me not only back out of the school but off the campus, I couldn't get any information from anyone else, either. If anybody had seen anything unusual on Tuesday, I'd be the last to know.

Since I wasn't allowed to set foot on campus unescorted by a security guard, I positioned myself across the street and watched the school's front entrance. I felt frustrated that I wouldn't have access to most of the kids and hoped Candy would do better. Seconds later, what seemed like a million kids of all colors, shapes, and sizes converged, leaping and bounding as they made their exit like a jubilant mob.

A few had to pass where I stood and I flashed Jeanine's picture, asking if they'd seen her after school on Tuesday. A couple of kids stopped and actually listened to me, but no one knew anything.

To most of them I called out, "If anyone knows the whereabouts of Jeanine Lawson, please call me. My name's Mavis Davis. I'm in the book under investigations."

Several kids seated themselves on the stairs and pulled out their books, beginning their homework. I ached to cross the street to speak with them but spotted a security guard with his eye on me. Finally, I leaned against a light post, catching a lingering kid or two walking my way as I waited for Candy. The sun beat down on my head, perspiration dampened my pits, and the concrete sidewalk burned through my shoes. About fifteen minutes later, Candy came jogging up, out of breath. "What took you so long?" I demanded.

"Like I was doing my job, Mavis. I got a lead. A kid saw Jeanine get into a car with some dude."

Chapter Three

"So where's the kid?" I straightened up and started for the car.

Candy followed me. "He had to jet out of here. His mom kept honking for him."

"Why didn't you come get me? I've been out here for ages." We stopped on the sidewalk. I was about to reach for her neck but caught myself. After all, she was just a child. She couldn't possibly know that security barred me from the campus or how frustrated I felt.

"Don't worry, Mavis," Candy said. "I've got it all down right here." She made a production of pulling out a spiral notebook that heretofore she had concealed inside her binder. "When I get some bills paid, I'm going to get one of those PDAs. So much easier to carry around than paper notes, don't you think?"

"No, I don't think you need to spend a couple of hundred dollars on a PDA." I tapped my toe and held out my hand. "Hand them over, Candace, dear."

"It's getting so you can't take a joke, you know, Mavis." She slapped the notebook into my hand, her bracelets jangling. "And, like, I think they cost three or four hundred, just so you know in case you want one for yourself."

"I have no sense of humor after waiting in the sun. I feel like a grilled T-bone. Probably smell like one, too."

Her notes read: "White dude, 40s, white Saturn sedan, Texas plates, around 3:30 Tuesday." Below, she had added: "She hugged him."

Candy shifted her weight over to one foot, crossed her arms around her binder and books, and pouted at me.

"You done good, kid."

She beamed. "Thanks, but could you do me one favor?"

"Name it." I hooked my arm through hers as we walked the rest of the way to the car.

"Don't ever call me Candace again."

I would have laughed but for the deadpan expression on her face. "Now who can't take a joke?"

"Like I mean it, Mavis."

With her hair green that day and matching eye makeup, numerous earrings, a patchwork denim jacket, and a multitude of chains hanging around her neck, it was hard to take her seriously. I refrained from saying anything insulting. "Okay, agreed. Buds?"

"Buds." She smiled and almost looked normal.

"So you want to interpret these notes for me while I drive to the office?" Once we were in the car, I turned the air-conditioning to high, a blast of hot air hitting us. To say that Houston, Texas, in the late spring, the summer, and early fall is not the most temperate of climates would be a gross understatement.

"Yeah. Like it was really cool, Mavis, you know? Maybe I'll be a real investigator when I graduate. Like, I was quizzing kids all day. Jeanine wasn't in any of my classes, but like some of the girls she hangs with are, so I talked to them before and after class, and, like, at lunch I asked around. Finally, as I shut my locker to go outside like at the end of school, this little kid came up. His name is William. He's a sophomore, I think."

"Is he in any of your classes?"

"My computer science class." Hardly being able to contain herself, Candy bounced around the front seat as though it was too hot to sit on, turning toward me, facing front, then toward me again. "Anyway, I nearly ran right over him, like he's such a little dude. He stood there holding his clarinet case and an armful of books and said he heard me talking, you know, and just wanted to tell me that he'd seen Jeanine get into that car with some dude."

"How come he noticed her?"

"Didn't ask. Like he probably has a crush on her or something, like that isn't too uncommon, you know, Mavis? A lot of the nerds like the popular girls. They're always watching them in kind of a spooky way, like stalkers or something, but they never talk to them or anything. Like they're in two different worlds."

"So if this kid's a nerd, why didn't he tell Tommy?"

"William's a sophomore. Even senior nerds don't hang out with sophomores."

I guess I would have known that if I hadn't been out of school since before time began, at least in Candy's mind. "What did the man look like?"

"He was an old white dude, probably in his forties."

I gritted my teeth, realizing where I fit in on the age spectrum.

"William couldn't see him very well, but he thinks he had gray hair. He wore wire-frame glasses. What really tripped me out was when William said Jeanine hugged him."

"Exactly what did he say?"

"Like she leaned in the window and said something to the dude and then opened the door and slid across the seat and wrapped her arms around him. Like they drove away."

"Strange. She must have known him."

"Yep, that's what I think."

"Did William say if he recognized the man or the car? I mean, could it have been one of her teachers?"

"Oh, I hope not since she hugged him. Besides, William would have told me if he knew the dude."

"Did you get a chance to talk to Tommy today?"

"Nope. I didn't even see him. Like, I looked for him all day to see if he had any news, but never found him."

We drove in silence for a few minutes, thinking our separate thoughts. There could be any range of possibilities, some I didn't even want to contemplate, like an Internet date. I would stay in the present moment, not get carried away before it was time.

"I'm going to drop you off at the office, Candy. Then I'm going to the Lawson's house. I think it's past time for me to talk to Tommy's parents."

"Can't I go, Mavis? Like, I won't get in the way. I'll keep my mouth shut. Please?"

I shook my head. "Not this time, kiddo. Margaret's got some typing for you to do. She's been alone all day. At lunch, when I checked in, there were papers to be served so she needs to go out. I want you there to answer the phone in case any of those kids call the office."

"Oh, right, but like you'll call me on your mobile and let me know for sure what's happening?"

"Of course. And Candy, good job today."

I dropped Candy off and headed for River Oaks, anxious to meet the Lawsons. I wanted to see if the kids' father matched the description William had given of the man Jeanine hugged. It made no sense that her father would drive a Saturn when he owned a home in River Oaks but anything was possible. If it wasn't Mr. Lawson, I needed to know what men the Lawsons knew who matched that description. Who would Jeanine get into a car with? My imagination ran wild with the possible explanations for what had transpired. I didn't like some of them.

I drove my Mustang down a long, well-landscaped driveway to a mansion set a good distance from the street. A huge, white, two-story colonial with pillars and a double-doored entrance, it resembled the White House. Many cars of the same make, model, and vintage of the day before filled the driveway. Looked like quite a gathering.

It took a lot of intestinal fortitude for me to walk to the front door alone. I often appear a lot more audacious on the outside than I feel on the inside. An older, rather bosomy woman, in a shirtwaist with a full-length white apron over it, answered. She wore her gray hair in a severe bun and smelled of lavender. Housekeeper-type.

I stuck out my hand, which she ignored. "Mavis Davis. I'd like to see Mr. and Mrs. Lawson and Tommy, please."

"Are you expected?" Her red-rimmed eyes gave me the once-over.

"No, but I need to talk to them. It's really important."

She cut her eyes at me in apparent disbelief. "They are entertaining right now, but I'll see. Have you a card?"

I resisted a snide remark and searched in my shoulder bag for a business card. When I gave it to her, she glanced at it and wrinkled her nose like the butler had the day before.

"Come in." She stepped aside and closed the door behind me. "Wait here," she said in a tone and with a look that led me to believe that if I ventured any further, I'd be shot on sight.

I stood in the entry hall and checked out the joint, which was every bit as elaborate as Melanie's folks' place. An aroma of lemon-oil furniture polish hung in the air. How rich did a person have to be to live in a place like that?

My heels clicking on the parquet floor, I walked to the entranceway to peek after the housekeeper. The hall opened upon a large foyer with a winding white, marble staircase leading up to the second floor. At any moment, I expected Grace Kelly to float down the stairs for her coming-out party. A crystal vase filled with tall, fresh calla lilies stood upon a small marble-topped table at the foot of the stairs next to the railing.

Classical music, laughter, and the murmur of voices drifted in from a distance. I heard a splash and a door slam. When I'd seen the cars outside, I'd expected something akin to a wake, but the noise I heard sounded more like a swimming party.

I looked around for a mirror so I could check myself out. At least I wore a cotton skirt and blouse and clean flats, and clean panties as my mother always told me to do in case I had to go to the hospital. I ran my fingers through my curls and pulled out a lipstick, swiping at my lips. My nails were ragged, but a manicure would have to wait until I made enough money to pay the other bills and the girls.

After a few minutes, a woman I took to be Mrs. Lawson sailed noiselessly toward me, the picture of elegance. An older version of Jeanine, she had coifed black hair and dancing blue eyes that I'd expected to be bloodshot from grieving. Instead, it looked like she'd been partying down big-time.

In one diamond-laden hand, she held an oversized, half-empty martini glass with three large, green, pitted, Spanish olives on a swizzle stick. In the other, a salmon-colored cloth napkin and a pair of what could only be designer sunglasses in black, rhinestone-encrusted frames. A long triangle of gauzy fabric in a Southwestern print hung off one well-tanned shoulder and barely concealed a black one-piece bathing suit.

She wore black, spiked-heel sandals and bright pink polish on her well-manicured toes and fingers.

She took my uncared-for hand with two fingers of the napkin-holding hand, her squeeze so light I thought maybe I'd imagined it. "Yes, Miss Davis?" Her voice came out melodious and light. "What may I do for you?"

"I wondered if I could have a few minutes alone with you and your husband and Tommy."

"Whatever for?" She smiled as she spoke.

The aroma of gin smelled as strong as a squirt of air freshener. As I stared down at her, I wondered what occupied the space between her ears. Was there more to her? Was this her public persona? This couldn't be real. "Tommy didn't tell you?"

"Tell me what?"

"He hired me to find Jeanine."

"My goodness." Except for her dark hair, Mrs. Lawson brought to mind the good witch in *The Wizard of Oz*. She had the same high-pitched, airy voice. "No, he certainly didn't. When was that, pray tell?"

Pray tell? That was my line. I studied her for a moment as she swallowed more martini, leaving lipstick smears on top of lipstick smears on the rim of her glass. "Yesterday afternoon. He came to my office with a girl who works for me part-time. I've been searching for Jeanine ever since."

"Pardon me," she said and put her hand to her mouth. I supposed she suppressed a silent belch; I didn't hear anything. "Are you in the habit of taking money from children?"

"No, Mrs. Lawson, I'm not, but Tommy's not exactly a child. He said he's eighteen. Perhaps you could call him in here so we can get this straightened out."

Mrs. Lawson stared at the olives in her glass. "I'm afraid

that's quite impossible. We've been checking on him the last few hours, but Tommy is unavailable at the moment."

"What do you mean unavailable?"

"It appears that he, too, has disappeared."

Chapter Four

"Disappeared?" I felt like my fingers had just been connected to a battery charger. "He came to my office yesterday with Candy."

"Who?" She stared at me, her eyes finally showing some sign of comprehension.

"Candace Finklestein," I said. "She's a student at Lamar. She works for me half a day. He wanted me to find Jeanine—"

"I've never heard him mention her—"

"He said you thought she'd run away, but he thought she'd been kidnapped. He said you thought she was mad at you and wanted to teach you a lesson—"

"Is she in some of his classes?"

"He even called Melanie before I went to her house yesterday evening—"

"Melanie? He didn't say anything to me—"

"I can't understand what could have happened to him—" I stopped. With both of us speaking at once, we were getting nowhere. "I apologize. You were saying?"

Her laughter was like the twitter of a little bird. "I guess I'm confused. Why would he go to you? I'd called the police."

"He seemed worried that no one appeared to be taking the situation seriously. He didn't think the police would do anything—that they would classify her as a runaway and that would be the end of it." She seemed bewildered. I *felt* bewildered. Who was confusing whom? Or whom was—never mind. "I can't believe after hiring me yesterday that Tommy would disappear today."

"Nevertheless, it seems to be true." She took another sip of her drink. "We contacted the school this afternoon when he didn't come home. No one has seen Tommy since this morning. He didn't attend his afternoon classes."

"Maybe he's out looking for Jeanine himself. Maybe he heard where she might be and went there," I said, ever the optimist.

She shook her head. "I think not. Security found his car still parked near the school."

"That doesn't make sense. Where could he have gone?" I glanced around, hoping she'd get the hint and ask me to sit down.

"I'm sure I don't know, Miss Davis. We were just discussing that when you arrived."

"Oh." I wondered who she meant by *we*. "Well, have you checked with Tommy's friends?"

"Yes." Her eyes swept to her empty glass and then vaguely over her shoulder.

"None of them have any notion . . ."

She shook her head again and stared at me with eyes that seemed to grow blanker by the moment. I wondered why she wasn't more upset. If it had been me—

"Hilary," a man's voice called. A large, rather attractive man in his late fifties appeared in the entry hall. He wore an off-white bathing robe and sandals. Twinges of gray graced his temples in striking contrast with the rest of his blue-black hair. A twinkle gleamed in his watery, bloodshot hazel eyes when he spotted Mrs. Lawson. He glanced at her, then me. "What's the holdup, dear?"

Hilary Lawson's face broke into a wide smile as she took

his hand and batted her eyelashes as only a Southern belle could do. "Harrison, dear, this is Mavis Davis, a private investigator. She claims Tommy went to see her yesterday and hired her to find Jeanine."

"Really?" His forehead knitted. He was sweating profusely. He dabbed at the corners of his mouth with a white linen handkerchief.

I pulled my hand from my skirt pocket, offering it to him. His ham of a hand was somewhat damp, but he had a firm grip. "Nice to meet you. I presume you're Mr. Lawson." On closer inspection, I saw that his pupils were dilated. I wondered what drugs he was on.

"You presume correctly. What's this about Tommy?"

"He showed up at my office yesterday with the high school girl who works for me half a day, Candace Finklestein. He gave me a two-thousand-dollar retainer to find Jeanine."

"Two thousand dollars?" He spoke with a slight lisp or else he'd had too much to drink and slurred his words, or both.

"He was pretty worried, Mr. Lawson. He didn't think the police were going to help find her and wanted me to drop everything and start looking for her immediately, which I did."

"Where would he get two thousand dollars?" Still slurring his words, he cleared his throat and dabbed his mouth again.

Mrs. Lawson shrugged and waved her glass in the air. "He doesn't spend his allowance as fast as Jeanine."

"I can give it back," I said. "I put the check in my safe. Hey, maybe you want to hire me to look for both of them?" That was bold, but I didn't mind taking money from adults.

Lawson swiped at his hair. "This is a strange turn of events, isn't it, dear?" he said to his wife.

"Yes it is, dear," she said.

"Why don't you come out by the pool and have a drink

with us and discuss it?" Lawson said. "We were about to have cocktails earlier when we discovered Tommy missing. We have friends over. We were just trying to figure out where the children could be."

Weird people. I wasn't sure that I didn't want to give the money back and shed myself of them. Who sits down to cocktails when their children are missing? "I don't know, Mr. Lawson. Why don't you call me and let me know what you decide."

He took my arm. "Now, don't be shy. Have a drink with us. We don't bite. It may be that we'll hire you ourselves." He chuckled. "Who knows what the children have gotten themselves into this time?" He glanced at his wife. Some nonverbal communication passed between them.

Mrs. Lawson patted my shoulder and said, "Yes, please do come in. This is nothing to be hasty about." She led the way out of the entry hall and toward the music.

Lawson held my arm rather tightly. We followed his wife past the staircase and a library every bit as elaborate as the one in Melanie's house, a baby grand piano the only apparent difference. It stood in front of French doors that I assumed opened onto a patio. White lace curtains covered the glass, preventing one from seeing through them at any distance. We traipsed down a long hall, Lawson stumbling once and seeming to rely on me to keep him on his feet. The music grew louder as we came to another set of French doors with sheer curtains. Mrs. Lawson pushed them open.

Clusters of men and women lounged on a patio and around a swimming pool so enormous it could have floated a yacht. Greenery and flowers that ranged in hue from white to dark purple served as the oversized yard's frame, the landscaping fantastic in its elaborate design. A complete outdoor kitchen, including a gigantic chrome grill, stood under a wooden gazebo. Two small Hispanic men with stained white chef's aprons wrapped around their torsos supervised the cooking of a slab of beef and shrimp shish-ka-bobs. If we had been inside, the air would have been thick and overwhelming. The chlorinated pool water and a strong sweet scent from the flowers in the garden mingled with slightly acrid smoke from the grill.

Adorned in various modes of dress from swimsuits to business attire, the Lawsons' guests sipped cocktails and chatted playfully. When they noticed our entrance, all conversation ceased. It was as if we were under a spotlight.

"Everybody," Lawson announced, "this is Mavis Davis, a private detective. Miss Davis, meet everybody." His chuckle turned into a wrenching cough, which he muted with his handkerchief. I felt like gagging. He dragged me to the bar on the far end of the outdoor kitchen where he finally let go of me and shifted the burden of his weight to a bar stool. A rather small, ugly, redheaded man served as bartender. He gave Lawson something to drink from a bottle under the bar. I didn't recognize the label, but that didn't mean much. I'm mostly a long-neck and wine drinker, myself. Lawson tossed almost half of it down his throat.

There must be a name for an outdoor kitchen, but since I didn't think I would ever own one, it was a moot point. I heard a woman say, "A woman private eye. I've always thought that to be a marvelous idea."

At that moment, I wasn't too thrilled, myself. Perhaps I should have gotten an innocuous position as a receptionist somewhere.

"Now what would you like to drink?" Lawson asked, patting me on the hand like he would an elderly aunt. "My bartender, Juan, can prepare most anything. Kelby, where's Juan?"

The man called Kelby said to Mr. Lawson, "Went inside for something. What do you want?" This last, to me.

I glanced at the man and resisted making a snide remark. Though the day grew late, the sun continued to beat down, the humidity never ceasing, it being Houston, Texas, only fifty miles from the Gulf of Mexico. I longed for something to quench my thirst and debated whether it would be ethical to imbibe alcohol on the job.

Lawson said, "There's a pitcher of martinis in the fridge. Also, a pitcher of frozen margaritas in the freezer, but whatever you want."

Hilary Lawson smiled her good-witch smile and held out her empty glass. The ugly man popped several olives into it. She must have eaten the others while I wasn't looking. He was about to pour the refill when Juan returned and took over. Juan filled her glass to the brim. She sipped until the level lowered about half an inch, smiled again, and tiptoed over to stretch out next to a woman on a chaise lounge.

When I turned back, Lawson stared my way, awaiting my decision. His coloring looked off, as though he were ill. Sunglasses concealed his eyes. Feeling like an exhibit in a museum, I said, "A bottle of water?" My voice croaked.

"Wonderful choice," he said, as though I'd made some stupendous decision. "Juan, give the lady detective a cold bottle of water." Immediately, conversations began again as if I'd never made an appearance. Lawson grinned and leaned on his elbow.

Juan handed over the water, which I swallowed almost half of before coming up for air. My face felt flushed. Hilary Lawson conversed with the leggy woman lying next to her as though her children were upstairs playing video games and not in parts unknown. Both watched me. It seemed exceedingly strange that she would abandon our conversation. Didn't she want to find her children? Or did she already know where they were? Why not usher me out the door?

The Kelby-man now stood with two other men next to the diving board. One gestured animatedly as he talked, the contents of his highball glass rolling from side-to-side like a sailboat in rough seas.

A man with smooth good looks seemed vaguely familiar. He relaxed in a lawn chair, alone, his eyes aimed toward Mrs. Lawson.

On the opposite side of the pool, three middle-aged women whispered among themselves. A couple of men sat on the side of the pool, dangling their feet in the water, deep in discussion. Kelby-what's-his-face now made his way to the other side and openly stared at me. He wore a gray pinstriped suit. He lit a cigar, the stinky smell wafting across to where I stood. As he headed our way, Lawson took my elbow, directing me elsewhere. As Ugly approached, he slipped in pool water and collided with us. Mr. Lawson's arm went to steady himself while I grabbed the back of a chair for support. The other man grasped at Lawson and they stumbled around for a few seconds in a clumsy waltz until both of them regained their balance. I had to bite my lip to smother my amusement. It's nice to know the rich can be as graceless as the poor.

"Damn, Kelby, watch it," Lawson said as he straightened up.

"Sorry, old chum. That water is really dangerous, you know. You should tell one of your Mexicans to mop it up." He picked up his cigar from where it had bounced on the concrete and landed against the bar.

Lawson said something to Juan in Spanish. Juan left. Lawson made his way haltingly behind the bar, pulled out a folded, white dishtowel, and blotted the remainder of his drink off his clothing. "Good thing my glass was almost empty. This is Kelby McAfee, Miss Davis," Lawson said, indicating the little ugly man. "He's a business associate of mine. Kelby, shake the lady's hand if you can manage it without knocking her down."

McAfee switched the cigar to his other hand and shook my fingers. The cigar stench clung to his clothing like fabric softener gone bad. "Nice to meet you." I suppressed a shiver and wondered why Lawson hadn't introduced us in the first place.

"Same here. What is Harrison hiring you for?"

I glanced at Lawson, but he had bent over behind the bar. He straightened up, his face red, and began sloshing more liquid into a glass. "He hasn't hired me to do anything, yet."

"Then what are you doing here?" The deep voice came from behind me.

I turned and came eyeball-to-eyeball with the owner of the familiar-looking face. He wore a sports shirt that matched his swimming trunks. The way he held his drink, I could see an impressive diamond pinky ring and a diamond-and-gold watch—which must have cost thirty thousand if a dime—on his left wrist as though deliberately on display.

"James Rush," he said, and stuck out his hand.

"The lawyer. I knew I recognized your face." My hand slipped into his. His shake wasn't bad. Firm, not bone-crushing, but there was something about him . . .

"It's nice of you to say so." He bared what had to be chemically whitened teeth.

"Not at all. I've seen your picture on the news and in the paper several times. Didn't you win a huge verdict recently? What was it, some millions of dollars in a mass tort claims case?"

"Two hundred or so, but what's a mil or two one way or the other?" He cocked his head as he smiled at me.

I laughed. "I can see why it wouldn't be impressive to you, but to me, that's a lot of money."

Lawson came from behind the bar with a full glass. He still seemed tentative on his feet.

"After a while, money doesn't mean much," Rush said.

"Says you," I said. "I know a lot of people who wouldn't agree."

"What he means is, the greatest joy is in the winning," Lawson said in a dour tone of voice.

"It's the battle—the challenge of seeing who's going to come out on top." More slurred words from another man who had just walked up. Looked like Lawson wasn't the only one who'd had a bit too much.

"This is Clayton Hadley, Miss Davis, another business associate," Lawson said haltingly.

"How do you do, Miss Davis," Hadley said, "miss" sounding like myth. A short, pudgy fellow with a bushy mustache, tiny dark eyes, and a pockmarked face, he and McAfee might tie for the grand prize in a hideous man contest. Where were all the beautiful people?

I held out my hand once again. Hadley shook it, barely touching it before pulling his hand away. I wasn't sure I wanted to make contact with the fellow anyway.

"Can I get a refill, Harrison?" Hadley asked.

"You stay where you are, Harrison, and visit with your guest. I'll get it," Rush said, taking the glass and walking behind the bar as though it were his own.

Juan had finished mopping up but hadn't returned from storing the mop. Rush dropped a couple of cubes into Hadley's glass, searched around under the bar, and poured Johnny Walker Black.

"It's just a game, is that it?" I asked, looking from man to man.

"That's it, all right. Fun and games," Rush said as he handed Hadley his glass.

Something was going on, only I wasn't in on it. I glanced at their faces again. Their smiles went no further than their mouths.

"So you're going to hire this young lady to find the missing children, is that it?" Rush asked Lawson.

"Seems she's already been hired by someone else," Lawson said. He grimaced and put his hand to his stomach.

"You don't mean Hilary?" asked McAfee.

"No, I mean Tommy. He hired Miss Davis yesterday. Isn't that right?" He nodded at me.

"Yes, sir. That's correct."

"Tommy's always been imaginative," Lawson said. "Seems he thought something had really happened to Jeanine and went to Miss Davis's office after school. Paid her a two-thousand-dollar retainer."

I cringed. Talk of money—where it concerned me at least—was embarrassing. I wanted to scoot right out of there before those rich snobs made me feel any cheaper. I couldn't do that so I addressed the issue head on. "You're obviously not worried about either of your children."

Lawson chuckled, though it hit an odd note. Again it resulted in a wrenching cough. Again he wiped at corners of his mouth and blotted his forehead. "No, my dear, I'm not. They'll come back in good time. You know how hot-headed teenagers can be."

I studied his face. He looked strained and his words didn't ring true. "I've never had children, but Tommy didn't appear hot-headed to me, Mr. Lawson. He came across as a deeply troubled young man." I began to get hot-headed myself and not just from the searing Houston heat. If he'd forced me outside in front of all his friends just to make me feel like a fool, he was succeeding.

"What did he think Jeanine was up to, Miss Davis?" McAfee asked.

"He didn't know." I turned to him. "But he thought she would have called him if it was an act to get attention."

"And she hadn't?" Rush asked.

"No." I drank more water. "At least not the last time I talked with him."

"Well, I think I know my own children better than you do, Miss Davis," Lawson said loudly, "and believe me, they're just trying to punish us for some imaginary offense." He backed closer to the bar and leaned his weight on his forearm.

As loud as he'd been, Lawson had caught most everyone's attention. The talking stopped again, all eyes turned toward our little group. My face grew hotter.

"I'm sure you do, Mr. Lawson." I saluted him with the water bottle. "I'll send Tommy's check back in tomorrow's mail." I gave him a cutting glance and started to leave when he reached out for me.

"Hold on, Miss Davis." He emitted a groan. "Nothing to get offended about." He swallowed again from his glass.

I started to give him a tangy retort when his glass fell out of his hand and shattered on the concrete. Like a slow-motion movie, he clutched his chest, his eyes rolled up, the whites shining, and he slumped to the ground. "Arrgh."

"Mr. Lawson!"

Everyone gaped as if they'd swallowed too much pool water. Crouching over the man, I could see his skin had a sickly pallor.

"Somebody do something," I yelled. "Call nine-one-one."

"Move out of the way." A man shoved me and bent over Lawson, putting his ear to Lawson's chest. Then he felt Lawson's wrist for a pulse. He started CPR.

"Call an ambulance," a voice said.

I grabbed my cell out of my shoulder bag and punched in nine-one-one. A group of people encircled Lawson. I saw other people on their cells as well—the man McAfee, two almost pimply-faced young men, a couple of women I hadn't been introduced to—but completed my call anyway.

The man continued trying to resuscitate him for several minutes. Finally he rocked back on his heels and shook his head. "He's dead."

Chapter Five

"Harrison!" Mrs. Lawson shrieked from where she lay. Several women rushed to her, preventing her from getting up.

"Holy shit," a man behind me said.

"Are you a doctor?" I asked the man who'd tried to resuscitate Mr. Lawson and made the declaration of death.

"Afraid so," he said.

"Can't you keep trying? Do something?"

"Lady," he said. "He has no pulse. Get me something to cover him."

"How do you ring for the help?" I asked McAfee, whose eyes bulged out of their sockets.

"Huh?" He appeared dazed.

"A blanket. I need a blanket. How do I ring for the help?" I looked to Hadley and back to McAfee. They both stared blankly. I couldn't tell if it was the booze or shock. The circle had broken with people moving away from the body with apparent revulsion.

"There's a buzzer here on the bar, Miss Davis," James Rush said. He had one hand on a liquor bottle. "I've already pushed it, but I gave Juan instructions." He poured himself another belt.

"You're a cool one." While I waited for a response to his buzzing, I noticed his hand shake as he lifted his glass to his mouth.

The women gathered around Hilary. The doctor proceeded to her and took her hand. Her face was as pale as printer paper.

As I watched, several of the men tossed off their drinks. The people in the pool climbed out and covered up.

The housekeeper came outside. I said to her, "I'm afraid Mr. Lawson's passed away. We could do with a blanket to cover him up."

The older woman stumbled, but I caught her.

"I'm sorry," I said and led her inside. "Could you tell me where they're kept?" I wondered where Juan had gone. Now that I thought of it, the other two Hispanic men had faded from the scene as well.

The housekeeper looked at me for a moment, eyes blinking rapidly.

"We don't want to leave him just lying there," I prompted.

She cleared her throat and fanned her face with her hand. "I'll . . . fetch . . . it," she said, stared at me a few seconds longer, and crept from the room.

I walked back out to the pool. "Don't anyone touch anything," I said in a loud voice, though I'm not sure anyone was listening.

The doctor looked at me from where he sat with Hilary.

"Do you want to call in a prescription for Mrs. Lawson or something?" I wanted to get him alone and find out if he would guess at the cause of death.

"Good idea. Joan," he said to the woman who looked like an overaged cheerleader, all blonde hair and animation, "sit with Hilary."

As we left, I saw several people move closer to the body, staring down at it. I swear, if Mr. Lawson hadn't already passed on, he'd have died of asphyxiation.

Inside, the doctor rummaged around in the desk in the library, excuse me, media center, until he found a telephone book. "What do you think he died of?" I asked as I watched the doctor calmly punch in some numbers on his cell phone.

He cocked an eyebrow and shook his head. "Don't know. Looked like a heart attack."

"Well, was it a heart attack? I thought it might be a heart attack, but I thought heart attack victims made more weird noises when the attack came, like a squeal or a grunt. I was near a man who had one once, and he cried out something awful and jerked around like a fish out of water."

He rolled his eyes, and then identified himself into the telephone and gave an order for some medication to be sent to Mrs. Lawson. When he hung up, I said, "Well, could it have been maybe a stroke? I've never been around a stroke victim. Except I had a friend who got sunstroke once."

"Miss Davis," he said with a sigh, "I don't know. There will have to be an autopsy."

"If it's a heart attack, why would there have to be an autopsy? Can't the family waive the autopsy?"

He sighed again and acted annoyed. "I don't know. You have to ask the medical examiner or someone in that field."

"What kind of doctor are you? Aren't y'all supposed to know these things?"

"Look, I'm a plastic surgeon. I haven't seen a dead body since medical school."

"Oh. Well, you're a friend of the family, right? Did Mr. Lawson have a history of high blood pressure? How were his cholesterol and triglyceride counts? High?"

He gave me an exasperated look as he started to edge away. "I don't know, Miss Davis. Can't this wait?"

I shrugged. "I guess so. I just wondered if there would be any reason to suspect murder." That just slipped out, surprising both of us.

He gave me a furious look. “Are you saying you suspect someone here of killing him?”

“You never know,” I said and backed away, wishing I’d kept my mouth shut.

“You’re not going to suggest such a thing to Hilary.”

“I’m not?” He said the wrong thing. I hated it when people, especially men, told me what to do.

His dark eyes grew darker. “Give the poor woman a break, will you? Her kids have run off, and now this—”

“Say,” I said, “do you think the two events could be related?”

“I’ll be damned if I know.”

“How much do you know about the family?”

“Not much, really.” He headed toward the pool area. “I know them socially and Hilary’s been a patient of mine, but never confided in me. She keeps her problems to herself,” he said. “Unlike most women.”

“What’d she have done, a boob job?”

“Really, Miss Davis.” He opened the door to go out.

“Just asking, Doc.”

Someone was coming inside. It was the woman, Joan. “She asked for you, Bart. Maybe she should be taken upstairs to lie down.”

“I’m coming.” To me, he said, “Do me a favor, will you, Miss Davis?”

“Anything.”

“Try to be a little more discreet with the others than you have been with me.” He left to go to Hilary.

I stood back and observed the people lingering over their drinks. Rush dallied behind the bar, freshening up cocktails as glasses were shoved under his nose. He looked right at home.

McAfee lounged off to one side, puffing on his cigar and

staring at Harrison Lawson's body. He had a wandering look in his eyes and a thin frown upon his lips.

Hadley's beady eyes concentrated on his drink as he shifted unsteadily from one foot to the other, still in approximately the same spot as when Lawson had dropped.

The doc assisted Hilary into the house and, presumably, upstairs.

The housekeeper returned with a blanket and began straightening it over Lawson. She sniffed and stopped to wipe her eyes with a tissue she pulled from the wrist of her sleeve.

An older, dowdy woman swooned. Two men caught her and eased her to a chair.

"I wonder if they need help," I mumbled.

"No," came a throaty female voice from beside me. "That's Yvonne Rigby. She always makes a scene, though it was nice of her to wait until Hilary left. Usually, she tries to get all the attention right off the bat."

It was Joan-the-cheerleader-type standing beside me. She dabbed at the corners of her bloodshot blue eyes and attempted a smile. Her mouth quivered as she spoke. "I'm Joan McAfee, Kelby's wife." The alcohol on her breath threatened to overwhelm me.

"I'm Mavis Davis," I said. "Nice to meet you."

"What did Bart mean when he said for you to be 'more discreet'?"

I stared down at the short, blonde woman. I had a good fifty pounds on her. She wore excessive rouge and bright red lipstick. Her pancake makeup and mascara had smeared together so that she looked clownish. I didn't know how delicate or sensitive she was, though I suspected she was pretty tough. I shrugged. "I was just asking him some questions."

"About Harrison?"

"Yes. About his health."

"He'd had a heart attack before, but he was basically healthy. Worked out every day with James, Kelby, and Earl. I know, because sometimes Kelby gets carried away with racquet ball and doesn't come home on time. I have to call down to the club after him."

"I see. So you think it was a heart attack, too?"

"What's that supposed to mean?" Her eyes held a curious, though watery, look.

"I'm sorry if I sound strange. I'm just speculating. Could something else be the cause of death?" I can't help it; I have a suspicious mind. PIs are supposed to be the suspicious type. It says so in the rule book—rule fifty-five, I think.

Joan put her face very near my ear and whispered, "You think it was other than natural causes, don't you?" Her voice trembled.

"Do you?" I whispered back.

"I don't know. There's always more than meets the eye, isn't there?" She was still whispering.

"It certainly seemed to be that way when I came in."

"You're the expert," she said. "What do you think happened?"

I was pleased to be called an expert. I'm afraid I preened a little. "I'm not sure. It was odd that he would take a drink and drop down dead like that, though he didn't look up to snuff when I met him." Up to snuff, hell, I didn't want to tell her but ever since I came in I noticed something wasn't right about the man. His pupils had been dilated, he'd been sweating profusely, he kept dabbing at the corners of his mouth with his handkerchief, his speech was slurred, his hand was damp, he was unsteady on his feet, he'd clutched at his stomach as though in pain, and had a wrenching cough. No, I didn't think he'd had a heart attack. Something was wrong, though I didn't know what it was.

"Poison? You think his drink was poisoned?"

"There's always that possibility," I said. I wanted to laugh, I don't know why. "Tell me, Joan—is it all right if I call you Joan?"

She nodded vigorously.

"How did Mr. and Mrs. Lawson get along?"

Her eyes darted around and, as if she were judging whether or not she could be overheard, she looked from Kelby, who was closest to us, to me, and back again. Then she led me a couple of steps away.

I played her conspiracy game, hoping she would tell me something—anything—waiting anxiously for her next words.

"Things were not going well lately, I understand."

I was able to pin down the aroma on her breath to gin, a popular drink with this set, apparently. "From whom?"

"Everybody knew it. Relationships built on a lousy foundation often have trouble making it. Don't you agree?"

"Mmmm . . ." I wanted to hear more about the lousy foundation.

"I don't see how they lasted this long." She gave me a knowing look.

"But they've been married, what, nineteen or twenty years?"

"Oh, no, darling, barely twelve." Her eyes suddenly dried up and became bright.

"Then the children—"

"Adopted, you know."

I nodded as if I had. "What about all these other people, do you know them?"

"Certainly. Hilary and I are the best of friends."

If that was her best friend behavior, I'd hate to be her worst enemy. "Who's that man, something-or-other Hadley?"

She slurped from her drink. "Clayton. He's in real estate. Harrison and he invested in some big commercial properties together."

"And that tall, blond man at the far end of the pool." I indicated one of the two men I'd seen engrossed in a conversation earlier.

"Earl Smythe. He was Harrison's stockbroker. They had a falling out back when the stock market had that large dip—let's see, when was that?"

I shrugged and nodded. How would I know?

"But I think things are on an even keel now," Joan said. "Although, you never know." Her eyes flashed.

"And the man Smythe was talking to when Mr. Lawson died?" I pointed out another man. This was great. The woman was a wealth of information.

"Hmmm . . . let me see—"

"Joan, dear," a woman in a black swimsuit padded up to us. "I'm so sorry." The woman kissed the air on each side of Joan's face.

"Thank you, Gladys," Joan said and smiled.

I have to repeat, a lot was going on that I didn't understand. But, I was trying. Seeing as how Gladys didn't appear to want to fade away into the sunset, I excused myself and walked to the doorway where the man about whom I'd just asked Joan stood. I'd find out for myself.

"Hi, I'm Mavis Davis," I said as I approached the man with my hand outstretched. He wore a navy sport coat, tan slacks, and tan loafers, and shifted from foot to foot as he stood back and observed the milling about. I thought he must be reaching heat exhaustion in those clothes. He switched his glass to his left hand, wiped his palm with his cocktail napkin, and shook my hand. His clasp was cold, but dry.

"Weylin Scott, National Insurance Trust."

"Pardon?"

"Sorry," he said, looking sheepish. "I said 'National Insurance Trust,' but I didn't mean to. It's a habit with me. Always selling, selling, selling—but then, that's what got me here in the first place."

"Insurance?"

"Yes," he said. "I work for Harrison. Mr. Lawson?"

"Oh, yes, at the company." I pretended I knew what the hell he was talking about.

He smiled. It was a nice one, broad straight teeth that showed off his olive complexion. "Your first cocktail party here, Miss Davis?"

"Yes and undoubtedly my last. What about you?"

"Yeah, same here. Now that Harrison's dead, they'll probably be at the McAfee's in the future. That is, if the board promotes him. I haven't been there long enough to even be considered for it, but salesman of the year is a good start, don't you think? That's how you get promoted, sell, sell, sell."

"Is that why you're here? Salesman of the year?"

"Yes. That's how it starts, see. They look you over after you get salesman of the year, and if they like you enough, then you get bumped up. I only wish I had a wife. It helps, you know."

That sounded old-fashioned to me, but I nodded. "How long have you been with the company?"

"Eighteen months. Harrison handpicked me himself. Recruited me right off the Rice University campus."

"Lucky you."

"It was quite a break," he said. "I haven't let him down, either, but his dying like this has let me down. Now that I think of it, I'd better go speak to Kelby. Pardon me," he said and cut through a group of people who stood between us and the bar.

I observed everyone for a few minutes, wondering who among them would have a motive for murdering Mr. Lawson. I know, my imagination was getting the better of me. Okay, if in fact it was a murder. It could have been nothing more than heart failure. My thoughts wandered to the two missing—adopted—children. And why was Gladys giving her condolences to Joan? Was Joan his sister or something? She didn't look that broken up and there was no family resemblance.

From my vantage point, I could see everyone except Hilary Lawson and Doctor Bart, who, no doubt, were upstairs in her room. It was quite a crowd. Insurance people. Real estate people. Stockbrokers. What I knew about them could fit on the head of a pin. I didn't even have any. Insurance, I mean. I'd better not tell Weylin that or I'd be signed up before I could think twice. I didn't have any real estate, either. Or stocks, bonds, or mutual funds. Just the working poor, that's me. While I stood pondering, the front door apparently opened to let some other people inside, because the next thing I heard was a rude voice that said, "Well, if it isn't Mustang Sally."

Chapter Six

I cringed as I turned and saw ludicrous Lon, the worst of Houston's finest, breathing hot and heavy, his fat face flushing, followed by an entourage of boys in blue and a couple of EMTs.

"There goes the neighborhood," I said.

"Ha ha, very funny," he said as he wiped his brow on the sleeve of his jacket. Huge circles of sweat stained the fabric under his armpits, which emitted an odor I'd rather not describe. "Okay, men," Lon barked, "get to work. Herd all those people inside and don't let any of them leave without talking to me first." Turning to me, he said, "What the hell're you doing here, Mavis Davis?"

I cringed again. There had always been something about the way he said my name that made me feel like my ears were going to shrivel up and fall off. Our historic mutual contempt dated back to when I was a probation officer with a mission and he was a rookie cop on an ego trip. "Working," I said. "And you? Who called the police?"

The EMTs hurried to the body while we talked. I watched them do an examination and shake their heads.

"Ha ha, very funny," Lon said again, underwhelming me with his vocabulary, as usual. His eyes gave the area a once-over. "That the stiff under the blanket?"

"Yes," I replied. "Harrison Lawson. In the midst of a conversation at the bar, he fell down, groaned, and that was it. Next thing we knew, he was dead."

"You ain't touched the body or nothing have you?" Lon did his best to give me the evil eye, but I am not easily intimidated and especially not by him.

"Lon, I swear, I've done nothing except procure the blanket." I held up three fingers. "Scout's honor."

"You shouldn't even of done that! You stay here. I'm gonna take a look." He shot me another dark glance that I suppose was intended to put the fear of God in me. The EMTs spoke to him and left. When Lon peeled the blanket back, his complexion turned something akin to sea green. He dropped the blanket into place and pulled out his handkerchief, picking up the largest piece of glass. He motioned for a uniform.

James Rush accosted me. "Did you call the police?"

I took it that he was having a fine time playing host and didn't want to give it up. I patted him on the hand. "Actually, no," I said. "But someone did. Who do you think it was?"

A frown pulled at his lips.

"Well, I'm sure it won't be long, Mr. Rush. There're enough officers here that they can be through quickly and you can be on your way."

He grimaced. From the looks of him, there was something on his mind, but I'm damned if I could fathom what it was. I slipped my arm through his and, when Lon returned in our direction, I introduced them.

"Detective Tyler, this is James G. Rush, the famous plaintiff's attorney. Mr. Rush, this is Detective Tyler, homicide."

"Oh, yeah?" Lon said, his eyes lit up and his face broke out in a crooked, toothy grin. He extended his hand in Rush's direction. "I read all about you. You just won some big case worth millions."

Rush, whose nose wrinkled up when he got close to Lon, nevertheless shook the man's hand and smiled as best he could. "You don't say."

"Yeah, what was it, ten or fifteen mil?"

"Close," Rush said as he pulled his napkin from around his glass, mopped his brow, and then wiped the hand Lon had shaken.

"Lon, how long's it going to be before you can release the Lawsons' guests? Some of them are pretty upset and would like to get out of here," I said.

"O—Oh." He looked over his shoulder as though just remembering where he was. "Well, glad to meet you, Mr. Rush. You hang in here a minute and we'll get your statement and then you can go." To me, he said, "Mavis, you come over here."

"Just what are you doing here, anyway?" he asked, his face close enough to mine that I got a whiff of breath so sour it would have curdled milk.

I'd been asking myself the same question. Who'd have believed it? I don't think the rule book for private investigators ever addressed the issue of what to do if a death occurred in one's presence.

"Investigating a runaway kid," I whispered into Lon's face. "I didn't know they'd have a party while their kid was missing, for Christ's sake, so I just came over and all these people were here and I was talking to the decedent and he fell down dead."

Lon's face looked like a curious Neanderthal's. He poked his stubby forefinger into my sternum. "You wait. I want to talk to you in a few minutes." He stalked over to the uniforms who had accompanied him.

I waited, not so patiently. The back door stood open and I could see people talking to the police, giving their names and statements, I suppose. James Rush stayed outside behind the bar. I noticed a small clear glass tube lying in a puddle of water. The tube was about the size of a cologne sample. I've seen Margaret use them at the office. The diameter is smaller than a pencil and the length, shorter than my pinkie.

Mrs. Lawson didn't seem to be the cologne-sample-type. Even if she was, she wouldn't bring samples down to the pool. Could it be? No. Well—only one way to find out.

Smiling my best, I wove my way from the lawn chair where I'd been planted by Lon, around the pool, to the bar. "Looks like I'm going to be here awhile. May I have another bottle of water, please?" I had the toe of my pump at the edge of the glass tube, but how could I pick it up without being conspicuous or smearing fingerprints, if any?

I placed my shoulder bag onto the bar and dug for my pack of cigarettes until I remembered that I'd quit smoking. Damn it. It would have fit perfectly. Well, if I could grasp the ends with my thumb and forefinger and slip it into my skirt pocket without seeming too obvious . . .

"What's that you're pointing at with your toe, Mavis?" Lon reached down and picked up the object in question and laughed at me as he dropped it into his own pocket. If there had been a print, it was gone now.

"I was wondering that myself, officer," I said. I pulled myself onto a bar stool and uncapped the bottle of water, taking another long swig. Why hadn't I just painted a sign in bold letters with an arrow pointing to the glass tube? Shit.

Chuckling, Lon stalked away.

Rush, I thought, had an odd look in his eyes, but he promptly mixed and tossed back another drink.

I chastised myself for being so obvious. I have a friend/former lover who works in a lab at the University of

Houston. His PhD had something to do with poisons. I'd thought of taking the little container to him for analysis. I doubted if it was only stomach acid that had given Mr. Lawson those symptoms.

I waited several more minutes before Lon finally came back. "Now, what was you sayin', Mavis?"

I gave him my brightest smile, anxious to get out of there. I figured I'd be able to get the guest list later, and I didn't think I needed to wait for the missus. She wouldn't be sober enough to talk even if she did come back downstairs, what with the alcohol and whatever drugs the plastic surgeon had in store for her.

"I was hired to look for a runaway daughter a couple of days ago—the brother hired me. I went to the high school and hit the streets but no luck. Then I thought maybe I ought to check it out with her folks, Lon, since I hadn't, so I came over here and the old man—I mean, the decedent—was sort of ragging me around and then he took a gulp of his drink and wham. Dropped down dead. If you ask me, I think something funny is going on." I let out a long breath and took another. "Furthermore, Lon, I think you've got some great suspects here—"

"Just hold your horses, Mavis. I'll do the thinking around here—Jesus Christ. Everyone says it was a heart attack."

"Well if that's all it was, why are you here?" I asked.

James Rush stopped what he was doing and glanced at Lon.

Lon cleared his throat. "Hey, I just got a call from dispatch. What do I know?" He shrugged.

The medical examiner arrived. The guests drew back the lace curtains and peered out the windows as the ME did a five-minute preliminary examination. I'm afraid I stared, too. When the ME moved back, other people stepped in with cameras and other equipment and did their bit. Finally, they put Harrison Lawson into a body bag and carried him out.

"What's it look like, Sam?" Lon asked. "Heart attack?"

"I'm unclear. I'll need his medical history, of course, and I'll have to do an autopsy to be sure. Pour me a belt there, will you, son?" Sam said to Rush who still played host. Sam turned his lined and worn face in my direction and nodded. I remembered the old man from when I'd worked for the county. He had to be close to retirement.

"Could it have been something else? Could there have been another cause of death?" Lon asked.

"Possibly, but like I said, the autopsy . . ." Sam said, as his eyes met Lon's.

"So you think it was natural causes?" Lon asked.

"How many times do I have to say it?" Sam said.

Rush handed a tall glass to Sam.

"That's a good boy," Sam said and emptied the glass with one long swallow. "Check with me later, Lon," he said. "I'll be able to tell you a whole lot more." He banged the glass down on the bar and left.

"Sure you don't want that drink now, Detective?" Rush asked.

"Can't—on duty. I'll take a water like Mavis. Now, you say everyone was standing around and all of a sudden the man just drops dead?"

"Yes. He groaned or at least made some kind of noise. He was in the middle of a conversation with Miss Davis here, swallowed from his drink, and fell down. Bart pronounced him dead," Rush said.

"Bart—that's the doctor that's upstairs with the missus?"

"Yes. Actually, he's a plastic surgeon, but he agreed to stay with her until her family physician could be reached to come over." Rush poured himself another generous ration of liquor and took a drink from it. Trying to fill up his hollow leg, I imagine.

"Tell me, Mr. Rush, who do you know that would like to have seen Mr. Lawson dead?" Lon asked.

Rush's harsh laughter surprised me. "Aren't you jumping to conclusions?"

Lon said, "Humor me."

"Well, that's hard to say, Lon. Any number of people who he stepped on during his rise to the top. You know he was president of the board and managing director of National Insurance Trust?"

Lon shook his head. He sat on a bar stool next to me. I thought he'd drool if he didn't quit staring at the booze bottles perched on the bar. He unbuttoned his collar and loosened his tie. "He had a lot of power."

"Yes. Actually, he'd mellowed quite a bit in the past ten or eleven years. He could still be brusque at times, but usually his heart wasn't in it." Rush looked at me. "You realize he was just giving you a hard time for the fun of it, don't you, Miss Davis?"

"It was a barrel of laughs," I said. I wanted a cigarette in the worst way. Or at least a piece of chocolate.

Lon ignored me and turned back to Rush. "Why do you think he'd mellowed?"

Rush tipped his glass up for another swallow before answering. "Simple. He'd gotten what he wanted."

"Well, I guess that's all, Mr. Rush," Lon said. "We'll be in contact if there's anything else. Don't want to keep you."

"Oh, I don't mind," Rush said with a smooth look. "All right if I stay around? You might need my help."

"Not at all," Lon said. "Be glad to have you."

I was trying to be patient while the mutual admiration society finished its meeting. It was obvious that Lon was in awe of this man—that he thought the G. in James G. Rush stood for God. It was also obvious that Rush was buttering up Lon. For what reason I'd have to get to the bottom of later. All I knew was that I wanted to get my turn over and get out. I still had children to locate.

Finally, Lon seemed to remember I was there. "What are you waiting for, Mavis, get outta here."

I grinned, left the bottle of water on the bar, and made haste toward the door.

"Just be available if I want you later," he called after me.

Without turning around, I waved. I wasn't giving him a chance to change his mind.

Chapter Seven

On my way home, I stopped by the office to check my messages. Candy and Margaret were still there.

"Couldn't wait until Monday, huh?" I said when I flung open the door. They were sitting at their desks behind the counter, talking.

Margaret's presence surprised me. Of late, she had been quick to go home in the evenings. Recently, she had acquired a boyfriend, but I think she thought that I didn't know that it was, for her, a serious affair.

Candy usually didn't waste any time leaving at five, either. Maybe her presence was a sign of maturity, that she was feeling some responsibility. I hoped so.

"Margaret, I'm glad you're here. Google heart attack symptoms for me, would you?" I asked.

Candy jumped up and ran to me. "Tommy called, Mavis."

Not sure that I had the energy to handle any more surprises, I sagged when I got to the counter. "What'd he say?"

Margaret interceded. "He said to tell you that he's okay, that you don't have to look for Jeanine anymore, that they're together, and you could keep the money." Margaret's eyes shot daggers at Candy. "Before I could ask him anything more, the phone disconnected."

Before I let them say another word, I locked up, stepped out of my shoes, and padded through the swinging door into the kitchen to light a fire under the kettle. There wasn't anything else they could say that couldn't wait until I brewed a cup of tea.

Candy and Margaret exchanged a few slightly heated words before following after me. By then, I had the kettle filled and on the burner and had propped myself up in a chair. I massaged my feet. Standing on that concrete around the swimming pool made the bottoms ache. "Is the computer still on?"

"Aren't you going to say anything?" Candy asked.

"Yes, Margaret, please Google heart attack symptoms for me, okay?" They didn't know it, but they were getting my reaction. I was tired.

Margaret left the kitchen. The silence was broken only by the gas flames hissing under the kettle and Candy's anticipatory breathing. Then the bell of the phone pierced the quiet. I snatched the kitchen extension, "Mavis Davis."

"It's me." Ben's low voice seemed to echo loudly through the line.

"Hi," I said, realizing there was a sigh in my voice. I must be more overtaxed than I thought.

"What's up? I tried you at home, but didn't get an answer." The note of concern in his voice made me feel good. "What are you doing at the office so late?"

"I know you're not going to believe this, Ben, but I happened to be in the wrong place at the wrong time."

"Uh-oh," he said. "What happened now?"

I hated to tell him, but it would not do our relationship any good for him to hear about it at the police station. "Well, you know that boy who was here yesterday?"

"Uh-huh."

Margaret returned with a handful of printer paper.

"Well—I was in the middle of a conversation with his father when the man dropped dead at my feet."

Candy sucked breath. So did Ben. The water boiled. The whistling of the kettle resounded off the walls. With the telephone receiver tucked into my shoulder, I grabbed my oversized teacup from the edge of the sink, pulled a teabag out of the box, filled the cup with water, and Ben still hadn't said anything.

"Hey. Are you still there, Ben?"

"Yep. What was the cause of death?"

"I don't know. Everybody said it looked like a heart attack."

"But you don't think so, is that it?" Ben asked. He knew me so well.

"Holy shit," Candy said and ducked when I frowned in her direction.

Margaret just shook her head slowly as she watched me. I scribbled the word *stroke* on a paper napkin and she left the kitchen again.

"I haven't done anything wrong, Ben. It just happened." I held the tea bag by its string and bobbed it up and down in the water, waiting for his next words, and thinking how good it would feel to pull the sheets up over my toes and drop my head to my pillow when I finally got home.

"I'm coming right over," Ben said.

"No—don't—"

The phone clicked, and the dial tone hummed. I held out the receiver so Candy could hear before I hung up. Discarding the tea bag, I dumped sweetener and milk into my cup and fell back into my chair.

"There are over three million heart attack sites on the Internet," Margaret said from the doorway. "I printed out some information from the first one. Strokes are almost as bad."

I snatched the papers from her hand.

"Tommy's case is getting to be a mess, isn't it, Mavis?" Margaret asked in a quiet voice.

"You said it." The hot tea felt good as it burned its way down my throat.

"Tommy's father died while you were at their house?" Candy asked.

"That's what I said, Candy," I answered a bit too sharply.

"Wow." She clutched her backpack to her chest.

Glancing at the first few pages, I saw that the symptoms seemed to match except for one or two things.

"What's wrong, Mavis?" Margaret asked.

"Something's not right here." I felt downcast, disheartened, and yes, still overwhelmed. "I don't know," I answered. "Margaret, could you Google poison symptoms?"

"So you think it could be murder?" Candy asked, jumping out of her chair and waving her arms about. "This could be our second murder case."

"I haven't been hired to solve a murder, Candy." I leaned back and envied her energy. "If it is a murder."

"Like you still have Tommy's case, though," Candy said.

"Not from what y'all said when I came in. He's fired me."

"Like when did you let a little thing like that stop you?" Candy asked, getting in my face. "Besides, you know, we didn't get a chance to tell you how mysterious the phone call was."

Margaret returned. "There's over a million poison Web sites."

"So how mysterious was the phone call, ladies?" I asked. I couldn't deal with the Internet when I was so tired. It would have to wait. Besides, Ben was fixing to arrive and jump my case for something I didn't do.

"The operator," Candy said as she put down her book bag and bopped over to the refrigerator, sticking her head inside.

"What operator?"

"You tell her, Margaret," Candy said. "Like Margaret took the call while I was in the bathroom." She pulled out a soda and popped the top on it, slurping from the can.

Margaret's eyes shined. She stood with importance, her hands folded in front of her. She wet her lips before she began. "Well, Mavis, I was just sitting here waiting for you to come back and tell us what had transpired at the Lawson home. Candy told me that's where you'd gone. This was after I got back from serving the subpoenas, after you dropped Candy off. I did get them served okay, by the way."

"Good." I wasn't sure I had the patience for this, but I smiled encouragingly at Margaret and nodded my head.

"Anyway, as I was saying, I was sitting behind the counter at the telephone. Candy had been answering it while I was gone and actually since I'd come back because she said you said for her to answer it because it might be one of the kids from her school, but Candy was in the bathroom, like she said. It rang and I picked it up and said hello." Margaret smiled broadly.

I could tell she was getting to the good part and watched her without enthusiasm.

"I heard some noise in the background—just briefly—and then the operator said, 'Go ahead, sir.' " She stopped and stared at me.

I stared back, my mouth slack as I waited. She didn't say anything else. My eyes went to Candy who was gulping down her drink. No one said anything. "Yes?"

"That's it," Margaret said.

"That's what?"

"Like, don't you get it, Mavis?" Candy cried.

"Get what?"

"The operator."

"Yes . . . the operator?"

"It was an out-of-town call, Mavis," Margaret said, her eyes as large as DVDs. "It wasn't on a cell phone or a regular phone line. It had to be some kind of assisted call."

"Okay. So?"

"So Tommy was like calling from out of town," Candy practically yelled. "That means that if he and Jeanine are together, like they're not home, you know, and like they're out of town, then it must be a kidnapping."

"How do you figure?"

"See, Mavis," Margaret started very slowly, patiently, like she was speaking to a small child. "We figure that the kidnappers gave Tommy exact change for a long-distance phone call. Then, they told him precisely what to say. Then, after he said it, they hung up the phone before he could give us any more information."

"Or any clues," Candy said as she tripped around the room.

"Oh . . . right," I said, my eyes rolling up to the ceiling in spite of myself.

"You don't think so, Mavis?" Margaret asked, sounding hurt.

"No, I don't think so," I said.

"Aw," Candy said.

"You guys kill me," I said. "Tommy said he was okay, right?"

"Yes," Margaret replied.

"He didn't say anyone was demanding money or anything, did he?"

"No," Margaret said.

"So what indication did he give you that he needed our help?"

"Well, why would he hang up just like that?" Candy asked.

I shook my head. "Did it ever occur to either one of you that maybe something is going on that we don't know about?"

They exchanged glances and bowed their heads. They were both pros at hang-dog looks.

"The whole family situation is more than a little strange," I said in defense of myself.

Both of them lifted their eyes to stare at me silently.

"Well, it is, whether you two like it or not. Number one," I held out a forefinger. "Tommy comes to us yesterday with a story about how his dear little rich sister with a bad temper is gone, and he thinks she's been kidnapped. Number two, her own mother says she thinks the kid's a runaway. Who knows better than a mother?" They exchanged looks again. "Number three, I get to the Lawson house, and they're having people over for cocktails and a cookout. Don't you think that's a little weird? Number whatever, something causes Mr. Lawson to drop dead, then Tommy calls here at about the same time. On top of that, some lady told me that those kids were adopted and implied that there was something significant about it. Come on, you two don't think there's more to this than meets the eye?"

"We just think Tommy's in trouble, that's all," Margaret whispered into her lap.

Candy nodded and actually squeezed Margaret's shoulder.

I gulped my tea and enjoyed feeling the warmth cascade down inside my chest as I studied their faces. "What's it going to take to convince you girls that we don't need to be involved in this?"

Candy jumped up. "A face-to-face talk with Tommy."

Margaret said, "I think you should at least go back and tell his mother that he called and said he's all right. The poor woman has so much on her mind right now—husband dead and children missing. Poor little thing."

"If you'd seen her, Margaret, you wouldn't call her that."

"Well . . . you're the boss, Mavis," Margaret said.

"Thanks a lot, Margaret."

There was a sharp banging on the door. I shook my head at them as I got up to let Ben in. "Don't say anything about what I said about Mr. Lawson. And Margaret, hide that printout and shut down the computer. Hurry."

I took my time peeking out to confirm it was Ben. He looked very handsome in a coat and tie. He must have had to testify in court. When I opened the door, offering up my cheek for him to kiss, he brushed past me, rather rudely, but not unexpectedly. Closing the door behind him, I pushed past him in return. "Come on in the kitchen and join the fun."

I sat back in my chair, pulled my feet up under me, and looked up at Ben. After he'd greeted Margaret and Candy, I offered him something to drink.

"Nope," he said, not quite harshly. He swung the fourth chair around backwards and straddled it. "Spill it, Mavis."

I began. I told him everything I thought he ought to know. His eyes did the narrowing bit as I recounted what had happened. When I was finished, he said, "That's not so bad. You're really not involved in murder, are you?"

"No, just runaways." I dared not mention that Candy and Margaret thought it was a kidnapping.

"Of course you'll back off that now, right?"

"What back off? I might have a fee to earn."

"Damn it, give me your word that you won't get involved in this case if it turns out to be more than a heart attack."

"There's still the boy and girl to find," I said.

Candy's face broke out into a grin, which she attempted to conceal behind her hand. Margaret quit chewing on her thumbnail and looked down into her lap. She had gotten quite good at that posture.

Here we go again. Ben on the issuing end of orders. Me on the receiving end. Story of my life.

"I don't think I can do that, Ben," I said softly, but firmly. "Tommy's my client. If his case is tied to some other complications, then I'm in."

"Why did I know you were going to say that?" His deep voice sounded like advancing thunder.

I shrugged for the umpteenth time that day.

"Why do I get the feeling that you're going to do whatever you feel like doing?" The thunder grew closer. Lightning was imminent.

I forced my eyes to form the most innocent of looks and shook my head. "Dunno."

He changed tactics on me. "I don't want to fight with you, Mavie," Ben said in his conniving, coaxing voice.

"Me, neither, honey," I said in a sugary voice that easily matched his. I slipped my left hand into his right as it rested on the table and intertwined our fingers.

"All right then," he said. "You just promise me that you won't get involved in any investigation unless you absolutely have to. And I mean absolutely."

"I promise I won't investigate Harrison Lawson's case unless absolutely necessary," I said, holding up three fingers. "On my honor."

He leaned forward and gave me a little peck. "Why don't you let me take you home now?" he asked, his lips turning up into a sly smile.

I knew exactly what he had in mind, and it was all right

with me. I'd find the energy for a little cuddle. "Why not follow me?"

After pulling on my shoes, I stood. We both turned to the girls. "Good night," we said in unison. "Have a pleasant evening."

Chapter Eight

The following morning, after a brief stop at the office to review the pages about heart attack and stroke that Margaret had printed out and left on my desk, I wended my way to the University of Houston main campus. I knew my friend, Stanhope, would be there. He was always there, either teaching or doing what chemists do in their labs. That's why our love life had been so lousy back when. And how we became mere friends. But that's another story.

Anyway, I found him, cockeyed as ever as he peered sideways into a microscope.

"Hey, guy," I called out. "Got time to talk to an old friend?"

His bald head popped up; he slid off his stool; and his face broke out into a grin as he lowered his glasses down to his nose. Leaning down to give me a hug, he said, "Always have time for you, Mavis." Which we both knew was a lie, but that's okay.

"You're lookin' good, big fella." Tall and as thin as vermicelli, Stanhope should have been a basketball player. "Need to eat more, though." I whacked him in the stomach with the back of my hand.

He feigned injury. "Did you come here to beat me up or some other ulterior motive as usual?"

"Awww—I like that. Can't a friend come visit a friend once in a while?"

Stanhope nodded. "Right."

"Well, since you asked." I pulled a stool over next to his and sat down. "I was at a party when this man drops down dead."

He rolled his eyes so far back in his head that for a moment I thought he'd become comatose.

"Now, just wait a minute. I had nothing to do with that. I was talking to the guy, though, and later, when the police got there, I saw a little bottle, but the cops got it. It was like one of those perfume sample bottles you get in a department store."

"Your point being—"

"I think he was poisoned."

He laughed. "Not much evidence to go on, Mavis. He drops dead. You see a bottle."

"Well, here's the thing. Everybody at the scene kept trying to say he had a heart attack, but the whole time I was there, he kept wiping his mouth and putting his hand on his stomach. He perspired a lot. He seemed unsteady on his feet. His eyes were like pools of bloodshot water."

He shook his head. "Still not enough to go on, Mavis."

"Someone told me that he had heart problems, but that he hadn't had a heart attack or any trouble in a long time. I was around a man who had a heart attack, years ago, and it seems to me they fall down and make heart-wrenching, no pun intended, noises. Am I right?"

"I'm a chemist, Mavis, not a doctor. What do you want me to say?"

I shrugged. "Okay then, tell me what the symptoms of poisoning are."

Stan screwed up his face. "Any number of things. It depends on what kind of poison. Cyanide, arsenic, drain cleaner—they all have some symptoms the same and some different. Nausea, stomach pains, diarrhea, vomiting, weakness, irregular heartbeat, dilation of pupils, dizziness—"

"Oh, I guess I wasted a trip over here. I just thought you'd be able to tell me."

"Sorry to disappoint you. Why don't you do an Internet search and you can read all about them and see if what you observed in the man matches any of them."

I jumped off the stool. "Yeah, I could do that. Or get Margaret to do it." I grinned. I wasn't going to tell him that Margaret told me how many sites there were. "I just thought it'd be easier to ask you."

"Well, thanks for your vote of confidence. See if you can figure out at least what type of poison it was, like one of the classic ones I mentioned or a household poison or a poisonous plant or a fungi or a medical poison or—"

"Okay, okay. I got the picture. Sorry to bother you." I kissed his cheek. "You're a doll, as usual. You could have just kicked me out."

"Hey, you want to have a drink sometime?"

"Aw, that's sweet Stan, but I'm still with Ben."

"Just as friends, then."

I headed for the door. "I don't think so, but thanks for asking." His offer was tempting but not enough to have to explain it to Ben.

On the way to the Lawson home, I asked myself what the heck I thought I was doing. Was I ready to commit myself to investigating Lawson's death? My imagination had run away with me. There hadn't even been an autopsy. No one had said he was murdered. It could have been a simple heart attack. After all, from the looks of things, he practically drank himself to death.

When I arrived back at the Lawson home, the housekeeper again confronted me at the door. This time, the woman wore an air of dejection like a thin coat. She'd lost her drill-sergeant attitude and didn't give me any trouble when I asked to see Hilary Lawson.

She put me in the library, but after she left, I went out by the pool. Every sign of the party the day before had been cleared away. The flowers and shrubbery served as a barrier to outside noise. My footsteps seemed to echo as I approached the bar and stood where I had been when Mr. Lawson met his demise. I tried to remember where everyone was, what they were doing, and how they had reacted when he dropped dead.

Out of more than idle curiosity, I opened the cabinet beneath the bar. To my surprise, the bottle with the foreign label from which Mr. Lawson had poured his drink was still there. Typical of Lon's police work. It was some kind of schnapps, whatever that was, imported from Germany. I wanted to take the bottle with me, but my bag wasn't large enough to hide it and then there was the small problem of an interruption.

"Miss Davis?"

I gave the bottle a last glance, noting that it had been opened but was awfully full, and closed the cabinet door, turning toward the voice. "Good afternoon, Mrs. Lawson." She stood in front of a gigantic philodendron, it framing her like a photograph.

Her spike-heeled black pumps made a sharp rapping sound on the concrete as she approached me with her right hand outstretched. In her left, she held a pair of black-framed sunglasses. A long-sleeved black sheath fell to mid-calf. We shook hands this time. Hers felt cold and dry, but she gave a decent shake and smiled a melancholy smile that didn't appear genuine. "Good afternoon, Miss Davis." Her clear blue eyes feigned puzzlement and a frown wrinkled her forehead.

"I don't want to take up a lot of your time, Mrs. Lawson, but we do have some unfinished business."

"Not at all, Miss Davis. Let's go into the resource room where we'll be more comfortable." She led me inside and indicated a hard-backed chair. "Please have a seat." I thought it was the old "put them in an uncomfortable chair and they won't stay long" routine. She positioned herself on the sofa, her hands folded over the glasses in her lap.

It's not that I'm suspicious by nature, but for a moment, she rendered me speechless. Her attitude—indeed, her whole demeanor—had done a hundred-and-eighty-degree reverse, which forced me to change my own attitude and try to be as good an actress as she appeared to be.

It seemed that we stared at each other for eons before I finally cleared my throat to speak. "Uh, I realize that you're going through a difficult time right now—what with the passing of your husband yesterday." I watched her face, not knowing what to expect.

Her eyes stayed on mine, unblinking, and she nodded her head.

"I'd like to offer my condolences to you in that regard." I felt as awkward as a fledgling.

"You're very kind."

"I didn't come here to discuss your husband, though, Mrs. Lawson. I wanted to talk to you about Tommy and Jeanine."

"Yes?" A hopeful expression sprang onto her face.

"Have you heard from them?"

"No . . . no, I haven't." Her lashes fluttered down over her beautiful blues.

"Tommy called my office yesterday."

"Is he all right?" She edged forward on the sofa and her eyes grew wide.

"I didn't speak to him myself. He called while I was here.

My assistant, Margaret Applebaum, talked to him. According to her, he said that both he and Jeanine were okay, that they were together, and that he didn't need my services any longer." I watched for a reaction, but she only appeared pensive. "I came over here to tell you that and to ask if you think they're really all right or if you think I should continue to try to find them."

While I spoke, I noticed her hands clench into fists and her knuckles turn very white. She refrained from speaking for a good thirty seconds. She gritted her teeth, the muscles in her jaws flexing, her mouth formed a tight, little line, her dark eyebrows drew together, then her face relaxed and two little tears rolled down her cheeks, one from each eye.

"What is it?" I asked.

She shook her head and put a small fist to her mouth, her eyes squeezed shut. Then she produced an embroidered handkerchief out of nowhere and dabbed at her face. I watched as she shivered and sniffed and then opened her eyes. She said, "I'm all right. I usually pride myself at being able to maintain control of my emotions. I'm sorry. Please forgive me." She looked as if the dam would burst at any second.

Who was the real Hilary Lawson? She appeared to be distraught, but how could I really tell? I wondered if she was still taking the medication the doctor had prescribed. It didn't look like it. Should I call for the housekeeper? I glanced around the room, wanting to do or say something helpful. "How about if I come back another time?" I stood to leave.

"No, no. I'm all right, really. Sit. Let me ring for tea," she said, her voice hoarse. I watched as she seemed to float behind the bar and back again to the sofa.

Shortly thereafter, the housekeeper appeared and Mrs. Lawson said softly, "We'll have tea, Frankie."

Frankie nodded, turned, and shuffled back out of the room.

"I didn't mean to be a bother, Mrs. Lawson," I said. "I just thought you'd like to know that we heard from your kids."

Frowning, she shook her head again. "No bother. I haven't had breakfast anyway. Frankie will bring something for us to eat with the tea." Her eyes steadied on mine. "Didn't Tommy say anything else, Miss Davis?"

"No, I'm afraid not, Mrs. Lawson. It was a rather short phone call. Margaret said he hung up abruptly."

Another long silence.

Eyebrows knitted together, she compressed her lips a moment and then said, "He didn't say where he was calling from?"

"No."

"No indication whatsoever?"

"No, ma'am, I'm sorry. Oh—it was long distance, though, if that's any help."

"Long distance—"

"Yes. Must have been a pay phone because there was an operator's voice before he began to talk."

She nodded, her eyes glazed as if she was deep in thought.

I heard slow footsteps. Frankie padded to the coffee table between us and set down the silver tray and tea service. She handed each of us a peach-colored linen napkin. Tiny sandwiches filled one plate, sugar cookies, another. Two sets of thin china cups and saucers and a fat silver pot took up the rest of the space on the tray.

"Shall I pour?" Frankie asked in an odd low voice as she crouched over the tray. I couldn't quite see her expression.

Mrs. Lawson's smile did not extend to her eyes. "That won't be necessary, Frankie. Thank you."

The old woman straightened up, smoothed her apron, ran her eyes across my face, and shuffled away.

Mrs. Lawson poured. "Lemon or milk?"

"Milk."

"Sugar or sweetener?"

"Sweetener."

I watched as she dipped a tiny silver spoon into a powdery substance and sweetened my tea, then a drop of milk. She handed me the cup. While I stirred, she poured for herself. It was gratifying to see that she dipped the tiny silver spoon into the powdery substance and sweetened her own tea or I would have been in an awkward situation, not knowing what was in store for me. Not that I have a suspicious mind, ha. She handed me an empty plate, took one for herself, placed some sandwiches and two cookies on it, and sat back. "Help yourself, please."

I hadn't eaten breakfast, either, yet considering the premises I hesitated to pig out.

"Please, Miss Davis, make yourself at home." She watched me, probably putting me to some kind of test. I just knew she was hoping I'd dump it. She smiled. I chastised myself for my ill thoughts. My awkwardness was probably the farthest thing from the poor woman's mind. Having convinced myself, I decided to eat.

I had just stuffed a sandwich into my face when Mrs. Lawson decided to pour her heart out. "I'm really concerned about the children, because if my husband murdered Harrison, the children may be next."

I almost choked. I hadn't said anything about murder. Chewing vigorously, my watering eyes affixed themselves on her now-vacant-looking ones. When I swallowed, I started to speak, but she beat me to it.

"I tried to tell the police yesterday, but they wouldn't

listen. You were still here then, weren't you?" She took a dainty sip of her tea and patted her lips with her napkin.

I shook my head. Was she loony? Her voice had a strange quality to it, like a child reading from a fairy story.

"They wouldn't listen," she said. Then she gave me an odd look and added, "James wouldn't either."

"I will, Mrs. Lawson. That is—if you want to tell me." And how.

She took another sip of her tea and munched a bit of cookie. Her eyes wore a distant look, as though she were caught in a daydream. "That's why I was angry with you yesterday."

Angry with little old me? "What was?"

"I was afraid he'd hurt them."

I tilted my head as though to clear water out of my ears. I didn't know what the hell she meant. I couldn't catch her eye as she seemed to be in a dream-like state, her eyes fixed in the distance. Someplace like Never, Never Land, I thought. "Who, Mrs. Lawson? Who do you think might hurt the children?"

"My husband."

We were getting nowhere fast. "He's de—de—passed away."

"No. You don't understand." She finally fixed her eyes on mine. "I mean Arthur."

"Arthur? Who's that?"

"My first husband." She looked at me as though I was quite stupid.

I almost did dump the plate as I half rose off the chair. I caught it with my left hand, still holding my cup and saucer in my right, and steadied myself while our eyes locked. Some of what I'd learned the day before from her friend what's-her-name was becoming clear. I smiled like I had no knowledge of the situation.

"Arthur Woodridge," she said.

"Your first husband?" I asked.

"Yes. The children's real father."

"You think he's got them?"

"I'm sure of it."

"Why's that?"

"There's no other logical explanation."

"For their disappearance?"

"And for Harrison's murder."

"I'm afraid I got lost somewhere in the shuffle."

"He said he'd get me."

"When?"

"Twelve—thirteen years ago."

"That's the last time you talked to him?"

"Yes."

"And where was that?"

"In the courtroom."

"In the courtroom?"

"After the trial."

"After you fought a custody battle?"

"No. Right after he was sentenced to prison."

"Your ex-husband went to prison?"

"Yes."

"For what?"

"Having sex with the children."

Chapter Nine

It was at this point that the plate of sandwich and cookies made like a set of skis, skidded down my lap, and landed at her feet. The cookies bounced, one landing on top of her shoe. In my attempt to catch the plate, my cup fell over, tea cascading off the saucer onto the carpet. I righted it before too much soaked in, but it was a shame about that chip.

Replacing the cup and saucer on the tray, I mopped at the tea with my napkin, grabbed the cookies, put them back with the sandwich, put it on the tray, and wiped off the top of her shoe. Brushing at my clothes, I sat back down and reached into my bag for a cigarette before remembering, again, that I had quit. I realized, then, how often I used my cigarettes to disguise or assist with something else that was going on. In this case, I needed a few moments to digest what she'd said. What an addict I am.

All the while, Mrs. Lawson sat watching. Then she said something about not being concerned about my little accident. I tried to stop my brain from calculating too quickly what could be in store for those two missing teenagers if what she said was true. Her ex a child molester? Would the kids be okay? Why would they go with him? Of course, the possibility still existed that they weren't even with the man. Then again, what if they were and prison had messed with his mind and he was a worse pervert than ever and . . . never mind, I must stay in the present moment.

After I settled back on my perch and apologized profusely a number of times, Mrs. Lawson said, "I'm sorry I got you so upset. For some reason, I got the impression that you knew all of this."

I wagged my head. No question she was as sharp as I suspected. "Lady, if I had known any of this, I wouldn't have been here sipping tea with you. I would have been moving mountains in search of your children."

She heaved a deep sigh and smiled. "I wanted to tell you yesterday. If it hadn't been for Harrison . . ."

I nodded. Sure she did. And it had only been the inconvenience of her present husband's death that had stopped her.

"I mean, I contemplated telling you when you first appeared at the door but didn't get a chance. You see, when Jeanine turned up missing, my first thought was that she was just angry and would return home. I began to worry when she didn't."

"I can see why." I nodded, noting her skill.

"Let me clarify."

"Sure." I put my hand on my knee to stop my foot from tapping. The whole scene made me a little nervous, but I was all ears.

Her face relaxed a tad, and her lips turned up at the corners as she looked at me. "It sounded crazy to Harrison, Miss Davis, but when the authorities began releasing so many prisoners so quickly in recent years—because of the overcrowding in the prisons, you know—I got worried that Arthur would be among them and would come and get us. He was very bitter about the jury's verdict. When he turned and looked at me in the courtroom that day—and said he would get me—I knew by the look in his eye that he meant it."

"How many years did he get for . . . that?"

"Fifty, but you know they get all kinds of credit for good behavior from what I understand. Remember a year ago they released that woman who hired that man to kill her parents? I read about that in the newspaper. She received two life sentences, but they let her out after ten years."

"It's called good time." I shook my head. "To think that he might be out after twelve or thirteen. Well, it shouldn't be any big surprise to me, but a convicted child molester . . ."

"You see, Miss Davis, Arthur used to work at the insurance company with Harrison. I did, too. That's where I met Harrison. He was my boss. After Harrison and I got married, I quit work so I could stay home with the children."

And to think I thought she came from money.

"When I first suspected what Arthur was doing with the children, I didn't know where to turn, so I went to Harrison who turned out to be a great help. He stood by me through the child welfare and police investigations. They found out that Arthur did some terrible things." She had that faraway look again.

"Anyway, after Arthur was convicted, it seemed only natural that Harrison and I should get married, so I got a divorce from Arthur after he went to prison. After our marriage, we decided that Harrison should adopt the children. We had Arthur's parental rights cut off, and Harrison adopted them."

"Then recently you got word that Arthur had gotten out of prison?" I asked.

"Yes, but not right away. It wasn't until Jeanine was gone overnight and then Tommy . . . I didn't tell the police what I suspected about Jeanine because I couldn't be sure, but after the school principal called, Harrison called our attorney who made inquiries." She picked up her teacup and sipped, patted her lips with her napkin, and continued, "We had just gotten word that Arthur had made his parole when everyone showed up for the party. Harrison said we should go on, business as usual. He didn't think Arthur would hurt the children. In fact, I was having trouble convincing him that Arthur took them. And then you came."

"And then he died—"

"Yes. I just can't figure out how Arthur managed all of it. I will, though, once I get my children back."

"So you think Arthur, the children's father, killed Mr. Lawson after he took the children? Do you have any proof, Mrs. Lawson?"

"Miss Davis," she said with that trance-like expression again. "I don't need proof. I know it in here." She placed her hand on her breast.

Oh, brother. I thought she'd not only had drama lessons but melodrama lessons. I nodded again. "What do you think he'll do to them?"

She sighed. "I don't know." Her blue eyes searched mine. She grimaced. "If he was sick enough to do what he did back then, there's no telling how sick he is now. I can't imagine what he's been through, there in prison."

"I can. I'm surprised the other inmates didn't kill him," I said, remembering all the stories I'd heard.

She sipped her tea, her eyes getting that faraway look again. The room grew still. A bird twittered outside. The air-conditioning kicked on. Cool air hit the back of my neck.

After a few minutes, our eyes met. She said, "Do you still want to find my children, Mavis?" She blinked rapidly. "May I call you Mavis? Because, if so, I'll pay you myself."

"Certainly." I stared down at my lap, determined to be in control of the situation and see what else I could find out. At the same time, I didn't want to tip her off that I didn't buy everything she was trying to sell. I got out a notepad and pen. "Tell me everything you can about your ex-husband. All of his habits. What he liked to do with his time off. Who his friends were. Where you think he might be. Everything."

For the next hour, Hilary Lawson and I had an in-depth discussion about Arthur Woodridge. By the time we were through, I felt as if I knew him as well as she thought she did. She even remembered that his folks used to own a cabin out in the woods in one of the counties outside of Houston, though she had never deigned to set foot in it. She thought his parents probably left it to him in their wills. She couldn't remember exactly where it was located, but if I could find it, and he did own it, it would be the most logical place to look for him and the kids. Kelby McAfee might know more about it since he and Arthur used to be such good friends before Arthur went to prison.

I was about to get into my car when Frankie beckoned to me from the side of the house. No one appeared to be looking out of the front windows so I went over to her. "What is it?"

She pulled rather roughly on my arm until we were out of view of the front windows. "Miz Davis, Arthur didn't have anything to do with Mr. Lawson's death." Her breath came in quick, short gasps as if she'd been running.

"How do you know that?"

"I know him. He wasn't the sort. All he wanted was to see the children." She seemed earnest. Her eyes didn't waver. But everyone seemed to have a motive for everything these days. I wondered what hers was.

"How did you know about the children?"

Frankie studied the concrete under our feet.

"Frankie . . ."

"So I talked to him, so I told them they should go see him," she said. "You won't tell on me, will you?"

I tried to hide my surprise. "Not if you tell me everything."

"There isn't time—she'll catch me."

"Who—Hilary? What could she do to you?"

"She'd let me go after all these years, and where am I to get another job these days at my age?"

"You're wasting time, Frankie. Just tell me what you know and I won't keep you."

"I know he didn't do what she said he did."

"How do you know that?"

"He told me so."

"Great."

"No," she said, grabbing my arm again. "You'd have to know him. He wrote to me."

"From prison?"

She nodded.

"What's he like?"

"A very nice man who ended up with the wrong woman." She frowned.

"Why didn't you come forward at the trial?"

"I couldn't, Miz Davis. I had no proof. I just knew he wouldn't do what she said he did to those babies, but who would believe me? I'm just a poor, old woman from the wrong side of town who's lucky to end up working in River Oaks. Besides, she had Harrison Lawson behind her and he was powerful even then."

"Did you know Arthur was getting out of prison?"

"He wrote and told me and asked if I'd talk to Jeanine and Tommy."

"So Tommy did know where Jeanine had gone."

"He wouldn't go at first, but she made him promise to keep it a secret. She was supposed to come back home."

"Why didn't she?"

"I don't know, Miz Davis. There's no predicting that girl. The way I figure it, she contacted Tommy and got him to come. I'm sure they're all right, though."

"You don't know that, Frankie."

"I do—in my heart."

"Not if Arthur killed Harrison Lawson."

"He didn't, though, not Mr. Woodridge. He never came near the house."

"But you think it wasn't a heart attack, too?"

"Mr. Lawson had a heart attack some time ago, sure, but since then he'd been taking good care of himself, eating right, exercising. No, someone did something to him, and if it wasn't Miz Lawson then it was someone who was here the night before, for dinner."

"Dinner? Why didn't Mrs. Lawson mention that?"

"I don't know. I guess she wants it to be Mr. Woodridge. All I know is, it wasn't."

"Who was here that night?"

"I can tell you who was invited. She gave me the night off—said since the kids weren't here if I'd cook dinner then I could have a night out. The Hadleys—"

"Hadley. He's the short, ugly man with the holes in his face?"

"That's right, Mr. Clayton Hadley. He's in some property doings with Mr. Lawson. I mean, he was. Then there was the Smythes—"

"The stockbroker."

"Yes. And the McAfees and Mr. Rush with some big blonde girl who was all over him so much it was embarrassing. He arrived early with her, just as I was leaving."

I laughed. "Is that it?"

"Yes. Ten, including Mr. and Miz Lawson."

"Well, thank you, Frankie. You've been very helpful." I took her hand and shook it.

"You're not going to tell on me, are you?" she asked, a note of urgency in her voice.

"No," I said. "Do you know where Arthur took the kids?"

She shook her head. "If they're not in that cabin, then I don't know. They haven't called. I guess they're afraid Miz Lawson will answer the phone."

I shouldn't have been surprised that she'd overheard our conversation. "Thanks. You've been a big help." I squeezed her hand. "Oh, one more thing. Mr. Lawson was drinking schnapps at the time of his death. Was that his usual drink?"

"Lord, yes. It's awful stuff and no one else will touch it, but Miz Lawson has to be sure there is always some on hand—I mean she did." Frankie shrugged. "Well, anyway . . ."

"Thanks again. You're a doll." The last time I saw her, she smiled for the first time since I met her.

Chapter Ten

I would have been chomping at the bit all weekend if Ben and I hadn't planned to spend it together. Not only did he sleep over on Saturday night, which was a rarity, but on Sunday we drove the fifty miles to Galveston Island and went to the beach, one of my favorite activities. I could only hope the kids were really okay, just as they'd told the girls.

Come Monday, since I was still hired to find the kids, I finally made it to the National Insurance Trust offices. They were all thick glass, deep pile carpeting, and huge green plants on the fourteenth floor of a building not far from the Allen Parkway. Outside, the building looked like hundreds of huge mirrors stuck together. I always wondered why they didn't reflect the sun so much that it blinded people or caused airplanes to crash, but apparently they didn't.

The front office had a receptionist that looked like a gazillion bucks. I asked for Kelby McAfee and, after a half-hour wait, she directed me through double glass doors, past rows of Danish modern desks with women listening to earphones and typing, and phones ringing incessantly.

Down a long aisle, around a corner, then another, and I came upon a kind of cul-de-sac with a desk, chairs, and other office paraphernalia positioned in the center. A middle-aged woman stood beside the desk as though waiting for me. She wore a dark brown long-sleeved jacket over a brown-and-white belted shirtwaist dress. Closed doors bearing nameplates encircled the area. The one directly behind the woman said HARRISON LAWSON in big, bold letters.

I handed her my business card. "I'm Mavis Davis. Here to see Mr. McAfee."

"Annette Jensen," she said. "Have a seat and I'll tell him you're here." I sat in a chair opposite her. She picked up a phone, pushed a button, and announced me, all very prim and proper. She wore her brown-and-gray hair cut short and sprayed back away from her face. She had long red fingernails and rings on almost every finger. "It's going to be a few minutes. He's finishing up a meeting. Would you like a cup of coffee?"

"No, thank you. I'm a tea sipper." Again I wished for a cigarette and wondered how long it would take to lose that desire.

"Suit yourself." She pulled open a drawer. "I have some tea bags in here somewhere."

"Oh, that's okay. Don't bother. Have you worked here long?"

"Twenty-five years." She smiled a small smile of pride. "I'm the office manager. Sort of like an assistant to Mr. Lawson." Her eyes met mine—suddenly I realized that she was barely holding herself together. "I hope I'll continue in that capacity."

I wondered if she meant by that last remark that she and McAfee didn't get along, but her face was void of all expression. "I guess you knew Mr. Lawson pretty well, didn't you?"

"I worked here when he got his first big promotion. Back then we were good friends."

"You probably know his wife then, too."

She frowned almost imperceptibly. "I know her. I used to

be her supervisor," she said with a contemptuous tone in her voice.

My ears pricked up. "It was pretty sad at their house Friday and Saturday."

"Humph." Her eyes cut from mine down to the papers on her desk. I wondered what was going on behind those lashes besides the fact that clearly she didn't care for Hilary.

"Will you be going to the funeral?"

"Yes. They'll let me off for that, but I have a feeling a lot of things are going to change around here." She cocked her head toward a door to the right of her desk. I couldn't read the nameplate from where I sat.

I leaned toward her, trying to create an air of confidentiality. "I heard that Mr. McAfee would probably be selected by the board to be in charge now."

Her eyes met mine again. I wondered what she knew. Probably everything of consequence that had ever happened at that company. We stared at each other for a few seconds, then she picked up a stack of papers and began straightening them. Finally, she said, "We'll see."

"I take it that you don't like him." I straightened the hem of my skirt where it lay on my calf, trying to act casual. When I looked up, she stared at me still, one eyebrow arched. "I'm sorry. I didn't mean to offend you."

She whispered, "It doesn't matter whether I like him or not. I just hope to keep my job. It would be hard to find another one at my age." She appeared to be somewhere in her fifties.

"It's hard to find a job anywhere these days in Houston."

"Too true."

I felt sorry for all the older women I was meeting who were worried about their jobs. "Has the crunch affected insurance companies as much as everyone else?"

"Yes. Even the sales of our top people are down. There seem to be more claims, too. I'm not sure yet why that is. Mr. Lawson was looking into it personally, he was so worried about it."

"I don't know how that could be related to the economy. Does this company write all kinds of insurance?"

She nodded. "Everything. Of course, we're stuck with a lot of it that we don't want—the pools, you know."

"Yeah, I've done some reading on them," I said. I didn't tell her that I thought the insurance pools were the best thing since Ben & Jerry's ice cream, which I sure would like some of since I couldn't smoke. "Things are tough all over. What did Mr. Lawson attribute the claims to?"

She blinked several times in rapid succession as her eyes met mine, and she started to say something, but the door next to Lawson's office opened and the murmur of voices became chatter as people came out in pairs and in threes, still talking. I could see a long conference table with chairs turned every which way. Several men surrounded McAfee.

"Goodbye, Annette," one of the women called. "Good to see you again."

Annette nodded and smiled, all business now.

An older, bald man wearing glasses and a five-hundred-dollar suit strolled out with Kelby McAfee. They spoke in quiet tones and shook hands. McAfee clamped the man on the arm, his mouth turned up in a huge grin. The man glanced in our direction as he passed by.

McAfee spotted me. Annette Jensen jumped up and went over to him. They exchanged a few words and then she returned to her desk and said, "He'll see you in his office in just a few minutes." I thought she looked kind of wistful, but she shrugged.

Both of us watched as McAfee hurried into his office and

closed the door. One of the lights lit up on the phone set on Annette's desk.

"Ms. Jensen, I'm not here about Mr. Lawson's death. I'm here about the children's disappearance. Did you know the Lawson children have disappeared?"

She grimaced. "No, I didn't."

I nodded. "The girl first, and the boy, a day later. Did you know the kids?"

"Yes." She glanced around as she spoke, as if to be sure no one was lingering. "Nice kids, but spoiled rotten. Still, what could you expect with a mother like that."

"Do you know anything about their being adopted?"

"Yes." She glanced over her shoulder at McAfee's door. "Their real father used to work here. He and Mr. McAfee came about the same time as I remember it."

"What did you think of him?"

"He wasn't much good at the insurance business, I know that," she said. "That's why Hilary had to work."

I nodded again. "Why did he give up his rights to his children? Do you know?" I wasn't sure I wanted her to know what I knew.

She blanched. "Don't ask me that."

"Why not?"

"I don't know anything about it, really," she said, and began to fidget with a pen. Her eyes darted around constantly. "It was a terrible thing."

"What happened?"

She shook her head. "Miss Davis, I liked the man. I was as surprised as the next person when Hilary said he'd done those things. All I know is—"

McAfee's door opened, cutting her off. She stiffened in her chair and said, "You may go in now."

McAfee's door was the one at which Annette had jerked

her head earlier. It said "Kelby McAfee," the print on the nameplate not nearly as bold as the one that said HARRISON LAWSON.

"Good afternoon, Miss Davis."

"Good afternoon, Mr. McAfee."

When he led me inside, I could see that his office was not nearly as pretentious as the one with the conference table, hardly twenty-by-twenty. In fact, it was more like twelve-by-fifteen, no doubt signifying his lower status.

It held a nice-sized mahogany desk, though, with a matching credenza, a couple of chairs, and a small love seat. A bookshelf stood to the left and an antique smoking stand next to the love seat. Various framed certificates of achievement hung on the walls, including a diploma from Texas A & M University and a yellowed certificate that said "Salesman of the Year" dated fifteen years earlier. Though it wasn't a bad office, I could understand his wanting to inherit a larger one, Lawson's, in fact. I would have loved to see Lawson's office, including the insides of the desk drawers.

McAfee eased into his executive chair with self-assuredness. He picked up his phone and said, "Coffee, please, Annette," and hung up. Finally, he looked at me.

I wondered what kind of game we were playing; clearly we were playing something. Maybe he was showing me how important he was.

"I'm surprised to see you here," he said, and kicked back in his chair. His faded red hair looked even lighter in the streaks of sunlight that sneaked through the blinds. His pale skin was like that of an albino. I hadn't really noticed that before. A genetic defect in some redheads. Quite unappealing on him. Lucky for me I was the suntan-and-freckle-type and my hair remained as red as when I was a child.

He wore a dark gray suit and had cuff links and a tiepin

that matched. His blue eyes were everywhere but on mine. Since I was already skeptical about him, when his eyes wouldn't come to roost, I became downright suspicious. There's something about shifty-eyed people.

"I guess I could say the same thing," I said, and crossed my legs as I leaned back and tried to look just as casual.

"Really. It was quite a shock, I'll tell you." He stared at his fingernails. They were shiny—like they'd been buffed at a salon.

"I heard a lot of interesting conversation at the Lawsons'." I stared at him hard. It took the longest time for him to glance my way.

"And this is something you think should be of some interest to me?"

"Maybe not, but I was curious as to why people should be giving their condolences to your wife. If I didn't know any better, I'd have thought she was the widow, not Hilary." I curled a strand of hair behind my ear and smiled my sweetest.

He bristled like an old boar. "Are you implying—"

"Mr. McAfee, if your wife had been having an affair with Harrison Lawson, it would have been plenty of motive for you to kill him."

His eyes met mine for a short time, the meanness almost leaking out. "You have quite an imagination."

Bingo. A bite. "You wouldn't kill for her?"

"Joan?" Laughter bellowed forth. It surprised me at first, but then I detected a bitter note.

"Did I miss something?"

He sat up when his laugh turned to a sputtering cough and choking sound. He pulled a handkerchief from his breast pocket and covered his mouth. His pale eyes reddened. He was okay after a couple of minutes and scooted his chair up to his desk, leaned his elbows on it, and looked me directly in the eye. His eyes were a faded blue, but pinkish around the edges. "She's screwed half the population of Houston and probably Harris County."

I don't know why, but his bluntness got to me. I sat there for a few seconds, my mouth open like a Venus flytrap.

"She's a nymphomaniac—always has been. Even in college. I'll bet she had every guy on the Aggie football team," he said, "not to mention the corps and the corps band."

I'd read somewhere that the term nymphomania wasn't in vogue with the experts anymore, but I didn't tell him. Instead, I asked, "Why'd you marry her?"

"Just stupid, I guess."

"I don't mean to pry—"

"Sure you do," he said. "That's your business, isn't it—sticking your nose where it doesn't belong?" His lids had fallen half over his eyes, but he was still staring, no—glaring—at me from under them.

"So you didn't have Mr. Lawson killed because you found out they were having an affair?" I knew I should let well enough alone, but sometimes my mouth seems to have a mind of its own.

"She said that, but it was the alcohol talking."

That was news to me. Good news. Even though, yes, I know, I was not investigating the murder. I tried to act as though I'd already heard it all before.

"She told them something like 'if he didn't die of a heart attack then I guess my husband killed him because he found out we were having an affair.' What a dreamer! I told the police that—the dumb bastards. Hell, I'd have to have more of a motive than that." He snickered. "Joan thinks she's a romantic, Miss Davis. Always looking for quote-unquote, love."

"But that isn't all they have to go on, is it? The police, I mean."

"What're you talking about?" He'd begun drumming his fingers on the desk pad.

"Don't they have more than that?" I was testing the waters—hoping he would let something slip.

"Like what?"

"You are next in line for Lawson's job, aren't you?"

He expelled a gust of air. Was there something I didn't know? "So?"

"So that's a motive, isn't it?"

"I've been next in line for several years, lady. If I was going to kill him, I'd have done it a long time ago."

"At least that's what you'd want me to think."

He cocked an eyebrow at me and sneered. "We were hunting buddies. Don't you think I could have arranged an 'accident' at the deer lease sometime over the years?"

My distaste for the man grew by the minute. Bambi's killer. Ugh. "I don't know. Could you have?"

"Hell, yes. Many a time he took the point. It would have been easy to mistake his back for a buck."

"It also would have been obvious."

His eyes perused me. "You don't know anything, do you?"

"What do you mean?"

He jumped up out of his chair, banging his thigh against the desk. "Does anyone know you're here? What are you doing here, anyway?"

I could see I wasn't going to get much cooperation out of this one. But my guesswork had at least paid a few dividends.

The look in his eyes unnerved me, but not enough to make me back down. "I . . . wanted to ask you some questions about Jeanine and Tommy and their real father."

"Arthur?" He became more tranquil.

"You knew him, right?"

"Sure—poor, dumb son-of-a-bitch." He sat back down and leaned back in his chair again, opened a drawer and got out one of those stinky cigars, clipped it, stuck it in his mouth, and lit it.

Smoke issued forth into my face. I wanted to vomit. "Hey, can I open a window this far up?"

McAfee laughed and reached over to his credenza, flipping on a smoke-eating machine, the whir of it soft. A lemon-lime scent filled the air.

"What do you mean 'poor, dumb son-of-a-bitch'?" I relaxed when he seemed to.

"Annette didn't tell you?"

"Annette—the lady out front—no." I sure wanted to get her alone, though.

The door behind me opened. A young lady I hadn't seen before came in with a cup of coffee on a saucer. She set it before McAfee.

"You want something?" he asked me.

"Got any diet drinks?"

"Yes, ma'am," the girl said.

"Please," I said. "Any kind. Or a bottle of water."

She left. McAfee and I didn't say anything. We just looked each other over. She returned with a can, a glass filled with ice cubes, and a napkin, and set them in front of me on his desk.

"Thanks," I said.

"You're welcome," she said and went out, closing the door softly behind her.

"Half-day high schoolers, they're slow," McAfee muttered.

"I have one, too." But I would never talk bad about Candy behind her back to him.

I poured my drink, took a sip, and waited for him to say something about Arthur Woodridge. He slurped his coffee, apparently going to make me ask again. Still game-playing.

"So what would Annette have told me had she been inclined to talk, which she wasn't?"

He smiled like a ghoul. "Well, Miss Davis, she was in love with Harrison, you know."

"Miss Jensen?" It was a good thing there weren't any flies in his office, I would have caught them.

"It's an old story. He never even knew it. That was years ago, though I imagine she still felt that way up until he died," he said, still smiling, sadistically, I thought.

"What's that got to do with Arthur?"

"Just that I was thinking, now that Harrison is dead, the old lady might spill her guts about how she feels about Hilary," he said with a smug look, and puffed on his cigar. "Guess she can't with the amount of stock Hilary'll come into."

"She did indicate that she didn't care for her very much." I longed for a cigarette so I could smoke in self-defense. At least that's the reason I gave myself.

"That doesn't surprise me. She hates her with a passion."

"For marrying him?"

"You got it," he said.

"She should have told him how she felt before he and Hilary got so involved."

"Annette never had a chance. He was so smitten with Hilary from the day she started working here that he was a lost cause. Hilary could do no wrong. Whatever Hilary wanted, she got."

"Geez."

"It was a relief when the whole thing got over and he married her."

"You mean the divorce?"

"Poor Arthur was a lost cause from the get go, too, but in a different way. He was just too dumb to know it."

"I don't understand."

"You really don't, do you?" He cocked his head and said, completely serious, "It was a setup, Miss Davis."

"What was—the divorce?"

"No, don't you see? You'd have had to know Arthur. He was trusting, poor soul. He never knew what was happening right up until they came back with the guilty verdict. You could see it in his eyes."

"Guilty verdict? What was she alleging, cruelty?"

"No—hey, what is this? I thought you knew about the kids," he said and sat up in his chair.

"Only that they were adopted."

"You didn't know Arthur was convicted of molesting them?"

"What?" I tried to sound shocked.

"Hilary accused him of molesting them. That's why his rights were cut off. I thought you knew."

I gave him my best dumbfounded look.

"Only a lot of us figured he didn't do it," McAfee said.

"That's impossible. I used to work there. Child welfare and the police would have investigated the case. They'd have found out if it was somehow a setup."

"Nothing is impossible when it comes to Hilary Lawson, my dear. When she sets her mind to do something, look out."

"How could she do it—her own husband? Are you sure?"

"As sure as my name's Kelby McAfee," he said pointing the cigar at me. "Listen, the kids were small. You must know how malleable kids are—if you've really ever dealt with them."

The thought that someone could get their children to say

what they wanted was one of the big fears of every child welfare worker. "That's horrible. But why would she do it?"

"To marry Harrison. He was rich and Arthur was a long time away from having any decent money—if ever. Arthur wasn't much good at the insurance business. She knew if she was caught having an affair with Harrison that she'd have trouble keeping custody of her kids. People were a lot more concerned about adultery back then." He let out a harsh laugh. "She had a very carefully laid out plan—and it worked. Woe be to the person who crosses Hilary."

"But if you knew about it, why didn't you do something?"

He shrugged. "None of us figured it out until it was too late." He swallowed some coffee. "And then, what could we do? Harrison wouldn't have listened to reason, she'd completely brainwashed him. We didn't have any real evidence to show the police. Those who were suspicious feared for our jobs. The evidence seemed overwhelming and people tend to believe that kind of thing even now, much less back then."

"It seems kind of far-fetched to me," I said. "Mrs. Lawson doesn't act like she's got that much on the ball."

"If you don't believe me, why don't you check it out? But be careful, you don't want to get on her shit list."

"I might." I studied his face. "I might just check it out. Now, about Mr. Lawson. If it wasn't a heart attack, who do you think killed him? Did Hilary do that, too?"

"First of all, is there any proof it wasn't a heart attack? Secondly, how should I know?"

"Could Arthur Woodridge have done it?"

"Possibly, if prison changed him a lot. In the old days, he wouldn't have had the balls even if he had the inclination."

"Prison does have a way of altering one's thinking."

"So I've heard," he said with another ugly smile.

"What about Hilary?"

"I don't know what her motive would be. He gave her everything she ever wanted and more." He grinned and I could see his yellow teeth. Yuck.

"Did you do it?"

He bellowed again.

"Did you?" I repeated when he'd stopped.

"Would I tell you if I did?"

"No."

"Why answer? You wouldn't believe me."

"Don't you have any suspicions of your own?"

"That's your job, lady, or at least it's the police department's job." He pushed his chair back and stood up. "Anything else?"

"Yes. Do you know where Arthur Woodridge's cabin is? Hilary says his family owned a cabin and that he might be holding the kids there."

"Um. One of the counties north of Harris, I believe. Or it could be east." He shook his head. "I'm not sure. I was only there once a long time ago. Wish I could be more help."

Like hell he did. I handed him one of my cards as I got up. "Call me if you think of any clues about where the kids might be, okay? Or even if you think of anyone who might have wanted to do away with Lawson."

"Sure. I'll do everything I can."

"I'm sure you will," I said, and smiled my sweetest at him as I went out the door, pulling it to behind me. I walked over to Annette's desk, where she was on the telephone, stuck my finger down my throat as if I was going to throw up, and pointed in McAfee's direction. She drew in a sharp breath and put her hand over the phone. For a moment, I was afraid I'd offended her, but then she smiled.

"Call me for lunch sometime, Annette," I whispered. "I need to confirm something with you."

She whispered back, "Okay."

I waved at her and found my own way out. I had lots of things to do. I had a date with Ben that night that I needed to get ready for. But the three big things were to find out if Harrison Lawson was really murdered, to find the children, and to confirm the story that McAfee had told me about Hilary Lawson. And not necessarily in that order. I also had to see the Child Protective Services file. And I would practically kill to get it.

Chapter Eleven

I went home and spread my Texas map across the kitchen table. The following day, Margaret and I would review tax and deed records until we found the Woodridge property.

Due north of Houston lies Montgomery County, county seat, Conroe, and the beginning of the Sam Houston National Forest. We'd start there and work our way around clockwise. When I got through mapping out all the places where Margaret and I might have to go, I had to hurry to get ready for my date with Ben. He'd asked me to dinner. He said he had something serious to talk to me about.

I was dressed to kill and when I opened the door for Ben, he had a murderous look in his eye, his face the color of a thundercloud. Were we in for another fight?

He stopped to kiss me on the cheek, though, before he stormed through the door. "You ready?"

"Quite." I've learned to respond in that fashion when Ben's in one of his black moods. Feeling guilty about snooping into the murder when I'd promised not to, I just knew I was the cause of his apparent foul temper.

"I'm not mad at you, honey," Ben said, his deep voice booming through the living room. "I'm just tired of being a go-between."

"What's the matter now?"

"The homicide captain's on my back about you again."

His eyes had that piercing, close-lidded look.

I remembered his saying he had something serious to discuss. Wasn't going to happen in the doorway. I grabbed his hand. "Don't let him ruin our evening, okay?"

He grunted.

I let go of his hand, snatched up my bag, and sailed out the door to the car before he could say anything else, determined to salvage the evening. Maybe he'd still come out with whatever was on his mind, even though I wasn't sure that night was the best time to discuss our relationship. And I just knew that what he wanted to talk about wasn't the weather.

After a dinner at which it seemed a dark cloud hovered over our heads, we patronized Starbucks for coffee, tea, and cake. He forced me to give up when he still wouldn't come out with whatever it was.

Finally, we arrived back at my apartment. I asked him in, as I always do. He leaned against the doorjamb and loosened his tie. "I don't know, Mavis. I'm tired and don't want to fight."

I looked into his large face, his eyes more soulful than angry. "Then don't, honey." I patted his cheek. "Just tell me you like my new dress." I twirled around. "And that you had a wonderful time." I stood on my tiptoes and kissed him lightly on the mouth. "And since I may not be around for a while, come make love to me." I smiled and crooked my finger.

He frowned as he reached his arm out and pulled me to him. His face came down close to mine. For a minute, it seemed like something out of a mushy novel. "You really know how to frustrate a guy, you know it?" His coffee-scented breath warmed my face.

I grinned, raised my eyebrows at him, and made a move toward the door.

He released me. "Where're you going?"

"Inside. It's stupid to stand out here talking in the humidity." I unlocked the door and pushed it open. Pulling on his arm, I said, "Come on. You can fuss just as well in the air-conditioning."

He shook his head. "Mavis . . ."

I walked inside.

"I meant, where are you going that you won't be around to make—are you going out of town again or what?"

By that time, he stood behind me and in front of the door. I circled around him and threw the dead bolt. "Yes."

He put his hands in his pockets and began jangling his keys. "Where?"

"Not sure yet." I sat on the edge of the easy chair, pulled my skirt up above my knees, crossed my legs, and started unbuckling my sandal.

"For what?" He stood over me, watching.

I slipped that shoe off and re-crossed my legs, starting on the buckle of the other one. I stared up at him, enticingly, I thought. "To find the Lawson kids."

"No," he said.

By taking off my sandals, I'd lost some advantage when I stood. "Yes. We agreed on Friday." I'm not exactly a squirt but had to crane my head back to meet his eyes once I had my shoes off.

"Friday I didn't know their real father was a convicted felon," he said, and crossed his arms. "Hell, I didn't even know there was another father."

"So?" I glared, my face defiant. Unfortunately, my forehead and his chin were as close as we got to being eye to eye.

"So he may be armed and dangerous, and you're not going to hunt for them."

"Why don't you take off your jacket and get comfortable?"

Ben cocked his head. "No you don't, Mavis. Let's have this out first."

I tugged gently at the knot of his tie, pulling it from around his neck. Then I began unbuttoning his shirt.

"You're not going, and that's final."

"Says who, darling?" I reached inside his shirt and put my arms around him. Shoot, if he was going to get mad, I might as well enjoy getting him that way.

"Says me and Captain Milton." He pushed me away.

"I'm only going to Conroe, that's all, Ben. I was just teasing." I laughed, trying to sound all sweetness and light like the ladies do on the soaps. Instead, it had a tinny sound.

"Okay. You can go right after you see Captain Milton in the morning," he said, smirking.

"What does he want now?"

"To talk to you about the alleged killer. Lon's brought him in for questioning."

Chapter Twelve

That bit of news made me feel like I'd just suffered cardiac arrest. I clutched Ben's arm, anxious to hear how they'd caught Woodridge so quickly. "Where did they find him? Are the kids okay? Have they sent them home? Where did he take them?"

"Hold it," Ben said, clamping a hand over my mouth. "I said the alleged killer, not the ex-husband."

I tore his fingers away. "Not Arthur Woodridge? But that's who Hilary Lawson says killed her husband." I was totally befuddled. "Just who did Lon bring in? And has the ME already done the autopsy and determined it wasn't a heart attack for sure?"

Ben laughed, obviously enjoying my confusion. "See, I knew you were involved in this case. If you'll calm down, I'll tell you."

"I'm calm." I wanted to shake him. "Tell me."

"First of all, Lon picked up Kelby McAfee this evening."

"McAfee . . ." I didn't want Ben to know I'd been to see him. "Was that the ugly guy with the faded red hair and shifty eyes?" I gave him the same dumbfounded expression I had used on McAfee earlier.

"Secondly, the ME's prelim shows that there was more to it than a heart attack. He may have ingested something."

"Yeah, yeah. Just what I thought! Someone did slip him something." Was I good or what?

"Captain Milton wants to get a statement from you about what you saw. He thinks you might be the only witness who is unbiased."

"I've got to get a drink." I made a beeline to the kitchen where I grabbed a beer out of the icebox, opened it, and chugged from the can. It felt good and cold running down my throat. I couldn't imagine how they'd figured it was McAfee. Where was their evidence?

"Got another?"

"Help yourself. There are mugs in the freezer." He did. "What I don't understand is how they knew this guy did it," I said.

Ben popped the top and poured the contents down his throat, squeezing the can in his fist when he was through and throwing it away. He wiped at his mouth, grinned at me, and said, "Good police work." He opened another can.

"Your ass, too," I said. "You said Lon picked him up?" He knew what I thought about the homicide division, or at least certain members of that group.

"Let's not get into that. I don't know what the hell's going on, except that I received a call this afternoon to see Captain Milton—which I did. He said Lon was bringing the guy in for questioning. The captain wants to see you in the morning. You might be a material witness since you were standing right there. Milton wants me to make sure you get to his office."

By this time, we were back in the living room. I curled up on the couch, pulling my legs up under me and put my beer on the end table. I seemed to think best curled up almost in a fetal position. What did that say about me? Ben sat an arm's length away.

"What about Arthur Woodridge? Hilary thinks he did it."

"Oh. It's Hilary now, is it?"

I shrugged. "Not to her face. Are you going to tell me about Arthur Woodridge or not?"

He drummed his fingers on the back of the couch. "I don't know what they're going to do about that. They didn't find out about him until after Lon went for McAfee and another uniform went over to the Lawson house later to tell Mrs. Lawson."

I ducked my head. "Then Captain Milton knows I've been to talk with her?"

He nodded. "He apparently went himself as a favor to James Rush and had quite a little visit with her earlier today."

"What evidence do they have against McAfee?"

"A fingerprint on Lawson's glass—an accusation against him by his wife," he said in a quiet tone.

"That would be the cheerleader-type—Joan?" As if I didn't know.

"Right. When Lon talked to her about the fingerprint, she got hysterical." He closed his eyes and shook his head. "She said she knew McAfee had found out about her affair with Harrison Lawson, but he didn't have to kill him."

That was pretty much what McAfee had said, but he hadn't been concerned when I spoke with him. This was all very confusing. I swallowed another mouthful of beer. "That's it?"

"No—he had more motive than that—"

"Wait." I held my palm up. "I know what it was. He was next in line for Harrison's job at the insurance company."

He stared at me as if to say that he wasn't surprised.

"Something someone said at the cocktail party," I said before he could get the question out.

"You're amazing, you know that?" He leaned toward me.

"Wait a minute, Ben. I'm still wondering . . . what are they going to do about Hilary Lawson saying her ex-husband killed Harrison?"

He scooted closer to me. "I don't know," he said, putting his second can of beer down on my coffee table. Then he took my beer away from me and set it beside his.

"Have they charged McAfee?"

"I don't think so, yet," he said, sliding closer. "They were waiting to speak to the assistant district attorney." His arm slipped across the back of the couch and down around my waist.

"I'm trying to think here, Ben," I said, pushing at his chest. "Aren't they the least bit concerned about Hilary's accusations?"

"Sure, sweetie. The captain's taking care of it." He put his face up to my ear and began nibbling.

"Ben," I said softly, pushing at him again. I giggled in spite of myself. It tickled. "How can they go on a fingerprint and an accusation? How do they think McAfee did it? So the ME must have determined for sure it wasn't a heart attack. What exactly did the ME say? Have the lab results come back already?"

He continued to come at me. "I don't know, Mavie." I was familiar with his approach. He was moving in for the kill.

"Are they going to try to find Arthur Woodridge and the kids?" I chuckled then. Let's face it; my resistance is not all that strong in the first place.

"Yes. That's why you're off the case. They're treating it like any other kidnapping." He reached for me with his other hand.

It was now or never. If I spoke up, I would ruin the best part of the evening. If I didn't, he'd assume that I was off the case, which I definitely wasn't. I needed that two thousand dollars. Besides, I didn't care for the way HPD handled kidnappings. And besides that, I had a head start on them.

But what the hell—we could fight later.

The next morning I awoke to the aroma of frying bacon and baking waffles. When I wandered into the kitchen, I found Ben in his bathrobe, which at some time in the past had found a home in my closet, spooning batter into the waffle iron. He had set the table and poured orange juice, milk, tea, and coffee. Crisp bacon lay on a paper towel–covered plate. It would take a real dunce not to realize what he was hinting at, but I wasn't buying.

Slipping my arms as far around his waist as they would go, I rested my cheek on his shoulder blades. "Good morning."

"Sleep well?"

"Mmmm."

"Your tea's all ready." He picked up the bundled *Houston Chronicle*. "Got your paper in."

"Thanks." I took it from him, pulling at the plastic wrapper. "I wonder if there's a follow-up on the story about Lawson."

"Didn't get a chance to look." He put the lid down on the batter and turned and kissed me on the forehead. "You go ahead and sit down while I finish cooking."

I smiled. I wasn't going to comment. I have to admit it was nice, though, having someone keep my feet warm during the night and wake up to in the morning. The snoring we'd have to deal with later.

I wandered over to the table and finished unwrapping the paper. Scanning the front page, I didn't see anything, but that wasn't unusual. The previous stories were inside. I thumbed through the sections that usually carried police and court news but couldn't find a mention of Kelby McAfee's arrest.

"They may not have charged him by the time that went to press," Ben said, coming over to the table with a platter of waffles.

"Yeah. I was thinking the same thing. It may not be as easy as they thought yesterday morning. What if Woodridge or somebody else did do it?" After smearing butter on the waffles, I turned back to the newspaper.

"Homicide doesn't need any bad press right now." He stood over my shoulder, looking on.

"True." There had been too many unsolved cases lately.

He leaned down and put his face to the back of my neck, inside the collar of my robe, rubbing his stubby chin on my bare skin. "What do you care anyway?" he said in a hoarse voice. "It's not your problem."

I didn't answer. I merely turned the page.

"You smell good."

I turned my head and smiled at him. "Don't start anything you can't finish."

"I don't go on until eight-thirty."

"It's seven-thirty now," I said. "We still have to eat."

He sighed exaggeratedly. "There's always tomorrow." He pulled out the chair adjacent to me. "I could come back tonight and we could go over what happened with you and the captain."

I cringed inwardly and turned another page.

He put a finger under my chin. "You are going to see Captain Milton."

"I haven't decided yet." My attention stayed on the news. "I've got a busy day ahead of me."

He jerked his hand away. "Doing what?"

"I have a client that wants me to check some records in some of the outlying counties." I put the paper aside and took a sip of orange juice.

"What kind of records?" His eyes narrowed suspiciously, just like in the movies.

I couldn't meet his eyes. I stared at the front page.

"Mavis . . ."

"Huh?"

"What kind of records?"

"Oh. Some deed records and tax records. They want me to find out the record owners of some property." I stabbed a waffle and dropped it on his plate and got one for myself.

"Oh yeah?"

"Yeah. I have to go to all the courthouses at the county seats surrounding Harris County." I poured syrup in circles on my waffle.

"For what?" There was a note of distrust in his voice.

"I told you," I said, glancing at him before I cut into my breakfast. "They want me to locate the owners of some property."

"For what, Mavis? What do they want you to locate the owners for?"

"It's resort property they're interested in," I said, pouring syrup on his waffle.

"That's no answer."

"Why are you giving me the third degree?" I asked. "I'm just trying to make a living."

"Because I know how you are."

"Thanks a lot." By this time I couldn't meet his eyes. "You're always so suspicious. Want more syrup?"

"Does this have anything to do with the Lawson case?"

"Why would you think that, Ben?" I stuffed about a quarter of the waffle into my mouth.

"Does it?"

I pointed at my mouth. Why couldn't he let it drop? Sometimes I thought he was a control freak. I chewed vigorously and washed the food down with some hot tea. "I'm going to check out the record owners of some resort properties, little cabins in the woods—that sort of thing. Why would you think that it has to do with the Lawson case?"

"Does Mrs. Lawson own some of these properties?"

"Not that I know of. I don't know who the owners are. I'm supposed to find properties that have improvements on them and get the names and addresses of the owners, that's all. Want some bacon?"

He scraped a couple of pieces onto his waffle and shoved the plate of bacon back at me.

"Thanks," I said, taking the plate from him and munching a piece. I grinned. "You're such a good cook. These waffles are wonderful."

"I want to know where you're going," Ben said and stuffed a piece of waffle into his mouth.

"Conroe, first. Margaret's going, too, only she doesn't know it yet." I continued eating.

"What are you going to do in Conroe?" he asked after he'd gulped down some coffee.

"Jesus. You're so suspicious. Okay, here's the blow by blow. First we'll look at one of those big maps they have in the county clerk's office, trying to locate the best places for cabins and such. Then we'll look further and see if the good spots are platted or whatever you call it. Then we'll go a step further and see if the plats have been sold, then the tax records to see who the record owners are of the ones that have the tax values for improvements. We probably will call any local owners to see if they're interested in selling and if so, advise them that they'll be contacted by a prospective purchaser."

He shook his head. "I don't believe you."

"Why would I lie about something as stupid as that? Ben,

the people want to know if any of the improvements are good enough for people to stay in without a lot of expense. It's an investment thing, see." I crossed my legs under the table. I would have crossed my fingers, but he would have seen.

"That is the stupidest thing I ever heard of. Anyway, if that's all you're going to do, why can't you go see Captain Milton first?" He scrutinized me as if I were a prisoner in custody. I was only glad he didn't start jumping up and down on my kneecaps.

I shook my head at him while I swallowed more orange juice. "It's not stupid, and I promised I'd start first thing this morning. It's important to my client." That part wasn't a lie. I drank down the rest of my juice.

"I'll take off and go with you then."

I'm afraid I spewed so much juice out that it splattered all over the front of his robe.

"See." He pointed his finger at me. "I knew you were lying."

I was coughing—choking—and he was sitting there pointing, an accusatory look in his eyes. He wouldn't even get up and come pound me on the back. No way I'd marry a person that wouldn't try to save me from choking to death.

After many minutes, and after I'd dried my eyes, nose, and mouth, and Ben was still watching, waiting for me to defend myself, I said, "I wasn't lying. It just went down the wrong way, that's all."

"You're going to see the Captain, Mavis."

"Am not."

"Are, too."

I shook my head. "Am not, and you can't make me."

Chapter Thirteen

Our relationship seemed to be degenerating again. Ben got angry and left without finishing his breakfast, which was okay by me, though he did tuck some hot waffles into his pocket when he unplugged the waffle iron.

I did not intend to go see Captain Milton. I wanted to find those kids and the truth about Arthur Woodridge before someone beat me to the punch. I might even figure out who killed Harrison Lawson along the way, since it seemed clear now that the police and ME thought he hadn't died of natural causes. I kept telling myself that no one had hired me for that onerous task, but myself kept replying that it could do no harm to my reputation if I solved it first. The murderer could be Kelby McAfee, but I'd be willing to bet the cops had no conclusive evidence. It could be anyone at this point.

Since I was running a little late, I called Margaret and told her to meet me at the office as soon as possible so we could get on our way. She said Annette Jenson had called late the evening before and left her number. I tried it but got no answer so I called National Insurance Trust.

When I got her on the phone, Annette spoke in a whispery voice. "Is this Mavis Davis?"

"Yes, I said it was," I said.

"There's something I'd like to talk to you about. Can you meet me?"

"I'm sorry. Not for lunch. How about later?"

"I didn't want lunch. We can't be seen together. How about your place this evening?"

"My office? Sure. What time?"

"No. Not your office. You might be watched. What about your house?"

No way. I didn't have a long standing policy of never bringing my problems home with me from the office, but I was going to start one. "How about we meet someplace else? You have a favorite bar?"

"I don't drink," she said, her words clipped.

"Good, then no one will expect to find you in a bar. Meet me at Lana's on Westheimer and Fondren. What time is good for you?"

"Miss Davis, this is important."

"I appreciate that. Lana's is secure. She keeps a shotgun and a baseball bat under the counter." I could picture her expression. She had appeared to be a proper lady.

"All right. Would nine be too late for you?"

"Nine is fine." The courthouses closed at five, and Margaret and I were sure to be back by then. "Is there anything I can do for you in the meantime?"

"Just make sure you aren't followed," she said and hung up.

First Ben, and then Annette Jensen. Everyone was getting melodramatic today.

That done, I dressed, but when I opened my door to go pick up Margaret, who should be sitting on the stoop and stuffing an Egg McMuffin into his face but lumpy Lon.

"The captain ain't as dumb as you think he is," Lon said, his full mouth revealing its contents. The big lout lifted his lard off my steps and grinned at me. It was not a pretty sight.

"Okay," I said, resigned to my fate. "Let's go." The idea of a ride downtown with Lon was not a pleasing one, but what could I do? If I ran, they'd think I was up to something, which I was, as we all know.

When we got to Captain Milton's office, he hadn't arrived, so Lon stuck me in a corner to wait. Watching the shift change, I nodded at some of the men and women that I knew as I sat and wished I'd never quit smoking. If ever I needed something to assuage my fears, to fill the void of empty time, or to just plain make me feel better, it was then. I knew I was an addict, but before the morning ended I didn't much care. I would have gladly knocked over the nearest convenience store for a smoke.

When Captain Milton showed up, he took one look at me, said, "Be with you in a minute," and disappeared behind his door for an hour.

I was steamed. After the first half hour, I called Margaret on my cell, advising her to meet me downtown. Finally, Milton opened the door and beckoned to me to come inside.

"Good morning, Miss Davis," he said as he rounded his desk and dropped into his huge easy chair.

"Is it?" I was not about to be any more polite than absolutely necessary.

"Never mind. I want to talk about the Lawson murder."

Alleged Lawson murder, I thought, as I stood silently before his desk.

"Sit down." He gestured at one of the lightly padded chairs that by design discouraged long stays.

"Thank you, but I prefer to stand."

"You're gonna get awfully tired."

"Aw c'mon, Captain. I've got work to do. I can't hang around here all day." I could visualize those kids and something happening to them while I went around and around with him. If only I knew for certain that Woodridge wouldn't hurt them.

"Just tell me what I want to know and you can go, so long as you're not investigating the Lawson thing."

"Which Lawson thing?"

"Any Lawson thing."

"What do you want to know?"

"Give me a blow-by-blow of how you got on the case and up 'til the time Lon showed at the house."

I sat. I told. I cringed inwardly.

"Did Mrs. Lawson tell you that she thinks her husband did it?"

"Her husband, sir?"

"Ex-husband." He frowned in my direction.

"Yes, sir."

"And you didn't call me?"

"I understand that you spoke to her after I did."

"That's not the point. If you have knowledge that would be helpful to the police, you have an obligation to spill it."

"I didn't have any hard evidence, sir," I said. I'm afraid my tone of voice was not what he was accustomed to hearing.

His fist slammed down on the desk. "That's what I'm talking about. If you want to get along as a PI around here, you're gonna have to cooperate. Just like that other thing. You never told us about all that stuff in Fort Worth."

"I tried to tell Lon, sir, but he wouldn't listen."

"Dammit, Davis. Next time, call me. I can't help it if I inherited people like Tyler. Listen, it's not only that you're interfering in an active police investigation, but it's for your own safety."

"Would you be concerned about my safety if I were a man, sir?" I grabbed the edge of his desk and glared into his eyes.

"Look, I expect to get the same cooperation out of you

that I get out of every other decent PI in this city. The only thing is, you're a woman. I don't want to see you get hurt." His expression grew fatherly, dumbfounding me.

"Is that all, sir?" I stood. A surly tone invaded my voice in spite of my best efforts to rid myself of it. "I don't want to be protected. I want to be treated just the same as anyone else, okay? Sir."

"No, it's not okay."

I stood there, bug-eyed. Damn. I knew I shouldn't have let Ben help me wrap up my first murder case. They probably thought I couldn't have done it without him. Well, I was going to show them. This time, when it was all solved, I'd let them in on it. Maybe no one had hired me to find the killer—the alleged killer. Maybe Tommy had only paid me to find his sister. Maybe Hilary had only hired me to find both kids. I didn't care. I moved toward the door.

"Sit down!" The captain jumped up and strode around the desk, sticking his big face in my own before I could find shelter. So I sat down. It was stupid, I know, because then he could hover over me and use psychological tactics to try to make me feel bad.

I crossed my arms about my chest and glared at the man. I didn't care if he was a captain. Nobody tells me what to do.

"Listen, Davis. We're doing all we can to find those kids." He stood over me, like before, shook his finger in my face, and tried to stare me down. "I've already sent a man to try to locate Arthur Woodridge's relatives, if any, to try to figure out where he could be hiding. There's a SWAT team on call for when we locate them in case he tries to hold them hostage. My men are contacting the authorities in every county surrounding ours, giving out descriptions and photographs, trying to find out if they've been seen. There's nothing for you to do."

"Are you checking the deed records, sir?"

"The what?" My question caught him off guard. He relaxed and rested his buns on the front of his desk.

"The deed records, the tax records. I was going to check them to see if there was a record showing his family owned any property in the outlying counties." I hadn't intended on saying anything, but I didn't want to get into permanent trouble with the police. I might need them sometime.

He gave a little. "I hadn't thought of that," he said in a milder tone. "I'll put some men right on it."

"Let me do that, Captain Milton. Let me do something."

He gave me a look that said he was considering it. I grabbed at my chance.

"I could search the records just as efficiently as your men. Maybe more so. I've done this type of work before, for attorneys." I stared at him, no anger and defiance now.

"I don't know, Davis."

"I would report back, sir. I promise. I've already done some research. I could leave now, start with Conroe—Montgomery County—"

"It's police business, Davis, and from what Mrs. Lawson said, he could be very dangerous. He's already killed one man."

I couldn't believe it. He'd already tried, convicted, and injected the man. "What happened to McAfee?" And what had happened to the presumption of innocence?

"We had to let him go. All we had was a fingerprint, and he had a reasonable explanation for that. Besides, he didn't have a strong enough motive."

Not to mention they'd picked him up before they knew about Woodridge, but I didn't say so. Instead, I said, "So you think Woodridge did it?"

"Mrs. Lawson thinks so, poor woman, and who would

know him better?" He shook his head. "I don't want anything to happen to you or those children."

"But I won't be anywhere around them, Captain. I'll be at the county courthouses in the county clerks' offices in the dusty, moldy, old deed record sections, unless, of course, they have everything on computer or microfilm, in which case—"

"Okay."

"I promise I'll call you as soon as I find something. I may not find anything. Your men may turn up something before I do, why waste your men when I could do the same job? After all, I am slightly better educated than most of them and know what I'm looking for." Stopping then, I hoped I hadn't overstepped my bounds.

"Okay, I said." He stared at me, his lips pursed.

I studied his face. Deep horizontal lines creased his forehead. His chin rested on his chest, giving him the look of a fat man, which he wasn't. He had a handsome face—for a cop—when he wasn't mad or anything. I remembered when I'd first heard of him, I thought he'd be an ogre, but since then I'd heard some good things. Like he was honest. Supposedly unprejudiced. Fair, but strictly by-the-book.

"Can I trust you not to run off if you locate them?"

"Yes, sir."

"I don't know, Davis. I shouldn't let you do it, but I suspect that if you don't have something to do, I'll be sorry later."

I grinned.

"I know how you are. I've checked you out. I know you're hard-headed and independent. And I remember the first time I saw you."

"What?"

"Years ago." He smiled. "At a political convention."

"I don't remember you from back then."

"You were at a microphone, trying to get some crazy, liberal resolution passed and arguing with the county chairman about some rule." He raised his eyebrows, his forehead wrinkling into three deep grooves.

"You were there? Which convention?"

"I'm not sure. It was many years ago."

"That was my wild and crazy political phase," I said, shrugging at the memory.

"Well, I remember—"

"You're not going to let a little thing like that make a difference now, are you?"

"I told you I checked you out," he said, solemn-faced. "I know how you can be." He pointed his finger in my face again. "I'm telling you, if you screw up, if you don't report back to me, this is the last chance you'll ever get. I'll make you so sorry that you'll have to seek another line of work."

I sprang out of my chair. "Thanks, Captain. I'm good, you'll see."

He straightened up, dismissing me. "I hope so, for your sake. Don't make a fool out of me. Now get out of here." He turned away, to go back around his desk, and loosened his tie as he did so. Last I saw, he was shaking his head and unbuttoning his collar button.

I closed the door behind me, smiling to myself, and headed to the first floor where Margaret should be waiting. I was anxious to literally get out of town.

As I started to get on the elevator, I spotted a woman I knew from when I used to work at what is now known as the Texas Department of Family Protective Services, I think, unless the legislature has met recently and changed the name again. Child Welfare or Child Protective Services. CPS for short. She started working there about a year before I left. We had been pretty good friends. A thick file under one arm, a shoulder bag hung over the other, she traipsed down the corridor and called out to me.

"Hi, Angela." I let that elevator go and walked to where she'd stopped.

"How are you?" She shifted the file to the other arm. "Long time no see."

"I know." I hugged her. "I've been meaning to call you for lunch. You look so good, what have you been doing?" She had lost a lot of weight and looked great in a tan pants suit with a small ribbon tied at the throat. Most of the field workers wore jeans and shirts unless they were going to court to testify.

She tossed her light brown head at me. "I got married and had a baby."

"Damn, it has been a long time. You could have called me, you know."

"I know, Mav, but I've been so busy. Between the kid and work, I don't have any time for myself."

"Yeah, I know what you mean," I said. I didn't, but what else could I say? "What are you all dressed up for?"

"I'm on office duty now. I'm a supervisor," she said with a flash of her eyes.

"Congratulations, when did that happen?"

"About eighteen months ago."

I frowned. "It has been a long time. What are you doing over here? Getting ready for court?"

"Naw. Just delivering an old file. The last caseworker on it retired and moved away a long time ago, and the old supervisor is gone. I'm the custodian of the records, you know how it goes."

A little bell rang in my head. "That wouldn't be the Lawson case, would it?"

"Why, you working on something? I've heard about you." She laughed.

"It's a living." I sighed dramatically. "Is it the Lawson thing?"

"No, sorry. It's really an oldie, Woodridge kids. This file's so old that it's probably even before your time," she said.

I grabbed her arm and pulled her around the corner. "That's the same case I'm working on, Angela. The kids are named Lawson now."

Her eyebrows shot up.

"Why are you bringing the file over here? Shouldn't it be sealed and in a warehouse someplace?"

She shrugged. "It was, but Mandy ordered it out."

I frowned. "Mandy's still there? I can't believe it. She must be a hundred by now."

Smiling, she said, "More like a hundred-and-fifty, but still as fierce as ever."

My mind raced ninety-to-nothing. "You going to turn it over to Captain Milton?"

"None other—except you know we never turn over anything. I'm to give it to him to copy and return." She looked hastily around. "But don't tell anyone."

"Right, confidentiality and all that."

Her dark eyes rested on mine. "So you're on the same case?"

"Yeah, and I could sure use a look at that file."

She shook her head. "Can't do it, Mavis. Not right now, anyway. What are you doing for lunch? I might get it back by then and happen to stop for lunch before I go back to the office."

"Can't. The generous Captain agreed not to lean on me too hard if I'd be cooperative and do some busy work for him. I've got to get right on it. Where are you going to be tonight?"

"I won't be able to get it out of the office. Sorry," she said, as she shifted the file to her hip. "Wish I could help you."

"I know. Well, it was worth a shot."

"Listen, I've got to get in there. I called him to tell him that we'd located it and I'd be right over."

"Sure," I muttered. "Just my luck."

"Let's really have lunch sometime, okay?"

"Call me next week."

She started down the hall, looking back at me. "If I don't, you can call me, you know?"

I flashed her a smile. "Right," I said. Then she disappeared through the doorway.

Chapter Fourteen

"Hey, Margaret." I found her sitting on a bench and thumbing through a well-worn magazine like you'd find in a doctor's office. She wore navy slacks and a flowered blouse with rolled-up sleeves. Her freshly washed hair fell into long, soft waves. She was pretty when she didn't try too hard to be something she wasn't.

Jumping up, she said, "What took you so long? I was starting to think I'd misunderstood you."

"Let's get out of here." I hooked my arm through hers. "Your car outside?"

"As near as I could get it." She shrugged. "What's going on?"

It was already well into the eighty-degree range by that time of day. The minute I stepped outside, I broke into a sweat. As we walked to her car, I explained what had happened and what the captain had said. Margaret listened attentively, shaking her head, and groaning as I described the situation.

"You're not going to let him boss you around like that, are you?" Gasping for breath, she took long steps in an effort to keep up with me as I hurried down the sidewalk.

I chuckled. "Hell, no. What do you think I am, a push-over?"

"Well, I didn't think so," she said with a huff. "Who does he think he is anyway?"

"Oh, he knows who he is. That's the problem."

"Oh . . . so what are you going to do, Mavis?" Fear had entered her voice.

I'm afraid I laughed outright. We had reached her car. As she unlocked the door, I couldn't hold it any longer. "Exactly what I said I was going to do," I said after I quit laughing.

Margaret didn't say anything else until after she'd started the car. "I don't get it."

"Take I-45 north, Margaret, and I'll explain on the way."

We sat in silence until Margaret maneuvered the car through the congested downtown traffic and onto the freeway. Margaret is not the type of driver that instills confidence. It's better to keep quiet when traffic is bad and let her focus on what she's doing. The good thing is, she knows it and, though she won't tolerate comments, thinks she understands what I'm doing when I sit silently while she drives. She thinks I'm letting her concentrate. I'm really praying and thanking God that she can't afford a large car with a V8 that could get away from her.

"Okay," she said, expelling the gust of air she'd been holding. We were now in the center lane, headed north.

I breathed a sigh of relief, too, and turned sideways in the seat so I could talk to her. "The deal is, we're going to do exactly what we planned to do all along. We're going to go from county seat to county seat, searching for that property, and hope we find them before the cops do."

"Two things," Margaret said. "One, you promised to call him. And two, if I'd known all this I could have spent Saturday or Sunday doing the research on the computer. I'll bet all those counties have their deed records on computer now."

"I keep forgetting about computers. You're right. I would

have felt a lot better last weekend if we'd found where Arthur is probably holding the kids instead of going to the beach with Ben." I grinned.

"Be serious, Mavis."

"I am. I really do forget about the darn things. As to your second concern, as soon as we find Arthur's place and go out and see if the kids are there, we'll call the captain."

"What if it's as dangerous as the captain says?" Her normally high-pitched voice sounded squeaky.

"We'll be careful, that's all. If it seems dangerous, we won't go in."

"Are you sure?" Fear had inscribed itself all over her face.

"Watch where you're going, Margaret. You want me to take the wheel?"

"No—not the way you drive." Her eyes darted back to the road.

"Thanks a lot."

"You're changing the subject, Mavis. I can always tell when something funny is going on, because you change the subject. I wish you wouldn't do that." She hunched over the steering wheel and frowned.

"Don't be scared, Margaret. I'm not going to let anything happen to you. I promise. If it looks dangerous, you can leave before I do anything."

"But I don't want you to get hurt, either."

"Now you sound like Captain Milton."

"But sometimes you do go off and do stupid things, Mavis. Things I would never even dream of doing."

"Not this time. I made a promise and I'm going to do my best to keep it."

"Well, just in case that's not entirely true, I brought you something." While staring straight ahead at the traffic in front of us, Margaret's hand snaked down beneath the front seat. She pulled out a smallish flannel bag that looked remarkably familiar and handed it to me.

"My .38. Margaret, I'm so proud of you." I squeezed her arm, careful not to distract her from driving.

"I didn't want us going out of town without any protection," Margaret said. "I know how you are."

I ignored that comment as I checked to make sure it was loaded and snapped the cylinder back into place. "You're showing a lot of initiative, kiddo. I appreciate it." I grinned at the thought of the soul-searching Margaret must have gone through in deciding to bring my gun. It must have been a difficult decision for her. "By the way, did you bring more than the five bullets it's loaded with?"

Margaret reached under the seat again and brought out a Ziploc sandwich bag. There must have been at least another two dozen rounds. Where did she think we were going, the Middle East?

"Just one thing, Mavis. Don't tell Ben. If he finds out, he'll kill us."

"Not if Arthur Woodridge gets us first."

"That's not funny and you know it." Margaret burst out laughing in spite of herself and I joined her.

We spent the remainder of the morning and part of lunchtime in Conroe. It's an almost quaint little place, compared to Houston, with friendly and helpful deputy county clerks. Unfortunately, we didn't find any record of anyone named Woodridge ever owning anything.

After that, we wolfed down a couple of burgers and headed east for Liberty County. The weather hadn't gotten so hot yet that everything had dried out. Some tall yellow flowers, red and yellow firewheels, and a few bluebonnets still poked their heads up on the sides of 105, which isn't superhighway, but isn't exactly a back road, either. I guess it could be called the scenic route since a couple of miles of it ran through the Sam Houston National Forest.

When we cut off to go south to Liberty, it was after two. The sun hid behind the clouds. A light sprinkling of rain fell. Margaret and I had long ago learned how to be together without chatter all the time. We both thought our separate thoughts and enjoyed the countryside.

I hoped we'd find something; hoped we weren't on a wild-goose chase or that we'd have to spend many more days searching records; hoped the police hadn't already gotten there; and hoped I'd be able to prove myself with this case.

In Liberty, we found the Woodridge property. It was almost five by the time we had studied the county clerk's plats and maps and purchased a map of our own. An A. Woodridge owned some kind of improved property on the Trinity River up near Moss Hill. We headed out highway ninety, north again on 146, then cut over to where we figured it was on the river. We got help reading the map from a young guy in a general store–type place.

When we found the turnoff, we drove through the brush on what wasn't much more than a path, parked the car in a curve behind a clump of trees, and, being careful to keep behind shelter, crept through the brush until we sighted the cabin.

It appeared absolutely vacant, but then it would if he wanted to make it seem that way. No vehicle was in sight. No sign of anyone. I wasn't quite sure at that point what to do. What if we had the wrong place? There weren't any signs or anything that said, THIS PROPERTY IS WHERE ARTHUR WOODRIDGE IS HIDING WITH HIS CHILDREN. There were no identifying numbers like in the suburbs, painted on the curbs. There were no curbs. No metal mailbox with the name embossed on it in black paint stood on a post at the end of the path. There weren't even any BEWARE OF DOG signs or POSTED KEEP OUT stretched over a razor-wire fence. I wondered how pissed off Captain Milton would be if he came to the wrong place?

Nevertheless, in keeping with my promise, Margaret and I drove back toward civilization until we could get a signal and called HPD. Captain Milton wasn't there. I left a very long, convoluted description of how to find the property and promptly went back.

Coward that Margaret is, I have to give her credit. When I told her to leave and park on the main street, she refused. We left the car behind the clump of trees again and slithered back toward the cabin like a couple of snakes.

As the sun began to set, the air grew cooler. A fresh aroma of green trees, rich earth, and no air pollution filled my lungs. The cabin, which on closer inspection looked fairly new, perched only a hundred feet or so from the riverbank in a small clearing. I wondered whether the original cabin had been seriously damaged or destroyed by the hurricane that had moved inland the year before. Could Arthur have rebuilt it so quickly after he got released?

Its rectangular windows faced the path leading to the front door. Unless we waited for nightfall, anyone watching would be able to see our approach.

"Margaret, why don't you go back to the car? That way, you're not implicated in anything and if the captain comes, you can direct him back here."

"You're out of your freaking mind, Mavis. I'm not leaving you alone out here. But how late are we going to stay? I did have a date tonight."

"Hopefully not too long, but you could go back near the highway and call him and tell him you might be late."

"I'm not leaving you," she said again.

I smiled my appreciation. We circled around, staying in the cover of the trees and brush as much as possible. Unfortunately, there were windows on every side. When we reached the edge of the clearing nearest the back door, we saw a short clothesline with laundry hanging on it. Farther back, closer to the river, grew a vegetable patch. Rows of plants, all about two inches high, were clearly set out and obviously carefully cultivated. I could see from the debris still clinging to many of the trees that the hurricane had brought high water well past the clearing where the cabin sat.

"I don't see how someone who has a vegetable garden could be a murderer," Margaret whispered, looking at me. "Do you?"

I clasped her forearm to steady my footing between the large tree roots and brush in which we stood. "Nevertheless, Margaret, it appears that it's at least a possibility." I, too, whispered. The environment seemed to call for it.

"Sure seems quiet around here," she said. "Spooky, almost."

"Yeah, I noticed that. The birds don't even seem to sing."

"Yeah," she whispered. "No crickets, no birds, not even a breeze, though I'm getting cold, Mavis."

"I wonder if they know we're here," I said. We had been down on our haunches. I shifted back on the ground until I was sitting cross-legged under a tree with low-hanging branches. I could see the cabin through the tall weeds, but hoped the occupants, if any, couldn't see us.

Margaret crawled over beside me and sat on some brush and pine needles. "You know what this reminds me of?" She was talking softly, her eyes glued to the cabin as were mine.

"What?"

"In the movies where the Indians would hide from the settlers and catch them when they were off-guard."

"Right."

"Or when other settlers would go searching for survivors of Indian raids. You know how sometimes the Indians would hide in the cabins after they attacked the settlers and then attack the next group that came along?"

"No, tell me. Did they do that?"

"I don't know, but it seems like I saw it in a movie." She glanced at me, subdued, innocent, and then back at the cabin. "I remember an old Gary Cooper movie where he and this lady he loved—that he'd saved from the Indians—found this cabin with no one in it. There was food still there and all—like the people had left in a hurry. It was creepy. The dog was still there, I think, and eventually he led Gary Cooper and the lady to the bodies of the settlers. Yuck."

"Don't get carried away, Margaret."

"I was just thinking about it, that's all."

"You sound like Candy. She got you watching that old stuff?"

"Yeah," she said and smiled, "most of it's pretty good, too. You ought to watch some of them, Mavis."

"Maybe I will sometime."

"There's this other one where—"

"Margaret."

"What?"

"I hate to interrupt your reverie, but don't you think we ought to give some thought to what we're doing here?"

"We're watching the cabin."

"Yes, Margaret, but I mean, what we're going to do next?"

"Oh, yeah, I guess so." She sounded disappointed.

"I was thinking that the more intelligent thing to do would be to wait until dark."

"There was a movie by that name."

"Please, Margaret . . ."

"Sorry." She leaned forward in a slouch, elbows on knees, and stared at the clearing.

Feeling like a tough taskmaster, I said, "It's just that we've got to have a plan, that's all."

She wouldn't look at me. "I know."

"Okay," I said, "stop trying to make me feel guilty. You're doing it, you know. Help me think this thing out."

"It's just that lately you never seem to want to talk," she said in a whiny voice.

"I'd love to talk, Margaret. Just not now. I'm a little nervous about this, okay? I thought you wanted to be in on things—well, now's the time. Let's make a plan." I knew I should have left her at home.

Her eyes lit up. "I've got it. After dark, we'll sneak up on him. We can separate. One of us can go to the front door of the cabin and one, the back. We'll rush him."

"Are you nuts? You want to get shot?"

Her face fell. "I didn't think about that. I just thought we could catch him in-between us."

"Wrong," I said. "In the first place, if he's a maniac, when he heard someone at the front door, he'd shoot without asking questions. In the second place, wouldn't it be better to try to get a peek in the windows and see what the layout is and where the kids are?"

"Oh, right, and then we can decide what to do."

"I was thinking that if the kids are all right, maybe we should wait for the police."

"Mavis, I can't believe you're saying that."

"I don't want to place Jeanine and Tommy in any jeopardy, Margaret. What if he hurt them on account of us?"

"Oh. I hadn't thought of that."

"It's settled then. In a few minutes, it will be dark enough to go take a look. One of us will have to do it."

"I'll wait for you here," Margaret said.

"That's what I thought. Better yet, why don't you go back to the car now, before it's too dark, and get your flashlight and come back here."

"Okay. You'll wait for me before you go?"

"Yes." I watched her as she wound her way through the trees and out of sight, giving me a wistful look—or was it fearful—before she left.

I sat in the silence, still staring at the cabin in the clearing, waiting for night to fall. When it did, it seemed sudden. I couldn't see the sunset through the trees. It did cross my mind to wonder what in the heck we were doing there, but I pushed that thought away. Amid much thrashing, Margaret reappeared, flashlight in hand, and in the wink of an eye, everything went dark.

No lights appeared in the cabin at first, then I could detect a dim glow, like that of a candle, shining through the window. The night sounds began abruptly. It was as though a conductor raised his baton and signaled the orchestra to begin. Who knew how many varieties of creatures and critters populated the forest and all of them sent a representative to play.

I gathered my courage and stood, brushing myself off. "Margaret, I'm going," I whispered toward her outline in the dark.

"Good luck," she whispered back.

I crouched and ran at an angle to the cabin, toward the corner between the front and side windows, praying no one was peering out. I held my shoulder bag with my left hand, my right inside on the butt of my .38.

When I got to the cabin, I tiptoed to the edge of the side

window and peeked in. It was the kitchen area, separated from the remainder by a shelf that blocked my view.

I tiptoed around to the front, crouched down until I got under the front window, and stood up only enough to get a view of the interior. When I did, what I could make out by the dim light was a total surprise.

Chapter Fifteen

"What I can't figure out," Margaret said as she drove back down the dark highway toward Houston, "is how they knew anyone would find them there."

To say that we felt dejected, disappointed, and disillusioned at finding the empty cabin would be grossly underestimating the true nature of our feelings. We didn't feel that good. I sat close to the passenger door, contemplating jumping out when she was going very fast, wishing more than ever for a cigarette or a beer or even a donut to feed my addiction and make me feel better, if only temporarily, my brain spinning around with horrible thoughts.

"Mavis . . ."

"I heard you."

"What do you think?"

"I have a lot of thoughts on the matter, Margaret," I said as I watched the landscape whiz by.

"Mind telling me?"

I sighed long and hard. "Seems like something fishy's going on, like they were tipped off or something. The question is, by whom?"

"I don't know. Who?"

"Well, I have several good ideas, Margaret. Like Frankie, the Lawson's housekeeper. They may have called her and she could have told them what Hilary has been saying about Woodridge."

"I've been wondering why the police didn't show up. Think they knew Mr. Woodridge and the kids were already gone?"

"Possibly. Captain Milton may have already known about the cabin and was just trying to get rid of me."

"I don't believe that."

Sometimes Margaret is unbelievably naive. Sometimes I am. This looked like one of those times. "Why not? It sure kept us busy for a day."

"Yeah." She, too, sighed. "It sure did."

"Then, there is the prospect of Arthur Woodridge never having been there in the first place, but that seems unlikely since laundry still hung on the line. So maybe he was there until the kids went with him and then blew it off. Maybe he's trying to keep everyone guessing. Confusing the issue."

"That could be it."

"Worst of all is the thought that maybe somehow, someway, Mrs. Lawson had something to do with it. She's the one that put everyone onto the cabin in the first place. At least she did me, telling me about the place and to talk to McAfee about it."

"Oh, Mavis. The poor woman—with her husband dead and all—I can't believe that."

"It is far-fetched, I'll admit, but it's a possibility."

"I'd hate to think it's true."

"Why do you say that? You haven't even met her. She's very strange. A very strange snob." I watched Margaret's face. Lights flickered on it as the cars flashed by us going the other way.

"But I feel sorry for her."

"Yeah. You would. She's really not as pitiful as you want to think, Margaret. I wouldn't be surprised if she was in this up to her hairline."

"But what about that McAfee guy? The police did pick him up. Maybe he had something to do with it."

"That's true. And you know, besides him, we still need to check out that Clayton Hadley. He's a real creep. And the stockbroker—Earl Smythe. I'm always suspicious of people with weird names. We need to see what they're really about. And then there's always the possibility of their wives. Maybe Lawson was having an affair with all of them."

"Oh—I don't believe that." Margaret laughed. "Mr. Lawson was getting kind of old for that much activity."

"You never know with Viagra."

"What if . . ." Margaret stopped in mid-sentence. She was getting excited. I could tell from the pitch of her voice and the way she breathed in and out quickly. It was bound to be something spacey.

I said, "What? What if he really died of a hard attack instead of a heart attack?"

"Ha!" Margaret burst out laughing. "A hard attack. That's a good one. Ha!" She chortled for few moments. That's one of the reasons I keep her around. She laughs at my jokes.

"No, really, what if . . . if one of those men really took the kids and Arthur Woodridge didn't do anything?"

Margaret really has strange ideas sometimes. Strange, but interesting.

"Why would one of them want the kids?" I asked, trying to remain calm and not break her face.

"If they wanted to make it look like Mr. Woodridge killed Mr. Lawson. One of them could have kidnapped the kids and killed Mr. Lawson and the kids. If he hid their bodies, then no one would believe Mr. Woodridge didn't do it, and he'd, Mr. Whoever, be in the clear and get whatever it was they wanted that they had to kill for." She glanced at me. She could probably see the look of disbelief on my face in the flashing light. Judging from what she said next, I think she did. "It was just a thought."

"Well, keep them to yourself."

"God, what a grouch."

"Aw, I'm just hungry."

The next few minutes passed in silence as we approached Houston and started passing the little shacky joints on the side of the road.

"Tomorrow, I want you to do some checking on McAfee, Hadley, and Smythe," I said.

"You mean you think what I thought could be true?"

"No, I don't think they have the kids, but any one of them could have killed Harrison Lawson. It could be totally unrelated."

"You promised Ben you'd stay out of that."

"No, I didn't. We need to find out what possible motives any of the three of them could have. We already have suspicions about McAfee, but do some more checking anyway. And on the others, too. Lawson and Hadley may have had some strange real estate deal going on, and Mrs. McAfee started to tell me about Smythe but got cut off. Something about the stock market."

"What do you want me to do?"

"Find out what you can about their criminal histories, and then get on the computer and search the real estate records. See what really big real estate deals have been going on recently."

"What are you going to be doing?"

"For one thing, I'm going to see what the medical examiner has to say. Then I'll just go see Smythe and Hadley and see what they have to say for themselves."

"Okay, Mavis. Is there anything special you want Candy to do when she gets out of school?"

"She could maybe call some of those kids back and see if there's been any more contact. Also, go ahead and print out at least some preliminary info on poisons like household, plant, common poisons, etcetera. Don't print the whole million pages, though."

"Actually it was more than a million."

Margaret can be literal. "Just a few on each, okay?" We were getting close to home. I was so frustrated that I thought I'd have a beer and then hit the sack. It was after ten so I'd wait until the next day to call Mrs. Lawson about what we didn't find. In fact, I might go pay her another visit in person and see if I could read her reaction. I also wanted to talk to Frankie again. Boy, did I.

"By the way, Mavis, did you ever call Annette Jensen back?" Margaret asked.

"Omigosh. I was supposed to meet her at nine at Lana's. Shit."

"Oh, no. You forgot her?"

I shook my head and didn't bother saying anything sarcastic in response. "Just get me home, Margaret. I'll go over there and see if she's still waiting."

"Oh, no," Margaret said again, her voice growing shrill.

That was going to be one angry lady, especially if any of the locals tried to pick her up. I laughed at the thought and Margaret gave me a weird look. As soon as she dropped me off, I drove like a maniac to where I hoped Annette would still be waiting.

Lana's was just getting going good at that time of night. It's a neighborhood joint where I sometimes go to have a beer and a game of pool. Lana's chili burgers aren't too bad, either. No hassles. We all live in the same vicinity and look after each other. If a stranger comes in, everybody's curiosity is aroused and no one settles down until the stranger is gone again or meets up with a local if that's his or her intent.

Once, years before my time, there was a shoot-out inside. The would-be robbers shot Lana's husband when he reached for his baseball bat. That's why she keeps a loaded shotgun handy now. On the bar, next to where one of the bullets ricocheted, there's a brass plaque commemorating the occasion. After Mr. Perez got shot, the neighbors jumped the guy who shot him and beat him to a pulp before calling the police. That's the kind of place it is.

After my eyes adjusted to the darkness, I did a visual search of the place. Annette wasn't there. Lana came out from behind the bar, a large, white dishtowel pinned around her middle.

"You lookin' for an old lady, Mavis?"

"Yeah. She was supposed to meet me here at nine, but I got sidetracked."

"Some long sidetrack. You see what time it is? The old lady was very upset. She give me this to give to you," she said, pressing a piece of paper into my hand.

"Shit," I said.

"Huh uh, I don't allow talk like that in my place and you know it." She wagged a finger in my face.

"Sorry, Lana." I shrugged. "It's been a bad day." Unfolding the paper, I saw Annette's home address scrawled on it in perfect penmanship. It said, "Please come right away."

"How long has she been gone?"

"About forty-five minutes."

"Thanks, Lana, you're a sweetheart. Hey, while I'm here, I wanted to ask you something. Have you ever heard of a drink called schnapps?"

"*Si*. The Germans or Austrians—same thing—drink it. Nasty tasting stuff."

"You carry it?"

She shook her head. "No one would buy it."

I nodded and patted her cheek before heading for the door.

"Next time we have a nice visit, okay, Mavis?" she called.

"Soon, Lana."

Annette lived in a neighborhood called Oak Forest. Not unlike my own, it had fifty-year-old homes and large trees pushing up sidewalks. The houses were relatively small, two- or three-bedroom, wood frames, most with carports instead of garages, but the lots on which they sat were large, the subdivision having been constructed before the oil boom when land wasn't so dear. I drove slowly down the road checking the numbers by the streetlamps that were spaced too far apart.

When I located Annette's house, there was a car in the drive, but the house was strangely dark, the porch light not lit. Perhaps she had given up on me and gone to bed. I couldn't blame her. I felt guilty when I thought about her having to wait so long while I was on a wild-goose chase.

I parked and walked to the front of the house. The screen door needed a fresh coat of white paint. I rapped on the wood frame; it banged loosely against the molding, unlatched. Pulling the door open, this time I knocked harder on the front door. No answer. I pounded again. Nothing. I turned the knob, but the door was locked.

I didn't know if I should go away and try to see her the next day, or call her on my cell, or try a window. Something about the place gave me an uneasy feeling.

I went back to my car and got a flashlight out of my trunk. Circling around the side of the house, I shined the light but couldn't see inside because the curtains were drawn. I worked my way around to the back door, rapped again, and the door came open. I wanted to run.

I reached in, feeling around the doorframe for the light switch. "Annette." I found the switch, but when I flipped it, no light. To say that I was tense from that moment on would not be an overstatement.

I shined my flashlight around the kitchen and took a couple of cautious steps toward the next room. My foot came down on an unmoving lump of something. Flashing my light downward, I saw a bulldog. It lay on its side like it was asleep, but when I crouched down I could see that it wasn't. Someone had bashed in its little head, and it lay in a puddle of still-warm blood. I felt around for a pulse but couldn't find any.

A shuffling sound assailed me from another room, then footsteps came toward me. Someone shoved me down on the floor. He, and I use that word advisedly, ran past me and out the back door. I tried to get to my feet but slipped in the dog blood. By the time I got my balance and ran around to the front of the house, whoever it was had gone. In the distance, I heard a car and knew it was useless to try to follow them.

I went back into the house, stepped past the dog, and tried the lights in the living room. Nothing. Whoever it was had taken care not to be seen by anyone. I shined my light around until I found my way into the master bedroom, searching for Annette. She wasn't there. I checked the bathroom and the spare bedroom and went back to search the living room. I found her crumpled on the floor in front of a swivel rocker. Her head was in much the same condition as her dog's. The telephone lay beside her, the receiver on the hook. I might not ever know who she was trying to call.

I checked Annette's pulse. It was faint, but still there.

With two fingers, I punched nine-one-one for an ambulance and the police. Then I called and woke up Ben. Then I retraced my steps to the back door, went outside into the yard, and threw up.

Chapter Sixteen

Poor Annette wasn't dead. Yet.

First, uniformed cops arrived. Then the ambulance. Then Ben. Then, of all people, Lon Tyler. If Ben hadn't been there, we'd have tangled more than we did.

I was a mess. There is something about dog blood that unsettles my stomach. After I threw up, I noticed that not only did I have dog blood all over my hands, but when I slipped and fell in it, it covered the knees and backside of my best polyester pants. And when I searched around in my car for my purse for something to wipe my mouth with, I got it on the seat, my purse, and my face. I almost got sick again the next time I saw it in the light when I realized it.

I was sitting on the floor next to Annette when the paramedics arrived and asked me to step outside, which I did. I had moved to the front stoop when Ben pulled up behind the ambulance.

"Mavis," he called. "That you?" Trudging in my direction, his flashlight illuminating my torso, he stopped a few feet away. "What is that on your clothes?"

"Dog blood. I don't think any of Annette's got mixed up in it."

"Annette?"

"The woman inside. The woman I promised to meet at Lana's and forgot about." I wasn't feeling so good about myself right then.

Lights blazing and siren wailing, a police car came to a screeching halt behind Ben's. Out jumped Lon, just what I needed, ha.

"Okay, Davis," Lon said when he waltzed up like the leader of the promenade, "what did you do now?" He wore a uniform that looked not only like he slept in it but smelled like he pulled it out of the dirty clothes hamper to put it on.

"Not a damn thing," I said. That happened to be my problem, but I wasn't volunteering anything.

"I heard there was a dead broad inside. You know her?"

"She's not dead." I stood and wiped my sweaty palms on the sides of my pants. "Go inside and see for yourself."

"I will." Lon trotted around to the back of the house when I pointed that way.

"He is such a pig," I said to Ben.

"I hate to tell you this, honey, but tonight you'd be in a tight contest with him."

"I don't need that. I've got to get out of here and go home and get a shower."

We stood looking at each other for a few moments. He didn't act as if he wanted to touch me and I didn't blame him.

The front door was thrown open and a paramedic backed out, pulling a gurney, bumping the screen door wide with his butt. When he and his female partner got Annette positioned on the porch, they lifted the gurney and carried her down the steps to the yard where they rolled her to the ambulance.

The lights lit up the house, followed by a patrolman coming from the other side and mumbling something about the breaker.

"Did you mess with the crime scene?" Lon stood in the doorway with his hands on his meaty hips.

I looked from Annette on the gurney to Lon. "Moi?"

"Yes, you. There's blood and smeared footprints everywhere, especially in the kitchen."

"Not intentionally. It was dark. I fell. After the paramedics came, I washed myself off with water and paper towels at the kitchen sink."

"And obscured the evidence."

I hadn't even known he knew that word. "I said it wasn't intentional."

"Sometimes you are so—"

"That's enough, Lon," Ben said.

"This isn't any of your business, Sergeant. What are you doing here anyway? This has nothing to do with narcotics."

Ben's face indicated that he was not at all pleased with Lon. "I'm making it my business. And you're not going to talk to Miss Davis that way."

"Miss Davis—" Lon's tone left something to be desired.

I said in a subdued tone, "You don't have to take care of me, Ben."

"Keep out of this, Mavis. I'm taking her home, Lon. She'll come down in the morning and make a statement."

"She'll go down and make it now," Lon said.

"I already cleared it with your captain," Ben said. "Come on, Mavis."

We headed for the sidewalk.

"I hope that's true, Sergeant," Lon called after us.

Ben said, "One of these days that guy is going to push me too far."

By that time, we were at the sidewalk and Lon couldn't have heard us. "I'm glad I'm not the only one who finds him annoying."

"Let's go in my car. I'll bring you back to yours tomorrow," Ben said.

I shook my head. "I appreciate it, but I just want to get a

shower and get in bed. But thanks for getting me away from Lon. I know I can't hug you or anything because of the blood, but thanks, Ben." I backed toward my car. "Don't be angry."

He smiled. "Guess I really didn't want you sitting on my upholstery anyway. Talk to you tomorrow?"

I nodded and headed for home.

My head hit the pillow well past the witching hour and, even though I was bushed, I couldn't do anything but stare at the ceiling in the dark, angry. Someone was jacking with me, and I didn't like it. I was sure it wasn't only the police. I suspected everyone with whom I'd come into contact. The whole setup, at the cabin and at Annette's, was one of the screwiest things I'd ever encountered and the people were some of the strangest. If being rich made a person weird, they could have it.

I must have finally drifted off, because the next thing I knew, I awoke to the ringing of the telephone. I found it and put it to my ear. The clock's little hand was on the two and the big one on the six.

"Miss Davis?" a voice I was too sleepy to identify said.

"Who is it?" I muttered.

"Are you awake?"

"Am now. Who is this? What do you want in the middle of the night?"

"It's Tommy Lawson. I need to talk to you."

Nothing like a shock to make one immediately alert. "Where are you?"

"I'll tell you that in a minute if you'll say you'll come and get us."

"Sure. Are you okay? Is Jeanine all right?"

"We're fine, but we want to see you as soon as possible. It's very important."

"Okay, but where?"

"Huntsville State Park. Right at the Sam Houston National Forest."

"Ugh."

"I know it's a long drive, Miss Davis, but please—"

"I'll come. Let me turn on the light and find something to write with—hold on." I scrambled around and found the stub of a pencil and an empty utility bill envelope. "Tell me how to find you when I get there."

"We're at a campsite." He described how to find their campground.

"Who else is there?"

"Father."

"Arthur Woodridge?"

"Yes, our father."

"Has he hurt you?"

"I can't talk any more right now, Miss Davis. I don't have enough change and our cell phones won't work. Just come, right away, and make sure you aren't followed," he said and hung up.

That last line was getting old. I wasn't exactly jumping for joy at the prospect of meeting Arthur Woodridge in the dark. I pulled on a pair of jeans, a shirt, tennis shoes, and grabbed my purse, which held my gun. I brushed my hair, ran a wet washcloth over my face, and was on my way, praying my sweet little Mustang would make it there.

If I thought Interstate 45 was dark in the middle of the night, it was nothing compared to the piney woods of Huntsville State Park. Some hour and a few minutes after Tommy's phone call, I arrived. Not knowing what the setup was, I didn't park where Tommy instructed me to. Instead, I cut my lights early and left the car near the main park road and walked, my gun drawn but down at my side so that it wouldn't be obvious.

The night noises again were loud. They brought back memories of camping when I was a youngster and how in the middle of the night when I had to pee I'd be scared something was going to eat me but had to go so bad that I'd brave the critters and make a run for the restrooms and showers. None of my brothers and sisters ever had to go in the middle of the night. When I'd wake them up to go with me, they'd threaten to kill me if I didn't shut up and go alone. When I couldn't hold it much longer, I would.

I never liked camping much. I didn't like sneaking about in the forest now, sure there was a bear hiding behind every tree and a snake hanging down from each branch, its fangs waiting to clamp shut on my jugular vein. My version of the ideal campsite was a Holiday Inn.

A lantern glow in the distance guided me. As I grew closer, I spotted the shadow of a tent. As I crept from tree to tree, I felt like one of the wolves in the cartoons. When they stalk their prey, their skinny little bodies tiptoe quickly to hide behind skinny little trees. Not that I could claim to be skinny.

A concrete picnic table came into view, then the outline of a person sitting on the bench, his back to me. I scurried to the shelter of a large tree. Their car sat several feet beyond the tent. It was Tommy sitting on the bench and a girl was sitting cross-legged on a sleeping bag on the ground. I could hear the soft murmur of their voices. The girl's laughter tinkled unmistakably in the dark.

"You won't need that gun," a deep voice boomed loudly next to my ear simultaneously with something jabbing me in the back.

I jumped at least a mile off the ground before a hand quickly closed over mine and took my revolver. "Don't shoot," I croaked. "It's me, Mavis." When I calmed down sufficiently to recover my wits, I was face-to-face with a man who, in the dark, fit the description of Arthur Woodridge, and I was defenseless.

He wasn't pointing my gun at me, though. He shoved it into the waistband of his jeans and took me by the elbow. It was one of the few times in my life that I was rendered speechless. He spoke softly as he escorted me to Tommy and the girl I assumed was Jeanine.

"I'm not going to hurt you, Miss Davis," he said, "but I can't let you go around wielding your gun at us, either." His voice gentle, his hand on my arm was the same. When we got closer to the light from the lantern, I saw a tall, very thin man with silvery-blond hair. State-issued wire-rimmed glasses framed his pale, washed-out blue eyes. He'd rolled up the sleeves of his blue work shirt; the tail tucked in neatly around his waist. A stereotypical criminal-type, he wasn't.

"Is this your Miss Davis, Tommy?"

Tommy turned toward me and smiled. "Miss Davis, did Father surprise you?" He laughed. "He's part Indian, you know."

The girl laughed then, too. So did I, albeit a bit nervously.

"I'm glad to see that you kids are all right." I sat on the bench next to Tommy and gave him a little hug. "You are Jeanine, aren't you?" I said to the girl.

"It's nice to meet you," she said. She was the spitting image of her mother minus the hard age lines around the mouth and eyes. The yellow hue of the lantern light made her look hardly more than a child.

"We were so worried about both of you. Your phone calls were so mysterious. Why didn't you tell Margaret what's been going on?"

I glanced from one teenager to the other. There really wasn't any family resemblance. Tommy had definitely inherited his looks from his father. Both kids wore work shirts and brand-new jeans and tennis shoes. They appeared nothing but healthy and happy, maybe a little tired around the eyes, but after all, it was the middle of the night.

Tommy laughed again. "I kept running out of change. Besides, I didn't know if the police were listening in or what, Miss Davis. This thing's become a big mess."

I looked at Mr. Woodridge who stood by the grill and poured what I assumed to be coffee into a cup from a tin pot. "Want some coffee?"

I shook my head and watched as he sat down on the sleeping bag next to Jeanine and sipped from his mug. I didn't know what he knew or what he'd done, except that he hadn't hurt the children. He looked perfectly harmless except for my gun sitting on the ground in front of him.

"You know your father is dead, don't you?" I asked.

Tommy stared at the ground. "You mean our adopted father," he said softly.

"Harrison Lawson is who I mean, and I can tell you already know about it."

"We read about it in the papers," Jeanine said, her voice defensive.

"Maybe I'd better just be quiet and let the three of you tell me what the heck is going on," I said, giving each of them a look that would have made Margaret and Candy cringe.

Jeanine and Tommy exchanged glances with each other and then with Arthur Woodridge.

"We need you to help clear this thing up, Miss Davis," Woodridge said.

"Yeah, the papers say Daddy kidnapped us," Jeanine said, "but he didn't. We wanted to come. Didn't we, Tommy?"

Tommy said, "I didn't know, at first, but now I do, Miss Davis. Frankie tried to get me to go see Dad when Jeanine did, but I was—I guess you could say—afraid."

I smiled. “I know. Frankie told me.” I looked at Mr. Woodridge. “She also told me she’d been writing to you.”

“Every week for all those years,” he said. “Since my folks died, hers were the only letters I got.”

“It must have been hard, being in there all that time.”

“It was, but it’s behind me now. What I’m worried about is the future.”

“Yeah,” Jeanine said. “What are we going to do about everyone thinking Daddy killed Mr. Lawson?”

“I don’t know, Jeanine.” I looked at Woodridge. “I’m not a coffee drinker, but I guess I will take a cup. I need something to keep me awake while we figure out what we’re going to do and get you all back to town.”

Woodridge set his cup down to get up when suddenly there were some crunching noises, like branches breaking, then a lot of footsteps pounding, and then a voice said, “Hold it right there. Police.”

Chapter Seventeen

The next few minutes were like a garbled nightmare. Everything happened at breakneck speed but seemed like slow motion. Terror flashed across Arthur Woodridge's face. His hand flew toward his waistband and then the ground in front of him.

An emphatic, male voice said, "Just try it, buster."

Woodridge raised his hands into the air. His look at me was one of confusion.

Jeanine stiffened upright, shock on her face, and glared at me.

Tommy cut his eyes at me and then shifted his body away. He didn't say anything but wouldn't look back at me, either.

A large number of men in various departmental uniforms converged upon us. Headlights flashed and engines roared as several cars pulled close. It seemed like a war zone.

Lon Tyler and Captain Milton in plainclothes trudged into the light. A man in a Walker County Sheriff's uniform strode forward with a shotgun pointed at Arthur Woodridge. He snatched my gun off the ground and handed it to another deputy, then the shotgun, and yanked Woodridge around, cuffing his hands behind his back. Woodridge never spoke. His chin rested on his chest.

"Thanks, Mavis," Lon said loudly, sneering at me.

"How could you?" Jeanine yelled in a strained, hysterical voice. She ran toward her father. Another cop pulled her away.

I started to go to her, to explain that I didn't, but Captain Milton grabbed my arm, restraining me. "Not so fast, Mavis. Stay right where you are."

"Tommy," I said, turning to the boy whose back was to me. "I didn't do it." I grabbed his forearm, but he jerked it away and walked over to stand next to his sister.

"Sarah," Captain Milton yelled. "Come get these kids."

A female police officer appeared from behind Lon and approached the kids. "You'll have to come with me." She took Jeanine's wrist, but Jeanine jerked away.

"Where are you taking my father?" Jeanine screamed at the deputy who held Woodridge by the elbow.

"To jail, kid," Lon said. "Where he belongs."

"No." She broke away from the woman and ran to Woodridge, throwing her arms around him. "He didn't do anything."

The woman followed Jeanine and pulled on her, but Jeanine held on for dear life, crying and saying, "He's innocent. You have to let him go."

Woodridge, his shoulders slumped, his head bowed, murmured something in her ear.

"Get that kid away from him," the captain yelled at still another deputy.

The female officer pulled at one of her hands, a male deputy struggled with the other, then Tommy hurried to them and said, "I'll get her." Tommy crooned to her, "Come on, Jeanine. It won't do any good. Come on. Let go. It'll be okay; I promise." Tears streamed down his face, too, and he reached up around her and pulled each of her arms from around their father.

She threw her arms around her brother, saying, "No," and sobbing.

Tommy glanced over her head at Woodridge. "We'll get help, Father. Don't worry. We'll tell them what happened."

Woodridge smiled a melancholy smile. "I know you will, son."

The deputy took Woodridge by the arm and led him away. All eyes followed their silhouettes as they trooped toward the headlights.

I heard more voices and saw a television camera on a man's shoulder. A very large man appeared at Captain Milton's side. I recognized the second man as an investigative reporter from one of the Houston TV stations. "Congratulations, Captain. One of the most effective operations I've ever seen. No one hurt. No shots fired."

"Thanks, Walt," Milton said.

"Want to say a few words before the camera?"

"Uh-uh. You just summarize the situation, okay?"

"Okay. Those the kids over there?"

"Yep."

"They okay? He do anything to them?"

"They appear to be fine. We'll have to have them examined by a doctor and get statements from them, but I think they're mostly all right. Just tired from the ordeal."

"Well, great. Just great. Good job, Captain."

Captain Milton nodded to the reporter. "Go on, Sarah," he hollered to the woman officer. "Let's get those kids home to their mother. Lon, radio Houston to call Mrs. Lawson and tell her the kids are all right."

"Yes, sir," Lon said. He was still sneering at me as he hustled off in the direction of the light.

"Come on, kids," the woman said. "The car's down on the main road. You got anything you want to take with you?"

Tommy still had his arms around Jeanine who wept softly into his shoulder. "No, ma'am," he replied. He stole a glance at me as they walked past. I could see the tearstains on his face and the frown lines around his mouth. The slant of his eyes told me that he thought I'd betrayed them.

"Some of you men gather up their belongings. We'll need it for evidence," Captain Milton said. "Christy, go down to that Walker County car before he gets away and get the keys to Woodridge's car. You can drive it back. And send Ben Sorensen up here."

That last was the worst of all. I wouldn't have felt a bigger jolt if lightning had struck me. I sank back on the picnic bench and hugged myself, feeling as though I'd been punched in the stomach by a pro. My mouth tasted sour.

The cameraman and the reporter positioned themselves to the left of where I sat so they could film the tent in the glare from the headlights. I heard the drone of the reporter's voice as he began his narration of events. Words like "kidnapper" and "alleged killer."

I looked at the scene as the cops dismantled it, piece by piece. One of the uniforms was searching the trunk of Woodridge's car. Another man yanked out the tent poles and set about folding up the tent. A third officer rolled up the sleeping bag on which Jeanine and her father had sat just a few minutes earlier.

I hadn't noticed before, but a Walker County deputy stood very near me. He wasn't doing anything except toying with a pair of handcuffs and watching the scene. I reached toward the table for my purse, but he jumped for it, grabbing it out of my hand. I realized then that I was in deep shit.

"I was only going to get a stick of gum," I said. He was a big one.

He pulled open my shoulder bag and searched it. Then he tossed it to me. "Okay."

I found a bent up pack of gum and stuck a piece in my mouth, my hands shaking. The cop took my purse and set it away from me.

"You going to arrest me?"

"Not sure yet. Just supposed to watch you until the HPD captain tells me different."

"What'd I do?"

"Accessory, I think."

"Oh." Accessory to what he didn't say. Other than when I was in college, I had never been arrested. That was just city court and a small fine for refusing to depart from a sit-in. I'd been in the county jail, though, many times. I used to visit my probationers when they'd violated their probation and been arrested. I didn't like the jail. The metal door clanging shut was such a final sound. It always gave me the creeps. The thought of spending a night there was not appealing. Even a few hours. My mind began running down the list of lawyers for whom we'd been serving papers, doing home studies, and interviewing witnesses. I tried to remember if any of them practiced criminal law or made bail bonds. I wondered if I would be able to get out of this mess.

I was still pondering my dilemma when up walked Ben. He sat down beside me on the bench, leaned back, his elbows on the edge of the table, and crossed his legs.

"I guess you're pretty sore at me, aren't you?" He stared at the campsite.

If looks could kill, Ben would have just uttered his last words.

"When are you going to accept the fact that it's my job? I have a duty to perform." His clipped speech sounded rehearsed.

I spit my gum toward the captain. The cop who babysat me shot me a dirty look. I crossed my arms about my chest and stared straight ahead.

I could feel Ben's eyes burning a hole in the side of my face. "I would have been derelict in my duties if I hadn't informed them that you were going to meet Tommy."

A prepared speech if I ever heard one.

"Besides, I was worried that you might be in danger. I knew you'd probably take your gun."

Was that concern in his voice? How touching.

"You were breaking the law by not calling us in the first place."

I'm such a hardened criminal.

"And you're not supposed to carry that gun. You don't have a license."

Armed and dangerous.

"Look at me." He grabbed my shoulders and twisted me around.

I was carrying knives, too. Daggers. They flew out of my eyes and pierced his.

"If you didn't have such a blabbermouth working for you," his voice was a fierce whisper, "this never would have happened. But look at it this way. That man could have killed you. You didn't know what the situation was. You could have walked into a hornet's nest."

A hornet's nest wouldn't have hurt me more than knowing that Ben betrayed the trust I thought we had. Mother always said, "If you can't say anything nice, don't say anything at all." This was one of those times, so I kept my lips sealed. I just sat there and shifted my mind to figuring out which blabbermouth he was talking about. I didn't even know I was going to meet Tommy, how could one of the girls? It had to be Candy. Margaret had been with me.

Tommy must have called earlier. Ben must have called, too, or else dropped by, and Candy told him. Candy was not long for this world.

So what did the cops do? Were they waiting for me when I left? Were they parked down the street from my apartment, and I never even noticed? Was I so sleepy that I couldn't detect a tail on me? Shit.

Ben's eyes searched my face, and from the look on his, he knew it was useless talking. We had been together too long for him not to know how I would react. What he didn't know, and I wasn't telling, was that I was as angry at myself as I was at him.

"Forget it," he said abruptly. "Just forget it."

I glanced up. What did he mean by that?

"You're in a lot of trouble, you know," he said.

I sighed and shrugged my shoulders. "Just go away, Ben," I said finally.

"I want to help you." His hand reached over and took mine, but I snatched it away.

I looked back at the campsite. It was mostly dismantled now. I heard a car start and saw the headlights of Arthur Woodridge's car come on. The officer called Christy was ready to leave for Houston.

Smoke trailed from the grill where a few moments ago someone had dumped the contents of the coffee pot on the coals. The smell of damp leaves and coffee permeated the air. The lantern and tent were gone.

Captain Milton came trudging over to us. "You're under arrest, Mavis," he said in a matter-of-fact voice.

I stood and put my hands behind my back.

The captain nodded at the cop who'd been standing by. After he'd shot me that dirty look, the deputy had stayed a little distance away. He came over, the handcuffs readied, and gave me an odd look. "Put your hands in front of you," he said, but he wasn't gruff about it.

"That's not necessary, is it, Captain?" Ben asked.

I stuck my hands out toward the cop, fully realizing for the first time that he worked for Walker County—that I would be going to the Walker County jail, not the Harris County jail which would have been bad enough. Glaring at Ben, all my anger burst forth. "I don't want your help, you son-of-a-bitch."

"Cuff her and get her out of here," Captain Milton said.

Chapter Eighteen

The last time I visited a jail, I had been a probation officer on the outside looking in. The view from inside gives one a different perspective. Since it was almost dawn when I finally arrived, most of the nighttime activity had ceased. The drunks were asleep. The puke had been cleaned up, but the odor still penetrated my nostrils like tiny arrows, the offending aroma not being completely disguised by the mop bucket of ammonia kept in the ready for just such occasions. My eyes burned even though I breathed through my mouth. Jail staff waited wearily for shift change, speaking in muted tones, energy levels low. A couple of deputies dozed.

After feeding the county computer all the information about me, taking my fingerprints, and processing the contents of my purse, the ID sergeant let me make my obligatory phone call. I called Margaret collect and urged her to find me an attorney and bonding company a-sap. A matron, or as they call them now, a female deputy, took me to a temporary holding tank. Later, they transferred me to a cell, which was like a hospital ward. Welcome to Bedlam, Texas, where ladies of the evening, drug addicts, drunks, petty criminals, and private detectives are all lumped together. If you aren't nuts when you arrive, you might very well be at departure.

Later that morning, the jail resumed normalcy. They served something they alleged to be breakfast on institutional plastic trays. I'm afraid I pined for my morning tea. Afterward, I listened to high-pitched female voices as they rose and fell, refusing to let anyone engage me in conversation. I wasn't interested in making any new acquaintances.

The doors clanked open to release those assigned to custodial duties around the jail and clanged shut again. Workers shuffled down the halls in their jail scuffs. Fresh uniforms were issued, the soiled ones collected for the laundry. No one seemed to notice that I wore my street clothes. Maybe they knew something I didn't. I sat there trying to be patient while female deputies took a few inmates at a time for their weekly trip to the commissary to purchase cigarettes, candy, and toiletries. The women taunted those left behind.

At ten-thirty, the iron bars clunked open and a matron took me downstairs. The deputy sheriff led me to an enclosed booth. When I opened the door, I saw a woman a bit older than me with a cigarette hanging out of her mouth. Yakking on a cell phone and doodling on a yellow legal pad, her feet propped up on a chair, she had made herself at home. She put the phone away and stood as I closed the door behind me. She was a heavyset, tall woman, dressed in slacks and a short-sleeved jacket. We stood eye to eye.

"Gillian Wright," she said as she stuck her hand out.

"Mavis Davis." I shook hands with her, happy to experience a firm, almost bone-crushing handshake. "And if you're an attorney, girl, I'm really glad to see you."

She had large hands with nails unpolished but clean, a wedding band and huge diamond on her left and on her right, two school rings. She grinned, showing even, very white teeth, pulled her hand away, and gave me her card. I glanced at it quickly, noted that hers was the only name on it, and sat across from her.

"A Margaret Applebaum called me," she said as she

picked up her pen. Under her lightweight, light brown suit, she wore a pink tank top. She had short, graying, straight brown hair, almost–navy blue eyes under thick lashes, a turned up nose sprinkled with freckles, and full lips. "I don't usually go out of county without a ton of money up front, but that woman made your situation sound so interesting, I couldn't resist." Her teeth spread into a grin again. I wondered if she always smiled like that.

"I appreciate your coming. How much did Margaret tell you?"

"Enough for me to know that you don't belong in this joint." She raised her eyebrows, her eyes growing wide this time as she smiled. She stubbed out her cigarette and reached for another one. "Why don't you let me jot down some information for my records and then you can tell me about it, okay?"

"Okay." I couldn't resist grinning back at her. I felt much more optimistic.

"I've got your name, how about your business and home addresses and numbers?"

I gave her what she asked, and then she asked a little more, date of birth, social security and driver's license number.

"Any priors?"

"Nope—except a fine for a protest once a long time ago."

"You, too?" She grinned. "Where was that?"

"In Houston."

"Oh. Mine was the University of North Texas in Denton."

She laughed again. It would have gotten monotonous except it was so contagious.

"You always this cheerful?"

"Nope. First thing this morning I won a big divorce case. And the drive up here afterward wasn't half bad."

"Oh. So you don't just practice criminal law?"

"Criminal, family, probate, and other odds and ends. Not too many people rely solely on criminal law to make a living. That okay with you?"

"Fine," I said. I could see she was trying to be serious. I hoped I hadn't hurt her feelings. I thought I might like to get to know her better when I got out of this mess.

"Married, kids, any of that stuff?"

"Divorced."

She laid her pen down and turned in her chair, leaning back against the cold, stone wall and propped her feet up on the chair next to her again. Shaking her pack of cigarettes, she offered me one.

"I'm trying to quit, besides, I don't think you're supposed to smoke in here." I wanted a cigarette something awful, but no way would I allow the addict in me to get the upper hand. I gritted my teeth and breathed in her second-hand smoke.

"Good for you, girl." She ignored my last statement as she lit still another cigarette, blew out some smoke, and said, "Why don't you tell me what the shit's been going on?"

"Aren't you going to tell me all that stuff about confidentiality and lawyer-client privilege?"

"Didn't figure I needed to, or am I wrong in assuming you know a great deal about criminal law?"

"No, you're right. How'd you know? Margaret?"

"Yeah, and after she gave me some background on you when she was trying to convince me to come see you, I checked you out with a parole officer I once had an affair with." She laughed again; it came from deep inside her and sounded good. I laughed, too.

So I told her all about the case, not leaving anything out, right up until I landed in jail. She was a good listener, stopping me occasionally to make notes, then laying down her pen and puffing on her cigarette while I talked. She asked appropriate questions at appropriate times. I liked her.

"So they said you're charged as an accessory? I'll check it out. Something doesn't smell right. Of course, if Woodridge didn't really kidnap or kill anyone, you might get out of this pretty easily."

"That's what I'm hoping, but I've got to get out of jail to be able to prove he didn't do it."

She waved her hand in the air. "Don't worry, I've got someone working on that as we speak."

"Good." I sighed so loudly that I'm afraid I sounded rather melodramatic.

"You didn't think I'd be wasting time talking to you if I couldn't get you out, did you?"

"What do you mean?"

"I'd be up in court annoying a judge. I'm trying to get you out on a PR bond. If not, then we'll get a bonding company."

"Oh, great, so it won't cost me anything?"

"Not much for the bond, just for me." She grinned again.

I cringed. "How much?"

"Five thousand if it's a plea or dismissal. I k now that sounds like a lot, but coming two counties north takes a lot of extra time."

There went my car repairs and a lot of other things I'd been hoping to afford some day. I didn't even want to hear how much she'd charge if we had a jury trial. "How do you want it?"

"What's your situation? Already spend your retainer fee?"

"No, but that's just about all I have right now and I'm not sure if I'm going to keep it." I explained about it being Tommy's money.

"Give me two thousand as soon as you get out, and the rest

you can pay by the month, okay? Treat me like an installment loan—kind of like a car note. Can you handle that?"

"Yeah." I tried to maintain my optimism, but it was difficult. At least I'd be out and have a lawyer. That's more than the women upstairs could say.

"You can serve papers for me sometimes in lieu of some of it, okay? But I've got to have the two thousand to start. Have to feed the kids and pay the secretary, plus the cost of gas . . . you know how it is."

"You do this and have kids, too?"

"Yep, two, and a husband. One's a teenager, sixteen. I charge a consultation fee just to pay him an allowance."

"How much is that?"

"What?" She glanced at me, her brow wrinkled up. "No, not for you, Mavis. An even five thousand. I like you. Maybe we can establish a working relationship. You could probably do stuff for me sometimes—if you get through this."

"What do you mean if?"

She chewed on the end of her pen and said, "I don't think the cops like you . . ."

"And?"

"And I want you to promise me something."

"What?"

"Be careful around James Rush. He's a powerful man."

"I know."

"I don't think you do. I've heard some things about him that I don't especially like. I know I wouldn't tangle with him if I could help it. He can be a real scumbag."

I studied her expression. "I don't think he's really got anything to do with the murder except for the fact that he may have been having an affair with Mrs. Lawson."

She nodded, but didn't say anything. "What I might do is check the index in the district clerk's office and see if I can find out who the lawyer was that represented Mrs. Lawson in the civil suit to terminate her husband's parental rights. That'll probably be difficult because the files are sealed, but I'll try. Some of the clerks owe me favors."

"Why? What do you think you'll find?"

"Well, if you can talk to him, you might be able to discover more about the case. If he won't talk to you, I'll check it out if I can. Those are confidential files and the information might be hard to get but if we can get it, it could be a real help. And I'll check the criminal index and find out who prosecuted the criminal side of the case and that might help."

"I don't know what all this has to do with Harrison Lawson's murder."

"I don't get you, Mavis."

"I don't understand."

"What I heard when you were explaining the case to me was that you think Arthur Woodridge was set up."

I studied her face. "Is that what it sounds like to you?"

"Yes, and if he was set up now, why couldn't he have been set up then?"

"It's funny that you would pick up on that, Gillian. I don't have any proof."

"I thought that's what you were getting at all along. I've seen it before, not often, but it's happened. In fact, there was an article published last year in one of the national legal magazines—I forget which one—about the large number of fraudulent claims of sexual abuse by a parent." She raised her eyebrows as if speculating on the possibilities. Hers was a face full of expressions. I wondered how well she did before a jury. She continued, "It happens a lot these days in child custody cases. The problem is proving the charges are false."

"The problem is going to be opening up a twelve- or

thirteen-year-old case. No one will want to say it was all a big mistake."

"Exactly. And politically, there will be a cover-up from all sides. Such a touchy subject." She glanced at her watch.

"That's part of what's got me worried."

"Right. Well," Gillian said as she pulled her briefcase from under the table and snapped it open, "you've got your work cut out for you. I'm not envious." She shook her head as she threw her legal pad and pen in the case. "It was nice meeting you." She held out her hand again and we shook. "You should be out of here in a jiff. I'll call and let you know the progress I make on your case. Oh—you won't have to make docket calls, either. I'll do that for you."

"Thanks for coming." I meant it. I wasn't often truly grateful for anything, but the fact that this woman, who was obviously successful, really bright, to whom I could talk freely, and with whom I was comfortable, came to see me, unpaid, made me appreciative. "By the way, how did Margaret get your name?"

"From Candy."

"Candy?"

"Yeah," she said as she reached for the door. "Candy's the daughter of one of my daddy's second cousins once removed or something like that." She shrugged. "He's a judge in Angleton."

"Who is?"

"My daddy. Candy's mother told her to call him and he told her to call me. They wanted someone they could trust."

Chapter Nineteen

Gillian Wright had given me a lot to think about. If I could clear Woodridge of the kidnapping-murder, I could clear myself. Just how I was going to do that, I didn't know, but after getting a taste of the jail, I had a lot of motivation.

I was so tired that if I didn't make a list of all the things that needed doing, I was sure I'd forget most of it. I hadn't slept at all. There weren't enough bunks in the cell for all of us and what there were, were occupied when I got there. With the hysterics of a girl who'd had a crack-up, and most everyone yelling at her to shut up, no one really slept much. The night had been spent with me sitting on the floor against the wall.

Probably the first thing I should have done was go home and hit the sack, but I didn't. I wanted to apologize to the Lawson kids for screwing up the night before and see if I could get back in their good graces. That would have to wait until later, though. I wanted to go to the insurance company and talk to McAfee again. I also wanted to talk to Hadley and Smythe. I needed to talk to Stanhope. Then there was that file at child welfare that I wanted to see. And I wanted to punch Ben in the nose.

After the judge gave me my magistrate's warning, I was told that my case would be filed in Harris County and not to come back to Walker County. Afterward, I was released on bail and found Margaret waiting for me. She threw her arms around me and hugged me as if I'd just been released from a dungeon after fifty years confinement. I hugged her back. It was nice to feel loved.

"Thanks for getting me a lawyer," I said when she finally let me go.

"Is she any good?" Margaret asked as she swiped at the tears spilling from the corners of her eyes.

I patted her on the shoulder and put my arm around her neck as I led her down the stairs and away from the jail. "She may not be Clarice Arrow, Margaret, but I'm glad she's on our team. She's smart, and full of distrust, and I think you'll like her, too."

"Good," she said and sniffed. "I was so worried." She started to tear up again.

"It's all right, Margaret. I'm not hurt. I even ate breakfast for once. At least they called it breakfast."

Margaret laughed. "You're so tough, Mavis."

I rolled my eyes. "Right, kid. Let's get my car so I can get home and change my clothes and hit the streets. I'll show them how tough I am."

"I've got some bad news for you."

Could my week get any worse? "Spill it, Margaret."

"Mrs. Lawson called this morning and left a message that you're fired."

"Oh, is that all? I guess we're never going to get to cash that check since Tommy is pretty angry at me as well."

"So Candy and I won't be getting paid any time soon?"

"Only if you can find the money someplace else. I need to scrape two thousand dollars together to pay Gillian."

Margaret drove me to the impound lot where I was able to get my car out of hock and drive home to my apartment. I sent her back to the office to check up on Hadley and Smythe while

I went downtown. It was so hot that it felt like someone had taken the lid off of hell. I wasn't looking forward to summer.

McAfee continued playing games with me. He kept me waiting a good while, probably hoping I'd go away. After the first twenty minutes or so, I figured as much so I put my head back and snoozed in the reception area. I guess my snoring was an embarrassment to them, because it didn't take long after that for the girl to show me in. I felt marvelously refreshed until I passed by Annette Jensen's glaringly vacant desk and went in to talk to him.

It was interesting to note that McAfee hadn't moved into Lawson's office. Upon my arrival, he didn't stand, or even offer a greeting, but that was okay. "More questions, Miss Davis?" he asked, faded-out eyebrows raised. I could tell I was a source of irritation.

I plopped into the chair opposite him and flipped out my notebook. I wasn't sure whether he knew I knew about Annette, so I saved that for later. "I was wondering if you could tell me whether Mr. Lawson's life was insured by your company, and if so, who the beneficiaries are."

His lips formed a thin smile. "Funny you should ask that, Miss Davis. I was curious about that myself and, in fact, was wondering why you didn't inquire about that the other day."

Good point. "You checked it out, then?"

He leaned back in his chair and started with the cigar business again. There was a sadistic streak in him a mile wide. After he blew smoke in my direction, he said, "Yes. I had Annette pull his file for me."

It occurred to me that the contents of that file were probably what Annette wanted to talk to me about. I smothered a cough, wondered if he intentionally mentioned Annette, and took the bait. "Where is Ms. Jensen, anyway? Is she sick or something?"

"She had a little accident."

"Oh. Sorry to hear that. What happened? Is she going to be okay?"

He puffed on his cigar. Lucky I left the door open or I'd have been asphyxiated. "Seems a burglar attacked her." He watched me closely.

"How awful."

"Yes, a terrible thing. She's unconscious at St. Joseph's Hospital."

"He must have really hurt her."

"Banged her in the head with something. From what I understand, it's still touch and go for her."

I cringed inwardly. If he knew I was involved, he sure knew how to hurt a girl. Maybe he didn't know. I couldn't tell from his expression. It wasn't any uglier than it had been the other day. "Poor thing."

"And he killed her dog. Beat it to death. Blood was everywhere, I understand."

My stomach heaved at the memory. The greasy alleged breakfast didn't help. "Yuck."

"Anyway, as I was saying, I had Annette check Mr. Lawson's file and I'd be glad to give you that information."

"Well, gee thanks, Mr. McAfee. I appreciate that."

"Mrs. Lawson was the primary beneficiary. She's to receive a million dollars."

"Whew."

"Each of the children is to receive two hundred and fifty thousand dollars."

"That's a surprise," I said.

"Not really. He cared a lot about those kids."

"I didn't mean to imply that he didn't. It just seems unusual to leave children that much money."

"Well, it'll go into trust for each of them until they're twenty-two."

"And who's the trustee, if I may ask?"

"Hilary."

"Wow, so she'll have over a mil and a half."

"That's correct."

A motive for murder if I ever heard one. No wonder Annette was so secretive. "As well as all his holdings—I guess she'll get all that, too."

"Probably, Miss Davis, but the will hasn't been read yet."

"What was he worth, anyway?"

"His net worth you mean?"

I nodded.

"Don't think it's been calculated, but I could give you an educated guess."

"All right."

"Another two-and-a-half."

"Million?"

He nodded. "At least, not including the house."

A whistle escaped me. Hilary Lawson would get three and a half million dollars and be in control of another half million. I wondered if the police knew that. I stared at him. "Do you know when they'll probate his will?"

"I imagine it'll be read after the funeral a few days from now. Rush likes all the formalities and he's notified several of us to meet him at his office afterwards."

"So James Rush was Mr. Lawson's estate attorney?"

"Right." He rocked back and forth in his chair, apparently enjoying himself immensely.

"That'll mean a big legal fee for him, won't it?"

"Yes, Miss Davis, but Rush doesn't need the money if you're thinking something is wrong there."

"Well, you know that old saying, 'You can't be too rich—' "

"I'm not fond of clichés myself."

"Sorry," I said. "I guess I won't take up any more of your time, Mr. McAfee. You've been more than helpful."

"Anytime, Miss Davis. Glad to be of help."

Liar, liar, I thought.

"By the way," he said as I started out the door. "I hear they arrested Arthur last night for Harrison's murder."

"Oh, really?" I tried to act totally surprised, but I'm not sure I pulled it off.

"You didn't know?"

"Why should I know?"

"Come on, Miss Davis. Stop playing games."

"I know they took you in for it, too."

He shot me a dirty look.

"If they let you go, Mr. McAfee, there's nothing to say that they won't let Mr. Woodridge go, also."

"So you don't think he did it, Miss Davis?"

"There's a little thing called motive, Mr. McAfee."

"Oh, I think all those years in prison were motive enough," he said.

"For killing Lawson? Ha. For killing Hilary, sure, but not Lawson. You just about said as much yourself."

"Maybe he got the wrong person by mistake."

"Wrong. There's also the small problem of opportunity, Mr. McAfee. How could Arthur Woodridge have gotten to Lawson? He couldn't have gotten anywhere near that house and you know it."

"Is there some reason you're getting so defensive, Miss Davis?"

I gave him one of my best "Go to hell" looks. "I'm sure if you know he was arrested, then you know I was, too. Right?"

He chuckled, clearly enjoying himself. I could tell.

"How did you like the Walker County jail?"

"About as much as you would."

"Seriously, Miss Davis, you are going to try to clear Arthur, aren't you?"

"Is that concern I hear in your voice?"

"Well, he did get a raw deal before."

"And someone is trying to give him another one now. I hope to figure out who." Or was it whom?

"Well, I'm glad to know someone is going to help him. Off the record, I wouldn't mind chipping in for his attorney's fees. I'd hate for him to get stuck with a court appointed attorney again."

I studied his face. Was he serious? "I hope it won't come to that, Mr. McAfee, but I'll pass the word along."

"Thank you. That offer's good for the kidnapping as well as the murder charge."

"The kids will clear him on the kidnapping."

"Maybe so, but Hilary will pursue that 'enticing' statute. Even if the kids clear him, which I doubt, she can still push the state to prosecute him for enticing them away."

I wondered if that was the same thing as interfering with child custody. I made a mental note to call Gillian and ask her about it. Anyway, if I could prove Hilary murdered Harrison, she wouldn't be pushing the state to prosecute Arthur for anything. She'd ultimately be pushing up flowers, I hoped. "Well, I'd better be going, Mr. McAfee," I said and turned back toward the door.

"Wait, Miss Davis. Don't you want to know who the rest of Harrison's beneficiaries are?"

"What?" I said, turning back again. He really was into messing with my head.

"The other beneficiaries, Miss Davis."

I took a breath of fresh air from outside the room and went back to my chair. "I thought that was all."

"Oh, no. There's Annette Jensen."

"How much?"

"Seventy-five thousand."

"He must have cared for her after all."

"Yes. She cried when she saw it."

"How sad."

"If you're a romantic. Stupid, is more like it."

God he was callous. "Does Hilary know?"

"No. At least not yet."

I was sure he'd make certain Hilary knew a-sap. "Hmmm. Were there any others?"

"One last one."

I waited, letting him play it out.

"Five hundred thousand dollars to Clayton Hadley."

Chapter Twenty

There should be some kind of limit. Only one motive per person per day. Like coupons. Or take a number and stand in line. The list was now up to four suspects and counting.

McAfee stared at me as I silently digested what he'd just said. I asked why Hadley had insurance on Lawson and learned that the policy had been in force for eighteen years. Lawson also had one for the same amount on Hadley. McAfee thought it had something to do with real estate. Then, without further ado, I took my leave as they say. The list of things to accomplish grew longer as the day grew shorter.

When I left McAfee's office, it was almost five. I called Angela, the children's protective services supervisor, when I got to the lobby. It was imperative that I meet with her about the file immediately. The woman who answered said she wasn't there but was expected to stop back by the office before she went home for the day. Did I want to leave a message? Not on your life. I knew if old Mandy found out what I wanted, not only would I never get to see the contents of that folder, but Angela's job would be on the line.

I called Margaret to hear what she'd learned about Hadley, Smythe, and McAfee.

"You're going to be surprised at all I've done so far, Mavis," she said.

"Good. Shoot." I walked outside and tried to hear what she had to say as I went for my car.

"Hadley is in real estate in a big way. I checked the deed records for the last twenty years. I can go back further if you want."

"We'll see. What did you turn up?"

"Well, it seems that he owns several large office buildings off the Katy Freeway. He and Mr. Lawson were partners in two of them and in a small shopping center at Sharpstown."

"That's interesting." There was an old, old Sharpstown scandal in the early 1970s or late '60s. I couldn't quite remember what it was about, but I wondered if Hadley and Lawson were involved in it. Weren't they a little young for that?

"I checked the tax rolls, and the two office buildings they're in partners on are valued by the central appraisal district at a half million each. The shopping center is valued at a million."

"Smart thinking, Margaret, but are you sure those are the correct figures? They're awfully low."

"Actually, there's a reason for that. When they bought them years ago, they were valued way below that. Then later, after the real estate boom, the values soared. Then within the last year, the appraisal district devalued them again. Someone obviously has or had some connections there."

"Were the taxes paid up to date?"

"No. They're a year behind. The billing address is to Mr. Hadley. You want it?"

"Yes." I wrote it down as she called it out to me. "Okay, Margaret, good work. Did you find out anything about McAfee?"

"Not really, Mav. I went ahead and checked the real estate records on him. He and his wife own a home in River Oaks, too. The taxes are up to date on it, by the way. Then he has some real estate holdings in his own name."

"What are they?"

"A couple of rental properties in the Heights and a restaurant on Westheimer."

"That all?"

"Yes, nothing grandiose like the others, but the restaurant does have a lot of value."

"Oh. What about Smythe?"

"Wait. Just want to finish telling you about McAfee."

"Okay."

"Taxes paid up on everything and the total values of his rental houses and restaurant are seven hundred and fifty thousand."

"Okay, Margaret, now Smythe?"

"Smythe is really interesting. He was listed in the grantor index quite a bit beginning last year. He's sold a number of properties."

"He's not in on any deals with Lawson or the other two?"

"Not that I could find."

"Well, you done good, kid. Listen, I'm going to run down to the welfare office and try to talk to my friend there. Then I'm going to talk to Joan McAfee. I probably won't make it to the office before y'all leave. If I don't, you don't have to wait for me. I know you've got to be tired from last night."

"What about you? You've got to be dead on your feet about now, Mavis. Can't some of this wait until tomorrow?"

"Don't worry about me, hon. I'm okay. I feel as though adrenaline is rushing through my veins."

"I don't like it, Mavis. I'm worried about you."

"Just get some rest yourself, Margaret. You never know what tomorrow holds."

"Well, be careful."

"Right." I hung up and called Joan McAfee. "This is Mavis Davis, Mrs. McAfee. I wonder if I could come by your house a little while later. There's something I'd like to ask you."

"Certainly, dear," her voice boomed into the phone. I could swear I smelled alcohol through the receiver. "What time?"

"Whatever time would be convenient for you, ma'am."

"Pu-leeze call me Joan."

"Yes, Joan. What time would be convenient for you?"

"Is this something you'd rather my husband not be present for?"

If she wasn't intoxicated, she was at least psychic. "Well . . . sort of."

She laughed so loudly that I had to hold the phone away from my ear. "How about six, then. Be prompt. He usually gets back around seven."

"Right. I'll be there with bells on." I couldn't believe I said that.

After we hung up, I drove over to the child welfare office and staked it out. The way I skulked around outside the building, hiding from everyone that came and went, I felt like a criminal preparing to do a mugging. I would be a criminal, if Captain Milton had his way and I couldn't prove Arthur Woodridge innocent.

My greatest fear was that I was wasting time for nothing. Since it was late in the day, downtown began to clear out. The weirdos were starting to come out of the woodwork, hanging around the sidewalks like low-flying vultures looking for prey. Angela might have skipped out and gone home without anyone knowing. It would be easy for her to cover for herself by telling everyone the next day that she'd gotten stuck at the police station or someone's home. We used to do it every once in a while when we were feeling so burned-out that we couldn't stomach the remainder of the day. Anyhow, I waited impatiently, thinking those thoughts, remembering why I quit the department, and sweating puddles until finally Angela showed up.

I came from around the corner and grabbed her arm before she could slip inside. I had learned that from the housekeeper, Frankie.

"What are you doing here?" She shook my hand off her arm as though I were a leper.

"I've got to see that file," I said as I pulled her away from the front door. "You got it with you?"

"No," she said. "I can't. You shouldn't come around here. You'll get me into trouble."

Her attitude had totally done a one-eighty since our last meeting. "What's wrong, Angela? Have I been blackballed or something? Shit."

"Look," she said, glancing over her shoulder and turning her back to the front of her building. "I don't know what you've done, but I've been warned to stay away from you. Mandy's been on my case. Called me into her office this morning. Said I'd been seen talking to you. Told me in no uncertain terms that if I was caught giving you any information, I'd sorely regret it. I need this job, Mavis."

"Damn. It must have been Captain Milton." I pleaded, "I've got to get a look at what's in that file. It could mean life or death to someone."

"Who, Mavis, you?" she said. "I don't owe you anything and I'm not going to risk my neck. What did you ever do for me?"

"Christ, Angela. What's gotten into you?"

"All you ever think about is yourself. I've got a baby to think of and bills to pay. Besides, I heard you were arrested for helping that kidnapper."

"He's the man I'm talking about, Angela. Listen to me. Something funny is going on or there wouldn't be so much pressure coming down from up high. Don't you get it?"

"Get what?" She was beginning to look interested.

"Why don't they want me to see what's in there? There's a reason." If she would only listen. She probably had the proof of Arthur Woodridge's innocence right in her hands.

"I don't know. What could be in a file that old that would have to do with a kidnapping that took place last week?"

"Have you looked at the file?"

She stared at me.

"Have you?"

"Well . . . no."

"Listen, you don't have to let me see it if you'll just promise me something."

She cocked her head. "I'm not making you any promises."

"No—no, that's not what I mean. You look at the file. You study it. I don't have to see it."

"You don't?"

"No. You read that file and study it closely. Read between the lines. I mean, look at everything that's in it, and look at it as if you were the mother and trying to set up the father for charges of sexual abuse, and then you call me. I'll bet you'll be as suspicious as I am right now."

She was chewing on her bottom lip, as if trying to decide.

"I don't want to get you into trouble, Angela, but I think you'll see something that will tell you I'm right. Now I think she's trying to do it again. Set him up, I mean. It turns my stomach every time I think about it."

"People didn't do that back then, Mavis. Not like everyone does now, yelling sexual abuse when they decide they want custody."

"Yes they did. I read about several cases, only they weren't carried to the extent that she went. That was the beauty of it for her, Angela. She not only got his rights terminated, she got him sent to prison so he couldn't ever bother her again. She didn't count on him being paroled before the kids left home."

She stared at me hard, as if she was trying to make a decision. I clenched my hands like I was in prayer and held them out to her.

"If anyone finds out . . ."

My hopes raised, I had to be careful now. "I won't tell a soul, Angela. I swear. I won't call you. You call me after you've read it. No one will know."

She sighed. "I don't know, Mavis." She ran a hand over her face and rubbed at her eyes with two fingers, leaving her eyeliner smeared at the inside corners.

I didn't know what else I could say that would convince her. I could only hope that she was still as fair-minded as she had been when she first went to work at child welfare.

"I don't even have any time to read it. My caseload is so heavy, and I've got supervisory duties as well."

I still kept quiet. The argument was with herself.

She turned sideways and looked back to her right at the front of the building. "I've got to go." She started edging away.

"Angela—"

She held up one palm. "I'll do it. Not going to promise you it'll be right away, but I'll look at it."

I expelled a deep breath. "Thanks. Just so long as it was yesterday." I grinned at her.

She shook her head in my direction and turned her back, swinging her briefcase as she headed for the front door. In a few seconds, it was as though we'd never had that conversation.

I hurried to my car and headed to River Oaks. When I found it, I saw that Joan's house was every bit as pretentious as the other two I'd seen, spacious landscaped yard, huge. It was decorated differently, though. Oriental rugs and screens combined with antiques.

Joan was pickled, to put it mildly. She sat at her piano, attempting to play, when the housekeeper led me to her. I heard her pick out a few notes, hit a bad one, then I entered the room in time to see her take a gulp of a drink and try to play again. She stopped when she saw me, for which I was truly grateful, and waved the housekeeper away.

"Hi-i-i-i, Mavis," she said.

She certainly was. "Hi, Joan," I responded. "Had a bad day?"

Joan slid off the piano bench and picked up her drink. "You mean this? No. Went shopping and my feet hurt, 'm tired. Thought I'd have a cocktail before Kelby got home."

I glanced down at her stockinged feet.

"But why am I telling you this? It's none of your business."

"I'm sorry. I didn't mean to insult you. I've sort of had it rough today myself."

"So I hear."

"Oh, you too, huh?"

"Yep. It's okay, though. I know you wouldn't do anything wrong. I liked you the minute I met you. Come sit down," she said, all of this in slurred words, as she led the way to a flowered sofa.

I sat at the other end. Just in case she got sick. You never know.

"Want a drink?" She jumped up again.

"No, thank you. Just a little conversation, if you don't mind."

She dropped down again. "Don't mind if I have one, do you?" Without waiting for an answer, she tilted up her glass.

"I was wondering if I could get you to finish telling me what you started the other day about Mr. Smythe," I said.

"What about him?"

"You said that he and Mr. Lawson had a falling out."

"They did. After the stock market did that loop-de-loop; Kelby tells me never to say crash."

"So you said, but could you elaborate on it for me?"

"You think Earl killed Harrison?"

"I don't know. What do you think?"

"Could have, I guess, but I'd put my money on Hilary."

This from the lady who a couple of days ago fingered her husband? "Why do you say that?"

"What?"

"You'd put your money on Hilary."

"She stood the most to gain."

"Mr. Lawson had a lot to leave her, didn't he?"

"Yep, but he was going to change his will."

"Excuse me? How do you know?"

"Told me so."

"Mr. Lawson told you?"

"Yep." She grinned.

"When?"

"Well . . ."

"I didn't mean that—I meant, recently?"

"Last week." She got up and almost stumbled as she went over to mix herself another drink.

"I wonder if Hilary knew."

Joan shrugged. "Who knows?" She pushed her sleeves up to her elbows and held out her highball glass as she poured vodka over ice, as if measuring. When she stopped, it was more than half full. Puke.

"I wonder if Frankie would know," I muttered to myself.

"What'd you say?"

"Nothing. But you still haven't told me about Earl Smythe, Joan. Is there something you don't want me to know?"

I watched while she poured a couple of inches of tonic on top of the vodka, then she dipped her finger in her glass and stirred. After she sucked off her finger, Joan came back to the sofa and smiled. "Sure you don't want something to drink?"

I know most alcoholics don't like to drink alone, but this was getting ridiculous. "I'm sure. I have to meet someone later. I'd hate to get stopped and smell of alcohol, but thanks anyway."

"You can't smell vodka, Mavis."

That's what she thought. "No, thank you. What I'd really like is to get out of here before your husband gets home. I don't think he likes me very much."

"He thinks you're a pain in the ass," she said. "But he thinks everyone is a pain in the ass."

The woman was a constant source of amazement. I couldn't decide if she was stalling or just lonely for someone to talk to. "About Smythe . . ."

"Well, since you aren't going to have a drinky with me, I guess I'll just have to tell you. Harrison lost a lot of money in the stock market. Earl was his stockbroker."

"I figured as much."

"Harrison got mad because he said if Earl was any good, he'd have known what was going to happen instead of just making money off his friends when the market was skyrocketing."

"Sounds like he was pretty angry, all right."

"Well, everyone lost money."

I didn't. For obvious reasons.

"Even Earl lost a lot of money. He made some of it up in the following months, but Harrison took his out on Earl's advice at that time and from what I hear didn't invest with Earl after that."

"But, Joan, they seemed to have remained friends. I mean, Mr. Smythe was over for dinner the other night, wasn't he?"

"You have been getting around, haven't you?"

I nodded. "Some."

"Yes, they still associate. That's because Earl lives around here and we all have the same set of friends. Harrison couldn't have just excluded him, you know. As it was, Harrison led Earl to believe that he wasn't investing in the stock market anymore, but that wasn't true. He just found another broker."

"Earl believed that?"

"Oh, I don't know, but Harrison is influential and has a lot of contacts, so I guess Earl decided to pretend like he believed it, anyway."

"So life went on as though nothing had happened."

"Well, Mavis, Earl thought so, but it wasn't true."

"What do you mean?"

"Earl was counting on their friendship and Harrison's contacts to a great extent. Harrison sort of made Earl in the stock market, so to speak. He picked him out years ago when Earl was fairly new, sent him a lot of business, and Earl got rich off it. They've only lived here a few years, you know."

A condescending tone had crept into her voice in spite of the fact that she was soused.

"No, I didn't know."

"Well, it's true. The last few years, Earl's business has tapered off and I heard that Earl just discovered that Harrison put the word out about him."

"What do you mean?"

"He nixed him—you know, spread the word that he was a lousy stockbroker. The guy's going broke, Mavis."

Chapter Twenty-One

Weariness was overcoming me, but I thought I might as well go see Frankie, as well as Jeanine and Tommy if they would talk to me, while I was in River Oaks. There was always time to collapse later.

It was still light so I parked out of sight a few houses away and went around to the back door of the Lawson home in hopes that Hilary wouldn't know I was there. I rapped softly on the screen door and waited. After a few moments, someone opened it a crack and an eye peered out. It was Frankie, up to her melodramatics, perhaps rightly so. Who knows? She never did open the door all the way or step outside.

"Frankie, I need to talk to you."

"Go away. Miz Lawson's on the rampage."

"I just want to ask you a couple of questions. Come on out." We were whispering so loudly I was sure Hilary would hear and come running anyway.

"No, I can't. I'll get in more trouble."

"What's the matter?"

"The kids sneaked out and she's blaming me. Now go away."

"Just answer me this. Did Hilary know Mr. Lawson was going to change his will?"

Her one eye flared at me. "She might have."

"Come on, Frankie. You've got to tell."

"No, I don't. I'm in enough trouble."

"Well, tell me this. Was Hilary having an affair with someone?"

The eye cast down toward the ground.

"Was it Mr. Rush?"

"How'd you know?"

"I didn't; I just suspected. Then Rush told her about the will, didn't he?" I asked.

"I don't know if he did or not."

"Mr. Lawson didn't know about the affair, did he?"

"No—yes—no. He knew there was someone—"

"But he didn't know it was Rush, did he? Or else he wouldn't have had the man write his new will."

"Your guess is as good as mine."

"Thanks, Frankie." I saluted her and heard the door close softly behind me as I jogged back toward my car. As I reached it, I remembered that I had one more question I had to ask, and I ran back to the house and banged on the door again. It opened abruptly.

"I told you everything I know," Frankie said.

"I just wondered. Did Hilary tell Captain Milton about the cabin?"

The eye bobbed up and down.

"Did you warn the kids and Arthur Woodridge that Hilary was telling everyone?"

"Yes," she whispered. Then in a loud voice she said, "I told you that I don't know nothin' and you shouldn't be askin'."

"Who's there, Frankie?" I heard Hilary say. "Who are you talking to?"

Frankie disappeared and the door jerked open all the way to reveal Hilary.

"Oh, it's you. What do you want, Miss Davis? Aren't you in enough trouble already?"

"I just—"

"No one around here has anything to say to you. Now get away from my house before I call the police." She seemed hostile, to put it mildly.

"Mrs. Lawson, you don't understand—"

"I heard about what you did last night. Didn't you get my message? You're fired. Don't ever come around here again."

I don't have to be told more than twice. I left. It was just as well. I was tired. I was confused. I was very hungry. I'd forgotten to catch lunch, and for me, that's saying something. My head throbbed, too. It was now time to go home and cave as I'd been promising myself. I'd just stop by the office to check my messages and then become a recluse for the evening.

Unfortunately, when I got back to the office, Tommy, Jeanine, and Candy met me at the door. Margaret was in the kitchen. The thought of what Mrs. Lawson would do if she caught the kids at my office was enough for me to turn tail and run. But I didn't. They could only execute me once.

Tommy looked contrite. "We came to apologize. Candy told us what happened, Mavis. We're sorry we jumped to conclusions."

"Yeah," Jeanine said, "and we're sorry you got put in jail. We want to pay for your lawyer and everything."

I looked from one to the other. How could I hold a grudge against children even if the memory of jail was still vivid? "I'm not sure what happened myself," I said, looking at Candy who, as usual, wore elaborate self-decoration.

Candy's eyes searched the floor, as though she was looking for a lost contact lens.

"Candy—" I started.

"Like, it's not exactly my fault, Mavis. Ben tricked me, you know?"

"I was just going to say that I like your cousin twice removed or whatever she is," I said.

"You do?" Candy smiled. "I'm not like real clear on that, either. I've never met her. I mean, why would I, you know? I've never been in trouble like with the law or anything like that. There's thousands of relatives I've never met. But, you know, I've met her dad. Mom took me down to Angleton once like when I was a child."

I encircled Candy with one arm, giving her a squeeze. "It's okay, kid. I'm too tired to fuss at you. Let's all go into the kitchen and get something to drink." I pushed through the door.

"Hi, Mavis. You do any good?" Margaret asked. She could be a sweetheart. She had my cup filled with hot tea and handed it to me. I nodded and smiled at her as I slipped off my shoes.

"Your mother know you're here?" I asked the kids. They had taken the chairs, and I was leaning against the sink, watching them.

"No, ma'am," Tommy said.

"I didn't think so," I said.

"She'd kill us if she did," Jeanine said.

"I know the feeling, Jeanine. I was just at your house."

"You were? You talked to Mother?" Tommy asked.

"It was more like she talked to me, if you know what I mean."

"We know what you mean," Jeanine said with a glance at her brother.

"As Frankie says, she's on the 'rampage' because you two got out of the house. How did you manage that?"

"Frankie helped us."

"So I thought. So what's up? You didn't come here just to apologize," I said.

"Miss Davis, will you help our father?" Jeanine asked.

"Mavis," I said.

Jeanine smiled. She would be a great model for a toothpaste commercial.

"Can you trust me now, Tommy?"

"I'm really sorry, Mavis," he said hesitantly and shook his head. "I trusted you before. It was just that with the police showing up and all . . . I couldn't believe you'd do that to us, but it sure looked that way."

"I know, but you can't jump to conclusions, Tommy. Even now, if I decide to help you, I might do something you don't understand, and I'll have a good reason for doing it. You'll just have to trust my judgment or I can't operate."

"We want you to help us, Mavis. We'll do anything you say," Jeanine said with a fierce look at her brother.

"Anything?"

"Yes, ma'am," Tommy said, ducking his head.

"Please, Tommy, I'm not your teacher. First thing, quit calling me ma'am, okay?"

Tommy looked at me, and I laughed. He laughed, too, and then the others, and when we were through, we were almost like a family, everyone comfortable with each other.

"We've got a lot of talking to do then," I said. "First off, who do you kids think killed your father?"

"You mean Harrison Lawson?" Jeanine asked.

"Jeanine, no matter what, he was your adopted father and he raised you. He loved you."

Jeanine shifted about uncomfortably in her chair.

"I know you're not happy with that thought, but if we're going to help your biological father, we've got to put aside our feelings and try to figure this thing out logically," I said. "Get me a chair, Candy."

"We've talked it over, Mavis," Jeanine said, "and we don't know. All we know is that Daddy didn't do it."

"How do you know that?" Margaret chimed in.

"We were with him," Tommy said.

"He could have hired a hit man or something," Candy said, dragging a chair into the kitchen.

"This isn't the movies, Candy," I said.

"He didn't have enough money for that anyway," Jeanine said. "No, I was with him a couple of days before, and Tommy was with him, too, on Friday. Besides, he just wouldn't do anything like that. It's Mother that Daddy hates, not Mr. Lawson."

"Tell you what, why don't we go back to the beginning? Why don't you kids tell us what you remember from when you were little and we'll work up to the present day," I said.

Tommy and Jeanine looked at each other and then at me. "I don't see how it could help, but we're willing," Tommy said.

"My memory is better than Tommy's, Mavis. I can remember things from when I was two," she said proudly. "Mother always says I'm strange. Anyway, Tommy didn't remember hardly anything until I reminded him of things. I guess you could say that he blocked it all out of his memory, sort of. I did, too, but when Frankie and I talked about it, and then Daddy contacted me the first time, it all came back in a hurry."

"When was that?" I asked.

"The weekend before I left with him. He called me that Saturday afternoon. At first, I was scared and I hung up on him. Then Frankie said I should talk to him when he called back, so I did."

I smiled at her, trying to be encouraging. "Okay, Jeanine, what is the first thing you remember from back when you were a little girl?"

"You mean from when all this started about Daddy?"

"Yes."

She looked at Tommy and her face flushed.

"Tell her," Tommy said.

Jeanine put her hand over her eyes. "It's terrible, Mavis."

I put my cup down and crouched in front of her chair. "It's all right, Jeanine. You can tell us." I glanced at the faces around the room. Everyone watched Jeanine, waiting solemnly for what would be the key to the whole sexual abuse case.

Jeanine removed her hand and looked at me with teary eyes. "I remember Mother talking to me one night. She pulled my pants down and took my finger and put it down there. She told me that was my tee-tee." She moved her hand to cover her mouth and looked at her brother again. He looked very sad. Jeanine said, "Then Mother told me Daddy had touched my tee-tee, and that he was very bad."

Chapter Twenty-Two

My first inclination after hearing the kids' story was to drive over to Hilary Lawson's house and slap the shit out of her. But I knew it wouldn't do much good, and I'd probably end up back in jail for assault. So what does one do? Trusting that the kids were telling the truth about what had happened ever how many years ago and that this wasn't some cockeyed story that they'd concocted with their father while on that little camping trip, I planned to see Arthur. But no way did I have the energy to make the drive two counties to the north that night. Calling the Walker county jail to verify visiting hours for the next day, I hooked up with a very helpful deputy who asked me, probably just out of nosiness, who I wanted to see. When I told him, he put the phone down and in the background I heard the clicking of keys on a computer keyboard. Moments later, I was informed that Arthur Woodridge was being transferred to the Harris County jail. Further, a Harris county deputy would be coming to pick him up early the next morning.

By the time I had time, I didn't feel like eating. I was a walking zombie and if I didn't get some rest, wouldn't be any use to anyone. Before calling the jail, I'd sent everyone home. After the call, I locked up and put the car on automatic pilot, ended up at my apartment, stripped off my clothes, and zonked out on the bed. I didn't wake up until just before dawn. My stomach rumbled like a huge diesel truck. Pulling on a pair of short-shorts and a T-shirt, I fried bacon and eggs and made a sandwich on whole wheat, poured a tall glass of milk, and went out onto the front porch to watch the sunrise. Nothing ever tasted as good as that first bite of sandwich and that first swallow of cold milk.

Houston isn't too bad in the early morning hours. It's not real cool, but we sometimes have clear skies and sixty- to seventy-degree weather in the late spring and early summer before the sun gets up good. I sat on the hard concrete stoop and leaned against the front of the building. I keep meaning to get a chair to sit on out there—one light enough to pitch inside when I'm not using it so the neighborhood youth corps won't make off with it.

There are some large trees where I live and sidewalks old enough to have cracks in them from the roots of the trees. From my duplex, I heard the vague roar of the early morning traffic. A slight breeze filtered through the trees and coupled with the humidity, blew my hair into little curls. Early morning birds twittered. I spent a few minutes appreciating my freedom and loving life.

I needed to simplify things—the Lawson-Woodridge case, my relationship with Ben. I needed to get away and longed for a vacation—another weekend on the beach at Galveston would do. Before I could go anywhere, though, I would have to earn some money and quick, or the summer would pass without my getting to lay my head on a beach towel again or wiggle my toes in the sand.

How I had become straddled with responsibilities and overhead I could barely meet, I didn't know. There were two salaries to pay in addition to my own. My debts were huge—including attorney's fees. The Mustang was damaged to such an extent that I was either going to have to get a new car or spend a lot of money overhauling it. Car payments were the last thing I needed. And, I realized, I was feeling awfully sorry for myself.

I brushed off my backside and went inside to the phone. Though it would be considered too early to call, maybe I could get some questions answered before Jeanine and Tommy left for school. Jeanine answered on the first ring.

"What do you do, sleep with the phone right next to your pillow?" I asked after I'd identified myself.

"Um-hmmm," she replied sleepily.

"Dumb question."

"Mom gets mad if my friends call in the middle of the night and it wakes her up. She got me my own phone line because of that, but she took it and my cell away the night before last when we came home so I had to take one of the downstairs phones, but she doesn't know it."

"Bad scene?"

"We're not speaking," she said. She breathed heavily as though she were stretching and waking up.

"I'm sorry, Jeanine." Somehow I felt responsible.

"I'm grounded, you know. She doesn't want me talking to anyone, especially you. Or Tommy, either."

"How'd you and Tommy get out of the house yesterday?"

"School. After we got home, we had friends help us get to your office. And Frankie. Mom can't keep us out of school or we'd fail and she knows it. But Mavis," I heard a yawn, "sorry. She's going to send us away."

"Where? When?"

"She can't right now. It's too late. Too close to the end of the year, but she's sending us both to summer camp the day after school gets out. She told us last night after she pitched a fit when we got home. Tommy has graduation, but there is a fish camp, for freshmen. She's making him go. After camp, she's sending me to boarding school."

"That's next week."

"I know. I'd run away again, but I don't want to fail, either. Oh, it's early isn't it?" she asked as if she just noticed the time. "I'm awake now. What did you call for? Any news? Did you see Daddy?"

"Yes. He's fine. Could you meet me, Jeanine? Before school?"

"Sure. Me and Tommy, or just me?"

"Just you."

"What's up?"

"I'll tell you when I see you. What time is good?"

"Seven forty-five. Across the street from the main entrance. You know where it is?"

"Yes. See you then."

We said our good-byes, and she hung up. I'm sure I heard another click a split second afterward. I hoped it was Tommy on an extension.

I got out my nine-and-a-half-foot-long jump rope that I'd promised myself I would start using to try to get into shape, skipped a hundred painful times, and then took a long, hot shower before driving over to Lamar.

A tight little group of girls stood on the sidewalk across the street from the school. Some were dressed in pastel walking shorts, blouses, and sandals, others wore pale-colored jeans and layered tops. They all looked a good deal alike to me. The in-crowd look. I recognized Melanie and said hello. The circle parted like the Red Sea, and out came Jeanine.

"What's going on? Why all the girls?" I asked after I'd pulled her away from the group.

"They're hiding me from security. I'm sure Mother is

having me watched. She's probably gotten together some dumb story about what happened and covered her ass in case I try to tell any of them what's really been going on." She sounded very wise for a sixteen-year-old. "But my friends know. And if anything happens to me, everyone will know."

"Don't get carried away, kid."

"Well, I don't trust Mother. If she could do that to Daddy, what might she do to me and Tommy?"

"Okay, okay. I'm not here to belabor your mother's virtues. I just want to know one thing. What was Melanie talking about when she said you and your mother had been fighting—before this whole thing came up."

Jeanine cut her eyes over her shoulder at Melanie and then back at me. "I caught her in a clench with Mr. Rush."

"What do you mean 'in a clench'? Were they . . . uh . . ."

"Like making out in the kitchen. Arms around each other. French kissing. His hand on her rear end."

"Um, right. So you took it upon yourself to speak to your mother about it."

She shot me a look that only teenaged girls can give. "Well, I couldn't tell my—Harrison about it, could I?"

I didn't answer.

"I didn't want to tell Tommy, either. It would have really hurt him, you know? I just thought she should know that she'd been seen."

"I can assume that she didn't take too kindly to your mentioning it?"

She laughed. It was an awfully bitter laugh for a young girl. "She sure as hell didn't."

"When was this? When did you see her?"

"A couple of weeks ago. No telling how long it's been going on. She said it was none of my business."

"Naturally. So you never told your father? Your adopted father?"

"No, why?"

"Just curious."

"Do you think she'll marry Mr. Rush? I've been wondering if she was going to divorce Harrison, Mr. Lawson."

"Would you quit that, Jeanine? It's really irritating me."

"Well, I don't know what to call him." She crossed her arms over her chest.

"Call him whatever you called him before. You've known all along that he was your adopted father. You loved the man, didn't you?"

Jeanine cast her eyes down at the books she held. "Yes. I just think he was a dumb jerk and my mother is a bitch."

"I don't approve of that kind of language in front of adults, either."

"I'm sorry, but she is. My real father is in jail, and the other one is dead, and my mother is going to send us off to keep our mouths shut while she goes scot-free."

"Hey, don't get all bent out of shape yet, kid. I'm working as fast as I can, but I have to eat and sleep, okay? Back off a little and be a kid for a while and I'll see what I can do. All right?" Talk about a bitch. In a few years, she'd be an A Number One if she didn't cool it.

She smiled then—her way of apologizing. "I know what you're thinking, Mavis. I can't help it sometimes, but I'll try."

I shook my head and tousled hers. "Go to school."

"You'll call me—"

"No. You call me. You never know who may be listening in on your end. Go on now. Good-bye."

She turned back to her friends, and I watched while they paraded into the middle of the street, stopping traffic. I wouldn't take one of Hilary's millions to be that age again.

While I was out and about, I drove to the Katy Freeway area to see what there was to see of Hadley's office buildings and past the shopping center at Sharpstown. I wasn't too surprised to find that the area looked relatively deserted—as opposed to how it might have been in the middle of the oil boom. It showed its age and wear and tear. The office building parking lots were almost empty when they should have been overflowing. A lot of the windows of the small shopping center were blackened and the doors had cards with leasing information taped to the glass inserts. Clearly, Mr. Hadley was in big financial trouble.

Chapter Twenty-Three

At the Harris County jail, I shut my ears to the clanging of the iron doors and tried not to shudder when I saw Arthur. He wore jail greens—the cotton suit that looks like hospital orderly wear. He shuffled in on thonged feet, perched on the stool across from me, and picked up the telephone connected by a wire to the one I held. From the stoop of his shoulders, he looked like a broken man. His wan smile belied his real state, his bespectacled eyes lusterless and ringed by dark circles. His spectacles, combined with the thick wall of glass between us, distorted his eyes. His face had a pale, unhealthy pallor, his wispy, gray-blond hair pasted to his head.

"The kids send their love, Arthur."

"They're okay?" Lackluster blue eyes stared through me.

"Yes. We've figured out how the police knew I'd be going up there, and they trust me now. Will you? I want to help. They want me to help. Is that all right?" I didn't want to tell him I already was, I didn't want him to realize what my motivation was.

"I don't think there's much you can do," he said. His voice sounded tinny and pathetic.

"So give up already," I said with a grin. That got a thin smile and a shrug out of him. "Come on, Arthur. You gonna let her whip you twice? The kids told me how it happened."

He spoke slowly, each word measured and painful. "I was

a stupid fool. Guess I still am. I loved and trusted her. She always had a way of twisting everything so it came out in her favor."

"I know. It's called manipulation."

"She can be so believable."

"Hey—I know."

"Do you think she killed Harrison?"

"I don't know. Right now, it could be anybody."

"If Hilary killed Harrison, they'll never be able to prove it."

"It won't be easy."

"You know, back then, I never figured out what she was doing until that last day in court. There was something in her face that told me she'd set me up. Until then, I thought she actually believed that I'd done those things to my kids."

I watched his face while he talked. I wanted him to get it out. In fact, I wanted him to get good and angry. He needed to fight this, but he was the only one who could give himself the will to do it.

"She came to see me one time after I'd been arrested. We sat across from one another just as you and I are now. I don't know why she came. She started crying and asking me why I did those things. She said I was sick." His eyes watered and his voice broke. "I tried to tell her that I didn't. I tried to convince her that I was innocent. I thought if I could just get out, that somehow I could prove it to her." He sniffed. "I begged her to make my bail. It was high, and we didn't have that kind of money, but she could have borrowed it. My parents had that little piece of property—you know—where the cabin is?"

I nodded. I remembered it well.

"My parents would have been able to mortgage it and come up with some of the money, but not all. She could have borrowed the rest. I didn't know that she didn't want me out.

She said she was afraid of me and what I'd do to the kids if I got out. Can you believe it?"

Sweet Jesus. I might go slap her yet. I shook my head, not knowing what I could do to comfort him.

"I never saw Tommy or Jeanine after my arrest. She wouldn't bring them here. They didn't come to court. Everyone just assumed I was guilty—even my lawyer. He was court appointed. He wanted me to plead guilty. He never even shook my hand. It was like he was afraid to touch me." A look of horror crossed his face. "I should have done it. Pled out. I would have gotten fewer years. No one wanted to try the case. But I wouldn't plea."

"Who was your lawyer?"

"A young guy. Rush. James Rush."

Well, shut my mouth.

"He hadn't been practicing very long and told me he was just taking appointments until he could get on his feet. He wanted to do civil work but had to do some criminal until he had some money in the bank to finance the other. He didn't give a damn about me or—"

"Arthur—"

"Hilary was the sick one—"

"Whoa, Arthur. Wait a minute."

He stopped and looked at me, as if he'd forgotten I was there. "I'm sorry."

"It's okay. I just thought there was something you might want to know."

"What's that?" His gray eyebrows knitted together.

"About James Rush."

"I know, Mavis. He's rich now. I read about him while I was at TDCJ."

"No, that's not all." I stared back at him. "He was at the house the day Harrison was killed."

He closed his eyes, his head wagging slowly from side to side. When he opened them, he smiled a Mona Lisa kind of smile. "She's slick all right."

"I'm not sure to what extent they're involved."

"No telling, knowing her."

"You think he was in on the setup back then?"

"God knows. I don't see how, though. He really was court appointed. I got a letter from the judge that said so."

"Maybe she got to him after the appointment. Maybe she paid him off."

"Do you think that's really possible?"

"Hey—anything's possible," I said.

"Then he could be in on Harrison's murder."

"What would he have to gain? He's a rich man . . ."

His eyes had begun to shine and the man actually grinned at me. "You're hiding something, Mavis. Tell me."

"Aw, shit. They're having an affair. I don't know how long it's been going on and I can't think what Hilary would have to gain from it. If Harrison had found out, she'd have lost her security."

"Yes, but the papers say that Rush is stinking rich."

"He is," I said. "Filthy, stinking rich."

"Maybe Hilary wanted her cake and to eat it, too. Maybe Harrison found out and she killed him for his money, just to be on the safe side, in case Rush didn't want her bad enough to marry her."

"Wait, we don't know for sure that Harrison discovered it. I could probably ask around. Annette might know. That is, if she gets okay."

"Annette?"

"The lady at the insurance company," I said.

"Annette Jensen? She's still there?"

"Yes. Did you know how she felt about Harrison? Kelby

McAfee says she adored him. That Hilary took him away from her."

"Kelby's still there? Amazing. I haven't heard all these names in years." His face looked like that of someone who had just walked into a class reunion.

"Kelby McAfee stands to take over for Harrison. President of the board. You didn't know?"

"No. I didn't think he was that smart. He was always sly, though. Stab you in the back first chance he got."

"He said that he and some of the others figured out what was going on in your case, but there was nothing they could do about it."

"He wouldn't lift a finger to help his own mother. Especially if he would benefit from not helping her. I can't believe he's lasted all these years. Nobody ever liked him back then. They only kept him on because he was a hell of a salesman."

"He's still not exactly appealing," I said, making a face.

Arthur laughed. "Does he still look like Mother Nature forgot to use her flesh-colored crayon?"

"Yep," I said and laughed. "Absolutely no appeal whatsoever."

"That's Kelby."

"Let's get back on track before we run out of time and they throw me out of this place." I picked up my pen and began making notes.

"What were you saying about Annette?"

"Someone clobbered her. She's seriously injured."

"Oh my God. Did they catch whoever it was?"

"No. Please, let's not talk about it, okay? I talked to Jeanine and she says she didn't tell Harrison. I'll ask around and see if I can find out. Joan McAfee might know."

Arthur nodded. "It might also be helpful if you could find out what Harrison died from."

"Yeah, I'm working on that." What with my current relationship with the police, I didn't know how I'd find out. Which reminded me, I needed to get back in touch with my friend, Stan.

"Are you going to tell the police that I didn't molest my kids, Mavis?"

"Do you think they'd believe me? Hell, they're convinced they've got a kidnapper-murderer in jail. Case closed. Why would they listen to me?"

"Oh." His face fell. "I just thought you had connections there, that's all."

"You already saw what good those connections did me."

"I'm sorry you got arrested. I never intended for you to get into any trouble." Arthur looked contrite.

"While we're on the subject, what exactly did you intend?"

He stared at the counter in front of him and picked at it with his thumbnail. "I wasn't sure how we'd work it out, exactly, but I thought we could hire you to find Harrison's killer and when you did, I'd be in the clear."

"You didn't plan on the kids notifying their mother that they were okay?"

"I was leaving that up to them. I really didn't kidnap them. I know I went about this in an awkward way, but I knew I'd never be allowed to talk to them if I asked Hilary first, so I didn't ask, I just called. Jeanine hung up on me at first, but later she talked to me. She's a headstrong girl. She remembered what had gone on; she said she wanted to come live with me. I told her no, that it was impossible, but she said if I didn't let her, she'd run away from home." He pounded the counter in front of him. "I agreed that we'd at least talk about it. It all got out of hand after that. I guess I'm not used to dealing with kids. I just let Jeanine have her way.

She contacted Tommy and then I went and got him. We were trying to figure out what we would do when we heard about Harrison. The next thing we knew the papers said I was a kidnapper and suspected killer. Everything just went haywire."

"Tell me about it," I said.

"I don't blame you if you're angry with us for dragging you into this mess. Tommy didn't know this would happen when he hired you."

"How could he? I'm not angry, really. Just a bit worn and tired. Sometimes I'm too sarcastic. I didn't mean to sound that way. Let's put that behind us and try to solve this thing and get you out of jail, okay?"

"Yes, ma'am," he said. "There's just one more thing."

"What's that?"

"I've got my arraignment coming up. Do you think you could get me a lawyer I could trust? One that wouldn't sell me out to Hilary?"

"Is a woman okay?" I asked, thinking of Gillian Wright.

"A woman got me into this mess, maybe a woman could get me out."

I grinned. "Right. I'll give my lawyer a call." I wanted to reach out and give his hand a pat of reassurance, but there was no way, not through the bulletproof glass. We said our good-byes and hung up. The deputy took him away. The bars clanged, the buzzer buzzed, and I went to the office, finally.

When I got to the office, Margaret had the coffeepot going and tea brewing. She must have really missed me.

"Message from the answering service, Mrs. Strickmeier."

"Strickmeier? Who the hell is that?"

"Don't know. The message is in there next to the computer. Why don't you call and find out?" Margaret said.

I went for the pink slip. It was the child welfare number. Angela got a new last name. I forgot. I got her on the line.

"I want to apologize for being so hateful yesterday," she said when I identified myself. "I'm on the rag. You know how it is."

I laughed. "Haven't heard that term in years, you nut. It's okay. I figured something was wrong. It's not like you."

"I was really a pisser. Can you forgive me?"

"No problem." I couldn't figure out the stall. What did she want that she was being so nice? "Did you get a chance to look at the file?"

"I'd like to make it up to you. Could I treat you to lunch today?"

"Is there someone standing over your shoulder?"

"Benihanna's? That would be fine. I'll meet you there at twelve-fifteen. Don't be late. You know how they fill up."

"I'll be there with bells on. Hope it's worth my while, Angela."

"Oh, it will be. The food's always good. See you later."

I laughed as I hung up. Either Mandy was practically sitting on her lap or they had a snitch in the office. Whichever it was, I couldn't wait for lunch.

I re-dialed the phone and Gillian Wright picked up. I'd always heard that after lawyers were hired, they were never in the office when a client called.

"This is Mavis. Would you like another client?"

"I can't give referral fees," she said. "It's prohibited by the code of ethics."

"I wasn't asking for that." I hoped she was joking. I was going to have to get to know the woman better so I could figure out what she meant half the time.

"A little humor never hurts. In this business, without it a person can't survive. Who are you talking about? Or shall I say in my best lawyer tone: To whom do you refer?"

She was a trip. "Arthur Woodridge. He's afraid his ex-wife will get to a court appointed lawyer."

"Like James Rush?"

"You know?" I was only mildly surprised.

"I'm earning my keep. You sent my money yet?"

"It'll find its way over there today."

"Woodridge got any money?"

I laughed. "You're brutal, you know that?"

"It's a cold, hard fact that teenagers have to have name-brand clothes."

"Thank God I don't have any."

"God has nothing to do with it these days. Just stay on the pill—or better yet use it in conjunction with a prophylactic, and you'll be childless and live a long life. You'll also be a lot richer."

"As long as I don't need a lot of legal help."

"Now you're getting the picture. Oh, by the way, the prosecutor back when is no longer with us. Died in a car accident the following year. Willowood, the custody lawyer, moved to parts as yet unknown. Can't find him in the Texas Legal Directory. How does that grab ya'?"

"I'm ecstatic."

"I knew you would be," she said. "Listen, I've got a client sitting here wanting to be serviced," she said and chortled, "so I'll have to talk to you later. Woodridge still in jail?"

"Yes. They brought him to Harris County this morning. So you'll see him then?"

"As long as you guarantee me my money."

"He's got some land he can sell if he has to."

"Let's hope he doesn't have to. Gotta go. See you in court," Gillian said and hung up.

I wasn't exactly having second thoughts because obviously she was actively involved with my case, but during the day, I did reflect on what an interesting person she was. Should have known that any of Candy's relatives would have a lot of character.

Now all I had to do was be patient until lunch.

Chapter Twenty-Four

After I finished reading over the mail from the past few days, returned the other phone calls, and made out a check to Gillian Wright, I decided to pay a visit to the University of Houston lab. I left Gillian's check for Candy to take over in the afternoon after she came in from school. Cousins, however many times removed, ought to be acquainted. Not that I felt that way about mine.

Stanhope was exactly where I'd left him. If he hadn't changed clothes, I would have sworn he hadn't budged. I shook him loose from his microscope and climbed up on a stool next to him.

"Stan, I've been reading about poisons. I still think Mr. Lawson was poisoned and the police do, too. Is there anything you can tell me that would pinpoint it?"

He smiled. "Yeah. I've been called in to consult."

"Cool. By the ME? He's a bud of yours if I remember correctly."

"You know that little bottle you didn't pick up? It was cologne after all."

"Oh. But they wouldn't have asked for a consult for that."

"No. You want the good news?"

"What? Have you been teasing me again?"

"They brought some tissue samples over for me to analyze. Seems some guy died the same time your victim did. Poison. They can't figure out exactly what kind."

My spirits shot up. "Was it from Mr. Lawson?"

He smiled. "I can't say." He winked.

"Great." I yanked on his shirt sleeve. "What was it, Stan? Tell me."

"So long as you didn't hear it from me."

"Not a word, I promise."

"It looks like a combination of poisons."

"That's weird. Like arsenic and something else?"

"Like from plants, common house plants like philodendron, oleander, calla lily, fairy lily, azalea, hyacinth, foxglove, yew—"

"Wait, wait, wait. Margaret got me some stuff from the Internet about house plants, but it can't be all of those."

"I'm not sure yet. I'm just naming some of the most poisonous plants around but definitely some of those. It would help if I knew what houseplants there were at the victim's home. Not that it would prove anything. Anyone could go about gathering up pieces of plants to make poison."

I thought about the beautiful landscaped properties of River Oaks. "There were calla lilies inside the house near the stairwell. Could that have been it?"

"Not by itself. Can you remember any others? How about oleanders outside?"

"Yes! Yes, oleanders out in the backyard by the pool. And gigantic philodendrons right outside the terrace door. I wish I knew my plants. No telling what I didn't recognize."

"Of course, just having a plant in your yard doesn't mean you used it to kill anybody," Stan said. "Still, it's a start knowing what some are."

"What a weird way to kill somebody. Don't you think so, Stan?"

"Yeah, it would've been much easier if they'd have just shot the guy."

"Yeah, quicker, but not by much."

"Why do you say that?" Stan asked.

"I was there, remember? However they did it, it was really fast acting."

"Hey, that gives me an idea, Mavis. Thanks. You've helped me narrow it down. How about I call you later after I'm able to narrow it down more?"

"Are you trying to get rid of me, Stanhope?"

"Good-bye, Mavis."

Angela waited surreptitiously for me around the corner of the restaurant and popped out just as I opened the door. I got the distinct feeling that she did that on purpose because of the way I behaved the previous day but didn't mention it.

Benihanna's is a Japanese restaurant smack in the middle of downtown Houston on the first floor of a major office building. If a person wanted to be covert, it was not the place to do it. Angela may have been of the opinion that the best way to conceal what one is doing is to do it out in the open to avert suspicion. I don't know. As soon as I opened the door, though, and the aroma of Japanese cuisine wafted out to me, the only thing I thought of was food. It seemed like a long time since breakfast.

I ordered steak and shrimp and plum wine. Ordinarily I'm not real big on wine, but that plum stuff—it warms the cockle berries of my heart, not to mention my stomach. I must have it when I eat anything Oriental. I'm not sure what Angela had. I was too immersed in myself.

The kimono-clad lady sat us at a table for six which promptly filled up with four men in expensive-looking business suits. An Asian chef bustled in, slapped a hunk of garlic butter on the built-in grill, and began doing tricks with his butcher knife and my shrimp, chopping off the tails and flipping them into the air and down onto my plate. I got to pig out while their meals were still cooking. When the chef settled down to shuffling the bean sprouts and onions around, and the edge of my hunger was gone, I came to my senses.

Obviously uneasy, Angela watched the door until the place filled up. Satisfied that she wasn't followed by Mandy or one of her spies, she told me in a low voice, "You were right. It could easily have been a setup." She smiled at the men sitting around us. They were intent on their own conversations and most likely didn't notice that her face looked like that of a girl trying to win Miss Congeniality. If anyone suspected she was up to something, she'd be a dead giveaway. The only thing missing was the canary hanging out of her mouth.

"What does it show?" I asked, being careful to follow her lead so I wouldn't piss her off.

"It was subtle enough, but you or I would have questioned it. I think the caseworker must have been either new or stupid."

"Or paid off," I said.

She grimaced. "You can't be serious, Mavis," she said. "It could be since I'm not involved, I can spot it more easily. People were more shockable then. It's easy to point the finger after the fact. A lot of the workers weren't degreed in the right fields, either."

"I know. Is it obvious enough to do something with?"

The chef had finished up and was portioning out the vegetables and entrees onto each plate. When he was through, everyone applauded, and he went away.

"It's not obvious at all. That's what I'm trying to say. It is to me, but it wouldn't be to an untrained eye or someone who wasn't interested or too horrified to look deeply."

"How did you figure it out?" I maneuvered a long slice of zucchini toward my mouth with my chopsticks. I pride myself on my ability to handle those two slim pieces of wood, but I'm not perfect yet.

Angela unrolled her napkin and meticulously straightened it out on her lap. She picked up her fork and stared at it as though her next words were written on the prongs. "It's 'the mother reported that the girl said this' and 'the mother reported that the boy said that.' Very few actual interviews with the children by the workers themselves. Or by the police. In fact, I don't think the police ever talked to the children at all." She pushed her food around on her plate before stabbing at a piece of chicken.

I needed more than that. I needed something I could take to Gillian or the police. "That's all?"

"Oh, it's a thick file. There are some quotes from the children from an interview someone did in the mother's presence on the very first day—the day she made the complaint. There was a physical done by a doctor. It says the little girl had a vaginal irritation and some scratches on her upper thighs. There's a report by a psychiatrist that says that the children wouldn't have used the terminology they used unless someone had interacted with them. It says they were too young to otherwise know the names for certain parts of the body."

"In other words, all the usual bullshit."

"Right," Angela said. "The police reported they searched the house and found some kiddie porn."

"That's a bunch of crap. She had to go to a lot of trouble to plant it."

"I know," she said. She sighed. "It makes me sick, Mavis.

No one ever talked to the children out of the presence of their mother. No one had them make any demonstrations with any kind of dolls, much less the anatomically correct ones. There was no videotape of the children. The report just says the kids were real emotional every time they were brought to the office and the subject broached with them. Especially the girl."

"Did anyone interview Arthur Woodridge?"

"A psychologist, not a caseworker. He was seen several times in the jail. The notes say that there was some hope that he could go into therapy and get straightened out and maybe the family could be reunited, but the psychological report says that he wouldn't admit his guilt and until he would do that, there was no hope of rehabilitating him. Then it says that the mother was seen by the psychologist and that she stated that she'd, and I quote 'lost all love for him and didn't think she could ever allow him back into her home again.' "

"Puke." The whole thing was making me lose my appetite. "Who was the doctor? I might want to pay him a visit."

Angela leaned over and reached into her purse. She pulled out a couple of pieces of paper and stuffed them into the side pocket of my purse. "It's all there," she said under her breath.

"What would it take these days to clear the man?"

She looked surprised. "You mean this man? Now?"

I nodded and took a sip from my midget glass of wine.

"It's never been done before—that I know about."

"Well, the kids will tell their story, but I know that's not enough because it's obvious how much they care for their father. They made a big scene the other night when he was arrested. The police will just think they are emotional teenagers trying to protect him. I've got to have more than that to clear him."

"Jesus, I don't know, Mavis."

"Would you make a statement? Would you give a deposition as an expert on what the file shows?"

"I'd lose my job. Besides, the department would never allow it to be made public that they'd made this kind of horrendous mistake. With all the problems CPS has been having the last few years like in San Antonio, they'd be afraid they would lose all credibility."

Why did I know that she'd say that? "What if I could prove that some of what's in the file was false? What if I could get a confession from one of the professionals that was involved that it was a weak case? What if I could prove that Arthur Woodridge's wife was having an affair with the man who was his defense lawyer back then?"

Her eyes widened at my last statement, but she shook her head. "I don't know. I feel sorry for the guy, but I can't lose this job. I know Mandy would fire me. I'd have to get her permission, and she wouldn't give it. If I went on and did it, I wouldn't stand a chance in hell of keeping my job."

I could feel myself coming to a slow boil. That was the kind of bureaucratic bullcrap that caused me to leave the department. "Would you at least come to the police department with me and talk to Captain Milton about it? Or have you already done that?"

"Are you nuts? All I did was take the file to be copied."

"Well maybe he wanted it so that he could do a little after-the-fact investigation himself. If you'd come with me, it might give him a boost if he's as suspicious as I was."

"Nah, Mavis. He wanted the file so that he could take it to the district attorney's office together with the old police file so that it would help get an indictment on the guy for kidnapping. They don't have enough for the murder indictment, but he doesn't want Woodridge getting out of jail and skipping while they're investigating."

"Shit. You've got to come with me."

"Shh," she said and glanced over her shoulder to see if anyone was listening. "No, I don't, and I'm not."

"Look at it this way, Angela. I've got a friend on the *Chronicle* and if you help me, I'll see to it that he'll write you up as the one who discovered the injustice that was done and righted it all these many years later."

Angela stopped eating and studied my face. Then she turned back to her plate, obviously struggling with herself. For once, I kept my big mouth shut. Let her struggle. Maybe she'd discover that she still had some integrity left, though God knows working for the government—getting along by going along—could destroy it in anyone. At that point I didn't know who was sicker, Hilary Lawson or the people who wouldn't take risks to help others.

I found myself dipping my chopsticks into my bowl of white rice and munching out while I waited for her answer. I don't even like white rice.

"Shelton says I should do something, too, Mavis, but I just can't do it."

"Your husband?"

She nodded. "He works construction and it's been slow. We're flat busted. He says we'll get along, but I just can't do it. I'd be blackballed at every agency in town." The mournful expression in her eyes made me feel guilty. I could understand. It wasn't easy, but I sure could understand her decision.

We finished what was left of our lunch in silence. When the geisha-type came with the check on the tray, I dropped a credit card on it. I may not have any cash, but at least I still had good credit.

As we were leaving, I told her that I was going to the police department and that she could come if she wanted to but that

I wouldn't count on it. She shook her head and told me she wouldn't be there. I thanked her for taking the risks that she had and then I watched as she walked slowly down the street. I could tell that the decision not to help was destroying her.

Chapter Twenty-Five

Lunch left me feeling lethargic. I would have much preferred to go home and nap rather than meet with Captain Milton but persuaded myself that it was essential not to waste any time. In a few days the Lawson kids would be gone to camp and Gillian Wright's job, as well as my own, would be much more difficult. Let's face it, I would procrastinate if I could rather than have another confrontation with a cop, but there just wasn't time.

When I stepped off the elevator, I took a deep breath and waltzed down the hall and into Milton's office with determined steps. I could see through his mini-blinds that he was occupied with someone but didn't let that stop me. I darted past his secretary whose desk stands adjacent to his office entrance and flung open his door before she could stop me.

"Captain Milton, I want my gun back," I said.

"You can't come busting in here," Milton said as he jumped up behind his desk. He'd loosened his tie, his shirt collar open. His face was a blustering red. I hadn't been there long enough to get him worked up into such a stew and wondered briefly at the cause of it. I looked to see who he'd been discoursing with and there sat Ben, slouched back in an armchair, his long legs stretched out in front of him, an amused expression dancing around his eyes. He gave me a cursory nod.

There was some background noise that I think was Captain Milton saying something, but it didn't penetrate. I was staring at Ben and had this wild desire to run to him and throw my arms around him. It was kind of like finding myself in a slow-motion film clip where the man and woman are in a field of wild flowers about a hundred yards apart, the woman in a flowery dress, carrying a floppy hat in her hand, and she begins running toward the man with outstretched arms, joy written all over her face. Then I remembered that I was supposed to be angry at Ben, so I turned my head and pretended I hadn't seen him. My stomach churned as I took an aggressive tact with the captain and squared off in front of his desk.

"You have no right to keep my gun. I want it back. It's not evidence of anything. I want you to make out a slip so I can go to the property room and pick it up. It's not safe for a woman to go about Houston without her gun." I was babbling, but it was all I could think of. I hoped it would stop him from throwing me out.

"What are you talking about, Mavis?" Milton asked. He came around toward me.

"Miss Davis to you, Captain Milton," I said. "My gun was in Arthur Woodridge's possession on the night you had him arrested. I want it back. I have no protection for my office." I knew I couldn't get it from him. Gillian would have to get the DA to authorize its release, but I kept on.

"Forget it," Milton roared into my face. His breath smelled like stale coffee beans. The office smelled like men's sweat.

"And while I'm here, I want to know what you're doing to clear up the false charges that Hilary Lawson filed on Arthur Woodridge thirteen years ago."

"False charges. He was convicted."

"So? They were false, and you know it. If you'd been the

captain on the case back then, you would have cleared him. You've seen the file. It's a pile of shit."

"Now wait a minute, Mavis. What do you know about it?" He was suddenly a tad calmer. Flattery will sometimes do that to a person.

"I was a child welfare worker, remember?" I wanted to say "remember asshole," but I didn't. "I know a put-up job when I see it. Besides, the kids told me how it all happened. And did you know James Rush was his defense attorney? Huh? Doesn't that make you the least little bit curious? So what are you going to do about it?"

I couldn't tell what Ben was thinking. While this exchange was going on our backs were to each other. He had gotten out of his chair and made a pretense of staring through the blinds at the main part of the office.

"What are you talking about?" the captain asked.

"I'm talking about the fact that Harrison Lawson's murder was conveniently executed right after Arthur Woodridge got out of prison. I'm talking about the fact that at the time of the murder, James Rush was present in the Lawson home. Rush, who is Mrs. Lawson's lover. Rush, who was Arthur Woodridge's criminal defense attorney thirteen years ago. I'm talking about the fact that anyone who isn't a fool can read between the lines of that CPS report and see that it was a setup. No one talked to the kids without their mother present then and no one will talk to them now, not if she can help it anyway. She's fixing to send them off to camp next week so you better hurry and do something fast." I stopped talking and planted myself in a chair next to an ashtray full of cigarette butts. That old desire reared its ugly head. Luckily, I wasn't in possession though the thought crossed my mind that I could dig one of the bigger butts out of the sand and light up. What an addict I was. There was something about the captain that made me lose all my resolve to quit, not to mention how I felt about being in the same room with Ben.

Milton grimaced as he leaned against the front of his desk and crossed his arms. He still had an angry look in his eye as he stared down at me. "Where do you get off coming in here with a story like that? These are highly respectable people. Do you know how important James Rush is? Do you know the kind of power he wields? Mrs. Lawson, herself, sits on several important boards in this town and has some powerful political connections. She even knows the mayor personally."

"I don't think His Honor the Mayor would approve of what Hilary's done," I said.

"Shut up, Mavis. Just shut up." He rubbed the stubble on his chin and stared at me.

"Fine," I said, standing. "Just thought I'd give you a chance to get the credit for clearing this thing up, that's all. You're going to be awfully embarrassed when it comes out and it appears you didn't do anything to help the poor man." I headed for the door.

Milton grabbed my arm roughly, jerking me around. "Don't threaten me, Mavis."

Ben was suddenly there beside me. "Now wait a minute," he said to the captain.

I shook Milton's hand off. "Don't touch me again, Captain, or I'll sue your ass for police brutality. I don't give a shit who you are or what your connections are. I'm not afraid of you or your big shot friends." I reached for the doorknob again.

"Everybody just calm down!" Ben shouted. He reached out, pushed the door and held it closed. "Don't you know you can't burst into someone's office and start a bunch of shit like this, Mavis? Sit down over there," he said, pointing to the chair from which I'd come.

There was a knock on the door, and Ben yanked it open. "What is it?"

The captain's secretary stood there with a shocked look on her face. She stretched her neck to see past Ben. "There's an Angela Strickmeier to see you, Captain."

Hope surged through me. "Send her in," I said. "She can help straighten this whole thing out."

Captain Milton gave me an ugly look. "I give the orders around here if you don't mind." Then he said to the woman, "Tell her to come in."

I suppressed a grin and stole a look at Ben who aimed a reproachful look at me. Angela came through the door. When she saw me, she smiled sheepishly and shrugged. Now her, I really wanted to run to and hug with all my might. She looked at Ben questioningly as he shut the door behind her, then at the captain.

"Mrs. Strickmeier, have a seat," the captain said and indicated the chair where Ben had been sitting.

Angela walked over to sit down and Ben stepped across the room and stood on the far side of the captain's desk where he could watch us. The captain pushed one of the phones back on his desk, making a space for himself, and halfway sat on the front of his desk, his legs dangling over the sides, one of them not quite touching the floor.

"This is Lieutenant Sorenson," he told her, indicating Ben.

Angela forced a smile at Ben and said something amiable.

My eyes met Ben's. He'd gotten a promotion and hadn't told me. I felt a twinge in my heart. Ben raised his eyebrows but didn't say anything. He nodded at Angela. I wondered if he was still a narc or had been moved to homicide.

"I suppose you're acquainted with Miss Davis, here," the captain said.

"We used to work together," I said.

"Shut up, Mavis," he said with a scowl. "I'm talking to this young woman right now. You'll get another chance to speak your piece."

I don't take kindly to being talked to like that, but I shut up. Angela shot me a sympathetic look, as if to say "I told you so."

I dug a piece of gum out of my purse, crossed my legs, and pretended I wasn't offended. Private detectives have to be thick-skinned. It says that somewhere in the unofficial rule book. Number thirty-nine, I think.

"I suppose you've come to see me about the case we discussed a few days ago, is that right?" the captain asked.

Angela smoothed her hair, pushed a few wrinkles around in her skirt, straightened the hem, and said, "Yes, sir."

"Have you taken it upon yourself to review that file?" he asked. "And if so, have you formed any opinions that you'd like to share with us?" He shot me a look that wasn't pleasant.

Angela glanced at me; I suppose for moral support. "Look, Captain, I didn't want to get involved, but there are some things contained in the file that make what happened to Mr. Woodridge questionable."

"And?" he asked.

"And if it were up to me," she said, "I'd reopen the case."

"Ah," he said and stood, rubbing his hands together like Simon Legree. "You would, would you?" He began pacing up and down in front of his desk, Napoleonic-style. I waited for him to stick his hand in his shirt breast.

She took a deep breath, gathering her courage, I think, and said, "Yes, sir. If you'll read each report, you'll see that Mrs. Woodridge, who is now Mrs. Lawson, exerted a great deal of influence over practically everything that was said and done. It began with the initial interview of the children and ended—well—when the case was closed after conviction."

"So you think there's some chance that Woodridge was innocent?" Milton asked.

"Definitely," Angela answered.

Milton ran his fingers through his hair and sighed loudly. "What a mess," he said, as if to himself.

"Yes, sir," Angela said. She was sitting on her hands, her knees hiked up, swinging her feet back and forth under her chair like a little kid in the principal's office. "What scares me is whether this has happened more than once."

Milton grunted and took his chair. "Let's take this one case at a time." He picked up a pencil and began chewing on the eraser. He glanced at Ben. "Technically, this doesn't even fall under my jurisdiction—except for that homicide. I think we ought to call in someone from Special Investigations. What do you think?"

"I agree, sir. It may not even be tied to the murder, but if we could get a man assigned to us, we could coordinate it all from here. We'd take up the homicide part and he could start checking out the allegations that these two ladies have made," Ben said. It killed me how he referred to me as he would any other woman. Was that all I was to him now? Had he written me off or what?

"We'd have to keep that part under our hats until we had something concrete to go on," the captain said. "No use asking for trouble."

Ben nodded.

The captain turned to Angela and me. "All right, ladies—and I use that term loosely when referring to you, Davis—let's get on with it. Let's hear what else you have."

I smiled out of the side of my mouth. If that's the only way he could deal with me, so be it. At least I was accomplishing what I wanted. I got up and dragged my chair to the front of his desk. Angela did the same thing. Then the four of us began a round table discussion that lasted until well after dinnertime.

Chapter Twenty-Six

I don't know quite how it happened, but somehow Angela, Ben, and I ended up going out to dinner together. I remember Angela calling home and asking her husband to pick up the baby from the day care center. The next thing I knew we were all three sitting in a booth in a little Mexican restaurant off Westheimer.

We had developed a spirit of camaraderie during the day. We had agreed with the captain that for obvious political reasons, the investigation into the Woodridge case would be a secret between the four of us and whoever the Special Investigations Division assigned. At least the sexual assault investigation would be. The homicide investigation was a matter of public record.

The captain was still not convinced that Arthur hadn't committed the murder. I had to agree that the man had plenty of motive. No manner of explanation into the character and personality of Arthur Woodridge would convince Milton that he couldn't have done it and not that the captain wouldn't have blamed him, he admitted, or at least he wouldn't have blamed him for murdering Hilary. At any rate, he agreed to keep an open mind and admitted that the investigations together might yield some interesting information about the true killer if it wasn't Woodridge. Many questions would be asked and many interviews conducted under the guise of investigating the homicide. I probably should have shared with him what I knew about the insurance policies, Hadley, and Smythe, but I didn't. Okay, I admit to having some character flaws.

The captain also made it very clear that I wasn't off the hook for the charges against me. End of discussion.

They set up a meeting for the next morning between Ben, Captain Milton, and the assignee, if you will, from Special Investigations where they'd review the case. The first thing one of them would do would be track down all the professionals who were used as expert witnesses in court, in hopes of finding out how everything had really transpired.

Lastly, much to Angela's relief, the captain requested that in light of the confidential nature of the investigation, it would be in the best interest of all concerned if Angela didn't mention what was going on to anyone in her office, including Mandy. No telling what political alliances people had that would cause them to tip off someone.

It was nice finding myself sitting across the table from Ben, discussing a case, one professional to another. We hadn't done that in a long time and I hoped it was an indication that our relationship was taking a new turn. I also felt reassured to know that he would be involved with the case. I knew that he was honest and wouldn't let anything get swept under the rug.

After dinner, Angela begged off and went home, leaving a few awkward moments between us. I started to make my excuses, too, but Ben wasn't having any.

"We need to talk," he said.

A knot made from refried beans and nerves formed in my stomach. "When did you make lieutenant?" My eyes flitted around the restaurant, meeting his, but not stopping for a visit.

"They announced it on Monday afternoon," he said, "but I never had the opportunity to tell you."

"And with it you got a transfer to homicide?"

"At least temporarily."

A silence followed. The waitress came to clear the table, and we ordered a couple more bottles of beer.

"I got a lawyer," I said. "Her name's Gillian Wright. You know her?"

"Heard of her. Don't know her." His eyes were all over me.

"She's neat. Different, kind of, from most of the ones I know. Older than me by maybe ten years."

"How'd you find her?"

"She's a distant relation of Candy's, a cousin thrice removed or something. Her father's a judge in Angleton."

He cocked his head. "Yeah, I do know her. She's kind of a nut, isn't she? Goes around making snide comments and laughing all the time."

"Yeah, but I like her."

He nodded. "You would."

I sipped from my long neck.

"I'll be making quite a bit more money," he said.

"That's good. What are you going to do with it?"

"Save it, I guess. Maybe take a vacation."

"I've been thinking I might go down to Galveston for the weekend when this is over."

"Be a tourist again?"

"Yeah. Just need to get away," I said. "Lie out on the beach again while there's still some beach."

"I know what you mean." He drank from his beer. "Next hurricane may take out the island. Their luck's got to run out pretty soon."

"Do you think the captain is worried about this case?"

"Yeah. He's bucking for deputy chief. Hates to make waves."

"But if he solves it, he'll be a hero."

"Not really. Rush has a lot of friends."

"At least I know something will really be done with you on the case," I said.

He looked at me with a melancholy little smile. "Thanks for your vote of confidence."

I shifted around on the bench and propped my legs up. "Ain't no big thang," I said.

He chuckled halfheartedly and tipped his long neck up, swallowing half its contents. Then he said, "How's Margaret? Is she mad at me, too?"

"She's been like a mother hen since I got out of jail. I think it scared her."

His lips formed a thin smile. "But it didn't scare you."

"Nope." I smirked. "I didn't like it, but it didn't scare me." There was a tone of defiance in my voice that I couldn't keep out.

"You're tough, you know it, Mavis?"

It was the first time he'd called me by name in a good while. It sounded strange. "Not so tough," I said.

"You'd make a good cop."

"I don't like taking orders."

"No shit."

We both laughed.

"I like this—being able to talk to you the way it's been today," Ben said, his face softening.

"I was just thinking the same thing."

"I guess I shouldn't always go around trying to tell you what to do."

"Sometimes it's like you don't give me credit for having any sense."

"When it comes to you, my thinking is somewhat antiquated."

"Chauvinistic."

"Don't get carried away. Outmoded—outdated maybe."

"Chauvinistic. You don't treat the police women you work with that way, do you?"

"No," he said slowly as he searched my eyes with his, "but I'm not in love with them."

That one caught me off guard. I almost broke out in warm tears. He took hold of my hand. It only served to make me feel worse. I couldn't speak for a minute. I couldn't look at him, either.

"Did you hear me?" he said in a low voice.

I nodded.

"How about we skip the apologies and go ruffle the sheets at my place?"

So we did. I followed him in my car. When we got there, it was just getting dark. He lived in a small apartment complex on the fringe of the Heights area. They reduced his rent in exchange for being on call for security.

His large, one-bedroom apartment was furnished with the remnants from his first marriage, which ended eons ago according to what little information I'd been able to glean from him since we'd started seeing each other. His living room furniture consisted of a worn sofa, a recliner, and a small TV/VCR/DVD combo. He used a large orange crate with a beach towel thrown over it for a coffee table. A cheap, plastic dinette and four chairs sat just off the kitchen. I think he bought that after the divorce because I have trouble thinking that any woman would have such poor taste.

Ben had apparently gotten custody of the bedroom furnishings. They matched. He had a king-size water bed complete with built-in bookshelves and stereo unit with speakers.

The music comes out on each side of the headboard. It's the kind of thing that a typical male would think sensual. That was where we made mad, passionate love that night to the accompaniment of a Houston oldies-but-goodies radio station. Afterwards, we split a beer and lay talking for a while. Then we made love again, this time it wasn't so frenzied.

The word contented comes to mind when I think of how I felt as I lay there dozing on and off while Ben snored loudly beside me. I was happy. I hadn't enjoyed being estranged from him. Those few days seemed like years. There was something about our semi-constant bickering that I'd missed.

I got up around ten and wandered into the kitchen for a drink of water. As I stood there, I pondered all the possible suspects in the Harrison Lawson murder. I think the count was now up to five, or was it six? Then I remembered Annette. I'd put her out of my mind. I felt too guilty.

I knew it was no burglar who broke into Annette's house and practically killed her. It must have to do with the murder, but how? Why? If it was the insurance, wouldn't she have known I could find out about the policies anyway? Maybe she knew something else. Did Harrison know about James Rush? Was that the clincher to the whole case? I knew she hated Hilary and would do anything she could to get her if Hilary killed Harrison.

I went back to bed still thinking about Annette. The least I should have done was go by the hospital to see her. I should have sent flowers, too. God, I felt responsible. I wanted to find out who tried to kill her almost more than I wanted to clear myself. If it weren't for me . . . I made a mental list of things I would do the next day. I'd go see Smythe, then Hadley. Afterwards I'd buy some flowers and take them to Annette at St. Joseph's. I fell asleep still feeling guilty.

Chapter Twenty-Seven

When I awoke late the next morning, Ben had gone. He'd left a sweet note on his pillow. I would have felt great except I remembered Annette and vowed to see her before the day was over. In the meantime, I wanted to see if I could make Hadley and/or Smythe squirm.

On my way home for a quick shower and change, I called Margaret and got the addresses of the two men. I'd hit Hadley first, since he was the farthest out. Then I could swing downtown to catch Smythe.

Hadley had an office on the fourth floor in one of his almost-deserted office buildings off the Katy freeway. The leather chairs in his reception area were worn and faded. The solid wood coffee and end tables were scarred and chipped. What I observed reinforced that which I'd already learned.

Handing the receptionist-secretary, a rather plump young woman in ill-fitting clothing, my card, I said, "I'd like a few minutes with Mr. Hadley."

She took the card and disappeared behind a closed door. About sixty seconds later, Clayton Hadley appeared, briefcase in hand. As he came toward me, I saw that he looked like he'd slept in his suit. The pockmarks on his pig-like face were like the craters at Yellowstone, the pupils of his dark eyes like pinpricks behind his eyelids. His gray-streaked black hair was pasted to his pate. "I'm afraid you've caught me on the way out, Miss Davis." His smile revealed abnormally yellowed teeth. "Another time, maybe."

"It'll just take a couple of minutes, Mr. Hadley." He passed me so I followed him to the door.

He glanced at his watch. "Can't. Sorry. I'm already late for an important meeting." He reached for the door.

"I'll walk you down to your car then," I said. "We can talk on the way." Persistence, I've found, is a good quality in a detective.

He grunted and glared back at the girl, opened the office door, and walked through the doorway in front of me. I followed him to the elevators.

"So what is it you want from me, Miss Davis? I understand the Lawson children have turned up." He frowned with his pig eyes.

"I guess you could say I'm looking into Mr. Lawson's murder," I said.

His eyebrows shot up. "Oh, really?"

"Yes, sir." The elevator arrived and I followed him inside even though I knew I would be at his mercy. Sometimes I'm not as bright as I think I am. I did stand next to the buttons, though, so I could push the red emergency one if he slugged me.

"Well, what do you want from me? I saw the same things you did. We were both there." He faced me, his eyes watching the numbers above the door.

"I understand you held a large policy on Mr. Lawson's life."

His eyes became little slits as he slowly turned them on me. I had my hands at the ready, one to block his blow and one to push the button.

"Now wait a minute. Are you implying that I had anything to do with Harrison's death?"

"I'm not implying anything. I'm merely conducting an investigation. It's odd, though, that Miss Jensen from the insurance company should be seriously assaulted after the murder. Like it leads one to think that maybe someone didn't want her telling anyone about all the beneficiaries." He didn't flinch. He didn't move a muscle. He didn't look surprised. He just continued to stare at me with what could only be described as contempt—no, pure hatred.

The elevator door opened on the first floor. Hadley still hadn't said anything. He walked briskly toward the exit. I followed.

"No comments, Mr. Hadley?" I called from behind him.

He turned on me when we got outside. "Get out of here," he said and headed toward some cars.

"What?" I was following again. It was no problem since his fat little legs had to take two steps to each one of mine.

He reached his car and hit the button on the key fob, unlocking it. I waited on the sidewalk for a response. It appeared he wasn't going to give me any. "I know you need the money, Mr. Hadley. I checked you out," I yelled as he was getting in his car.

He slammed the car door and started up, leaving me standing there watching as he drove away. Interesting response.

Earl Smythe was a totally different sort of fellow. I arrived at his office before noon. He worked for a large company in downtown Houston. A young woman who looked like she had just stepped off the cover of *Cosmopolitan* showed me to his office.

Quite handsome, Smythe couldn't have been a day over forty. He had large, straight white teeth and a captivating smile. Blond hair, sea blue eyes, strong nose, clean shaven, he looked like he should be on a tennis court with a sweater tied around his shoulders. Dark circles under his eyes were the only telltale sign of hard times. He wore an expensive three-piece suit, a signature tie, and pastel shirt with cuff links. He shook my hand when I entered. His hand warm, his shake was firm but not quite what I had imagined, a little wanting.

After I sat down across from him, I said, "I don't think we met at the Lawson's, Mr. Smythe. I arrived just before Mr. Lawson died."

"I remember you." He was solemn.

"I'm looking into Mr. Lawson's murder."

"They've decided it's murder then?"

"Yes. Poison."

He grimaced. "What can I do for you?" He started twisting his wedding band around on his finger.

"I hope you won't take any offense, but I heard that you and Harrison had a falling out."

"We did." He brushed at his hair and went back to fiddling with his ring.

"Could you tell me about it?"

"There's not much to tell. He lost a bundle in the market and blamed me for it." He stared at me, his somber eyes not wavering. "That was back when I had my own agency."

"You've only been here a while, then?"

"Since last month. My business fell off slowly and I couldn't afford the overhead."

That certainly rang true. "To what do you attribute that?"

"Harrison. He bad-mouthed me all over town."

I nodded. "When did you find that out?"

"I had suspected it for a long time, but someone confirmed it for me recently."

"Who?"

"I'd rather not say, if you don't mind."

"How recently?"

"Couple of weeks ago, after I got here."

"Oh, I see."

"Yes, I had a motive, Miss Davis, but I didn't kill Harrison." He leaned back in his chair and crossed his legs. "The thought did cross my mind when I first found out what he went around saying, but . . . I guess you could say I didn't have the guts for it."

"It seems to me that it takes more guts not to do something like that when you're angry."

He shrugged. "Let's say that I considered it very seriously. I might have done it if Joe hadn't given me a job here, believe me. I've been at my wit's end."

"Who do you think did it?"

"I don't know. All I know is it wasn't me."

I wasn't entirely convinced, but just the same I took my leave of him.

When I arrived at the hospital, Annette was just regaining consciousness. Her condition was still serious, the doctors allowing as how she might never fully recover. They permitted me to go inside her room when I showed them my identification and stretched the truth a bit by telling them I was investigating her case.

Her head had been wrapped in thick bandages. I needn't mention the guilt that I felt. I felt so inept, so useless, so incompetent. I had botched it; bungled it; blown it. I was nothing but a screwup and had almost cost a lady her life.

Annette turned her head toward me slightly, her eyes watching me.

"I'm so sorry, Annette," I whispered. "I should have been there."

She blinked her eyes at me and tried to say something.

"What?" I moved closer.

She was whispering. It sounded like "find the file."

"No, I didn't find anything, but I know what it was you wanted to show me. Mr. McAfee told me."

Annette shook her head.

"Yes, Annette, he told me about all the life insurance policies. I went to see Mr. Hadley this morning. And I know Mr. Lawson was going to change his will. I don't think he did, though. I don't think he had time."

"No," she whispered. She shook her head again and began to cough. A ragged sound came from deep inside her chest so I went for a nurse. The staff told me to leave, that perhaps I could see her tomorrow.

I took my misery and went to Lana's where I could be alone. When I looked up after my second long neck, I saw Lana wiping her hands on the ever-present dishtowel pinned on the front of her. She came toward me with a bottle in her hand. She eased herself into the chair across from me. I started to ask for another beer, but she cut me off with a sharp wave of her hand.

"Whatsa' matter with you, Mavis?" Her beady black eyes bored into mine. "You never drink so much in you life." She pushed strands of gray hair away from her pudgy face and wiggled around on the chair until her bulk came to a comfortable solution to a chair that is smaller than the bottom of the sitter. I had the feeling that she would stay so situated until I made a clean breast of it.

I told her. Not everything but enough that she got the idea. And I told her that the old lady I was supposed to meet could have died because of me.

"So you help her now by getting drunk on beer, no?"

"Go away, Lana," I said when I didn't get the sympathy for which I'd been hoping. "I've only just begun."

"No." She shook her head. "You need me to talk sense to you."

I stared at the bar. "The only thing I need is another beer. If you would be so kind as to waddle over and draw me one."

Out of the corner of my eye, I saw her head wag. "You be mean to me if you want, Mavis. It won't help the old lady."

My guilt was only exacerbated by my words and Lana's response, but I couldn't help myself at that point. "Nothing I could do would help her now," I said miserably. "Just bring me another beer, will you?"

"No." Lana crossed her flabby arms in front of her chest. "You want to get drunk, go someplace else. I not help you."

"Screw you, Lana." I started digging in my purse for money to pay my bill. "I will go someplace else. I'll never ask you for anything again."

"Tch, tch. I never know you were a quitter." It sounded like kweeter, the way she said it with her Tex-Mex accent.

"I'm not. The police are on the case. They don't need me."

"So why don't you find other work? You make somebody a good secretary or somethin'."

I knew what she was getting at, and it was working. I felt my mouth turn up in a crooked smile in spite of myself. My eyes I kept staring at the contents of my purse. I didn't want her to see that she was winning.

"What you say to that, Mes Davis—huh?"

"I say why you don't mind your own business?"

"My customers are my business. They help me. I help them. You wanna sandwich or somethin'? You can't go out to work on the old lady's case with nothin' but beer on you stomach."

She knew she'd won. I was feeling exceedingly stupid. "Yeah, give me a turkey—"

"With lotsa onions."

"Right." I looked at her as she lifted the heavy burden of herself and shook off the clinging chair. She smiled, knowingly, but not so big a smile. She was going to let me save a little, tiny bit of face.

"I got something for you first." She took a shot glass out of her pocket and poured a clear liquid from the bottle she'd been cuddling to her chest. "Sip. Don't gulp."

"What is it?"

"Just you drink it but slowly."

I sipped and almost gagged. Ugh. "What the hell is it?"

"Schnapps—I bought a bottle so you could taste."

That touched me; it really did. "Aw, thanks for thinking about me." That stuff was so bad no wonder Harrison Lawson couldn't taste the poison. Assuming the poison had really been put into the bottle. Ifs, ands, buts, and assumptions. A way of life for private investigators. It mentions that in the rule book, in a footnote.

Lana started across the room toward the end of the bar and turned back. "Mavis—did you find the envelope she had for you?"

"What envelope?"

She held her hands apart to indicate its width. "Big, yellow with papers for you she said."

"Shit." Whoever whacked her in the head had probably been looking for that when I'd arrived. I wondered if it was just copies of the policies or whether Annette had something else to show me. She'd been trying to tell me something at the hospital.

"I tole you no talk like that in my place," Lana said loudly, a scowl on her face and her finger wagging at the end of a short, flabby arm. She turned back to the bar.

"Make that a take-out order," I said. "I gotta go."

The Mustang practically flew to the office by itself. Candy

arrived at the same time and we entered together. Margaret was on the phone and printing out something from the computer. When she hung up, we had a meeting, the three of us in the kitchen again, gathered around the table.

"That was Ben on the phone," Margaret said. "He just wanted to let you know that there was no change with Annette Jensen."

"I know," I said. "I was there myself a while ago."

"Tommy called, too." Margaret held out a stack of pink slips. "He wanted to know what you'd come up with to keep him and Jeanine from being sent away. Oh, and Ben said to tell you the meeting went real well. He said you'd know what he meant. Are you and Ben on speaking terms again?"

I looked at Margaret and then at Candy. Couldn't fool either of them. "Yeah," I confessed. "Well—he's helping—you know."

"We know, Mavis," Candy said.

Margaret snickered.

"All right, you two. Enough of my love life. We've got to get down to business if we're going to make any headway with this thing." I tried to give them my reprimanding look, but it didn't quite come off.

"Come on, Margaret, let's get serious here," Candy said and put her hand over her mouth.

"Very funny, Candy," I said. I looked at Margaret. "Anyone else call?"

"Besides people wanting subpoenas served?"

I nodded.

"Your lawyer. They've already got you set for arraignment, she said."

"They're not wasting any time. Did you mark it down on the calendar?"

"Ummm," Margaret murmured, her forehead drawn together in a tight crease. "What exactly is that? I looked it up in the dictionary. What are you going to have to do?"

"I just have to go in and plead not guilty, Margaret, that's all," I tried to reassure her with a glance and a smile. "Don't worry. Gillian's going to take care of it. Speaking of whom, Candy, how'd you like your cousin?"

Candy sat upright in her chair. "Like she's pretty cool, Mavis. She was real busy when I got over there, but like she came out of her office and, you know, talked to me. She'd like to get to know me, she said."

"Great," I grinned at her. Maybe Gillian would be a positive role model for Candy. I hadn't been doing such a hot job lately.

"If anyone can get you like out of this, Gillian can," Candy said.

"I hope so, but we're going to have to do some of the work ourselves. I've been thinking while we've been talking that we need to try to figure out what was in the envelope that Lana said Annette was going to give me."

"What envelope?" Margaret asked.

"Oh, I forgot—" I proceeded to give them a rundown of the rest of the events.

"Do you think it had something to do with the Lawson kids being adopted and their father being put in jail?" Margaret asked.

"I don't know. It's a possibility. Annette could have found some papers about it in Mr. Lawson's office if she was cleaning it out after he died."

"Hey, you know, Mavis, maybe the old lady found some papers that show that Mr. Woodridge is like really innocent. Maybe some canceled checks showing that Mr. Lawson bribed some witnesses or something like that."

Candy flitted around the room like Tinker Bell. "That'd be great, huh?"

"Except every indication is that he didn't know Hilary framed her husband," I said.

"Aw, c'mon, Mavis. You don't believe that, do you?" Candy asked.

Margaret was quiet, watching us.

"What do you think, Margaret? Got any ideas?" It wasn't that I thought she'd come up with some brilliant notion, but I hated to let Candy overshadow her.

She turned her head to the side and chewed on her lower lip. "I don't think someone would kill Mr. Lawson for those papers, that's all. There had to be another reason."

"God. What a mess," I said. "We've got a frame for sexual abuse of a child thirteen years ago. We've got the mother probably having an affair with the man who was her ex-husband's lawyer. We've got a dead man who was having an affair with his employee's wife. There's a secretary with her head bashed in who was in love with the decedent. We've got people with motives coming out their ears."

"Don't forget the dead dog," Candy said.

"You're gross sometimes, Candy," I said. "But one thing about it is that the dog probably wouldn't have barked if he'd known the person who came to the house."

"Yeah, but who would go to her house anyhow?" Candy asked.

"And did they get the papers?" Margaret asked.

"Probably," I said. "I didn't see any and the police didn't turn up any that I know of."

"Maybe Miss Jensen mailed them to us on her way home," Candy said. "Or—maybe she mailed them to herself?"

I shook my head. "Only in the movies, Candy."

"She could have seen that in a movie," Candy said.

"Yeah, Mavis," Margaret said.

"I don't think the killer found them," I said. "Otherwise why would he or she have been there when I showed up?"

"See," Candy said, "they could be in the mail."

"It hasn't come yet, Margaret?" Let's face it, you never know.

"Nope. Anytime now."

"I vote that if the envelope isn't in the mail, we go out to her house and search it," Candy said.

My thoughts exactly. "I'll go out and search it."

"Let me go with you, Mavis," Margaret said.

"If anyone gets to go, it should be me, Margaret," Candy said. "After all, I'm the one who brought the case to the office. I should get to help investigate it."

"No one is going with me." I hated it when Candy got that one-upmanship tone.

"When are you going to go?" Candy asked.

"Tonight, after dark. The house is supposed to be sealed, and I don't want anyone calling the cops on me."

"You'll need someone to stand guard for you, Mavis," Candy said.

I shook my head and glanced at Margaret to see how she was reacting to all this.

"It's okay," Margaret said. "I couldn't go that late anyway. I have a date."

"With that dude, what's-his-face?" Candy asked.

"Yeah. It's okay, Mavis. I don't mind if Candy goes."

"You'll need me, Mav," Candy said as she gave me her most earnest look. "I can sit in the car and watch out for you. If anyone comes, I could honk the horn. We could park down the street a little from the house in front of another house and I could act like I was waiting for someone to come out. See, you need me."

"It's against my better judgment," I said. "It could be dangerous."

"Not if I lock myself in the car," she said. That whine of hers was starting to creep into her voice.

"I'm only planning to do it if the envelope doesn't come in the mail."

"Come on, please? I promise I'll do exactly what you tell me. I won't get in the way."

"Won't your mother wonder where you are on a school night?"

"She'll never know the diff, Mavis. I go out all the time."

"Great." There was a reason why Candy's mom wouldn't be named Mother of the Year.

"Please, Mavis? I promise I won't get into any trouble."

"I don't know, Candy. You're just a kid. I've got to take care of you."

"I'm eighteen now, Mavis. I'm fixin' to graduate. Besides, all you're going to do is search the place. What could go wrong?"

Chapter Twenty-Eight

I didn't relent. I just couldn't take Candy with me, and I could tell Margaret didn't want to go. I'd have to go to Annette's house alone.

The mail didn't contain anything from Annette. Margaret left to serve some subpoenas and run some errands. Candy stayed in to answer the phone and do a little typing job we'd gotten, another of our sidelines. I caught up on some paperwork.

Basically, when I'd started out, I'd intended to keep copious notes on every case. It would be accurate to say that I'm not the most meticulous record-keeper in the world. If I could but get a summary of recent events down on paper once a week I was doing good. The most logical thing would be for me to put it all on computer disks, but I had yet to be that ambitious with the computer. Margaret, and even Candy, knew more about computers and the Internet than I did, a situation I knew I must remedy. Perhaps I'd make it my summer project. Maybe I should take a course.

Meanwhile, under my old system, I would often keep a notebook or scraps of paper with information scratched down to formalize later for the file. And I wondered why when I was trying to articulate the problem or organize my thoughts they wouldn't come together. That was where I was in the Lawson/Woodridge/Jensen case. Lurking in the dark recesses of my mind was a question that needed answering or some information that needed questioning. Unfortunately, I couldn't for the life of me think of it. I spent the last of the afternoon carefully documenting the events of this weird case from beginning to present day. Still I couldn't fathom it.

Ben called to let me know that the investigator from the Special Investigations section was out tracking down leads. If they learned anything, he'd tell me later that night when we got together.

Having sent Margaret home for her date, I overcame Candy's arguments and made her leave at twilight. I stayed to catch up on a few more things before I left.

It was good and dark when the phone rang for the umpteenth time that night.

"Mavis Davis Investigations," I said.

"Stan, here, Mavis. Good news," his voice boomed through the wire.

"Great, Stan, give it to me."

"I've definitely isolated oleander and foxglove."

"I know we have lots of oleander bushes in the Gulf Coast area, but where would someone get foxglove?" I'd read about it. The flowers were pretty, like little fairies, but deadly.

"Hell, you can get anything you want these days if you try hard enough. It grows up north and on the west coast and Hawaii. I'm not exactly sure what kind of foxglove it was."

"There's more than one?"

"Didn't I tell you to do an Internet search on poisons? You didn't do it, did you?"

"Yes, I did, I told you. But I don't have time to read the minute details. After all, you did a doctoral program on it. I don't have three years or whatever—"

"Okay. Okay. I was teasing."

"I don't have much of a sense of humor these days. Anyway, how do you think they got him to ingest it?"

"Oleander would have to be disguised in something strong tasting. Foxglove leaves could be served in a salad."

"I didn't see him eat anything. He was drinking a lot, though."

"They found alcohol in his stomach for sure."

"Yeah, he definitely was drinking, and a lot, but if someone poisoned his drink, they could have killed anyone." Except, I thought, schnapps was not a popular drink and for good reason. I bet whoever did it knew that.

Stan laughed.

"What are you laughing at?"

"Nothing," he said. I could hear a female voice in the background.

"I'll let you go, Stan. Sounds like you're busy."

"Don't you want to hear my theory of the case, Mavis?"

"Shoot."

"I think the poison brought on a heart attack before the symptoms could really show up. Otherwise he would have had nausea, vomiting, maybe convulsions, stuff like that."

"Do you think they knew it would bring on a heart attack?"

"It's possible that they did, but given enough foxglove, a person can die in, say, twenty minutes or so."

"So what are you saying?"

"Well, if he'd eaten it earlier in the day, he would have died before you got there, unless they didn't feed him enough. So we can assume that either he ingested it earlier in the day and he didn't get enough to bring on the classic symptoms, but enough to tax his system so that he had a heart attack later in the day or the killer didn't give him enough at first, realized that, and put more poison, oleander at least, in his drink. The vic finally ingested enough to bring on the heart attack and would have died anyway from the poison probably ten minutes to an hour or so later."

That was one I'd have to mull over. I knew the police had not confiscated all the liquor bottles that had been at the party. A schnapps bottle had been there the following day, but was it the same one? Doubtful. More laughter erupted in the background. "I'll let you get back to whatever you're doing, Stan. Thanks for calling."

"If you need anything else, let me know," he said. "I'll be writing up a report and e-mailing it back." He hung up.

I replaced the phone. I was pretty sure I knew who did it, all the more reason to get to Annette's for whatever was in that envelope. I was convinced now that she must have hidden it, whatever it was, somewhere in her house and I had disturbed the search.

I started to pack up for the night when I thought I heard someone at the back door of the office.

It was a scratching sound, and it sent shivers down my spine. I knew we didn't have rats and I didn't have time to fool with a burglar.

Nevertheless, I tiptoed down the hall until I came to the door. I could hear it plainly now. Someone was trying to pick the lock. Oh, how I wished I had my gun.

The solution to the problem was simple. I'd leave and go down the street and call the police.

I tiptoed quickly back to the front of the office, grabbed my keys and my purse, and ran to the front door. When I opened it, I ran smack dab into Earl Smythe.

I thought I knew who committed the murder. Was I wrong?

"Miss Davis," he said, taking my arm, "I need to talk to you."

"Some other time, Mr. Smythe. I'm in a hurry." I could still hear the movement at the back door. Whoever it was, wasn't a pro or he'd have been inside long ago.

"No, it has to be now," he said, and I wondered if that was supposed to be a menacing look on his face or was he just worried about something. The thought occurred to me that whoever it was at the back door might be Smythe's accomplice. Needless to say, I felt a bit insecure at that moment.

I tried to jerk my arm loose, but his grip was firm. "I'm just on my way out to catch a burger," I said. "Want to accompany me?"

"Sure," he said easily. "We can talk while you eat."

"Well, shit, Earl, if that's the case, then would you mind checking my back door? I think someone is trying to break in."

"What? Oh." He looked at me. "You're serious?"

I nodded.

He glanced toward the back of the house, then back to me. I nodded again. He ran down the hall to the back door, his hard-sole shoes slapping loudly on the wood floor. I watched while he found a light switch and flipped it on. He jerked at the door.

"It's locked," he hollered loudly.

"You don't hear anything?" I walked toward him.

"Not now. Give me the key."

I handed him my keys and pointed out the right one. He put it in the lock and opened the door, stepping out onto the stoop. I followed.

"No one here now," he said as he stood on the stoop and looked around. He went down the steps and looked under the stoop and down the alley. "Whoever it was has gone."

"Thanks, Earl. I was just leaving to call the police from another location when you showed up."

He came back up and we went inside. I locked the door behind him.

"You know, you really should replace that antiquated lock. You need a double deadbolt."

"I know, but my theory is that if they really want in bad enough, nothing will stop them. Why spend the money?"

"It'll at least slow them down a little bit and force them to make some real noise," he said.

"I'll think about it." We started back down the hall.

"Were you really going out for a burger?" he asked.

"No, to get the police."

"Let's talk a minute, then."

"Okay." I looked up at him, waiting to see what he had to say. We stood near the open front door. I could hear the cars rushing past. Their lights flashed as they went by.

He looked suddenly sort of sheepish. "I was coming . . . my intention was to tell you . . . to reassure you that I had nothing to do with Harrison's murder."

"You already told me that, Earl."

"Somehow I got the impression that you didn't believe me, though," he said. "What would it take to convince you?"

I switched on the outside light, took Earl's arm, and led him onto the front porch, pulling the door closed behind us. "Well, for one thing, you just performed heroics for me." I smiled up at him. "And another, well, I know who did it."

"You do?"

"Yes. And it wasn't you."

"Who was it? Hilary?"

"I'm afraid I can't tell you just now. I'm still gathering evidence."

"Oh. I understand."

"It won't be long, though, Earl. I hope to get what I need

tonight." I patted his arm. "So you see, you made the trip over here for nothing."

"Not for nothing. I'll be able to sleep tonight, knowing that I'm not being investigated."

"Good," I said as I reached my car. I wondered why he was worried at being investigated. Oh well, that wasn't my problem. I had enough on my plate as it was. "Thanks again for what you did."

"My pleasure, Mavis. Good night."

"Good night." I stood there while he got in his car and drove away. Then I headed for Annette's.

I parked my Mustang around the corner and two houses down, grabbed my flashlight out of the trunk, and crept from the sidewalk to the back of Annette's house. The cops had indeed posted the place by pasting a paper sign to the back door glass. Crime scene tape hung off the porch.

I inserted the blade of my pocket knife between the edge of the door and the door frame, slipped the lock, opened the door and went inside in about forty-five seconds. I had learned that trick from one of my probationers when I was an adult probation officer. Once when I was on a home visit I got to talking to the guy about how he'd been able to commit so many burglaries without leaving hardly a trace of how he'd gotten inside, so he showed me. Given the right kind of lock, a credit card will work also. I'll never be as fast as Jud was, but most of the time I'm fast enough.

The house was hot and stuffy since the police had turned off the air-conditioning units after Annette had been taken away. I dripped like I was in a dry sauna. A strange smell permeated the air. I wasn't about to sweep the premises with my flashlight; I didn't want to know what it was.

Figuring that Annette had expected me to show up at her place sooner or later—rather than her adversary—I guessed that she hadn't had much time to think of a really complicated hideaway. I started in the most obvious place. The refrigerator freezer. I checked both but found nothing. I'd been hoping she would have slid it under the produce in the drawer or under her Tupperware containers on a shelf, but she didn't. My flashlight floated over her kitchen counters, the insides of the cabinets, the garbage under the sink—now I knew what smelled—and the oven. If the envelope was in the kitchen, she had hidden it ingeniously.

I stepped over the remnants of the dog blood and went into her bedroom. Surely she wouldn't put it under the mattress. Something made a noise in the stillness and it wasn't my palpitating heart. It sounded like it came from the kitchen. Were the floorboards creaking? I hadn't heard it moments earlier, but it seemed now somebody was inside with me.

Holding my breath, I snapped out my light and crouched down beside the bed. Whoever it was apparently didn't expect to find anyone around because they weren't being very quiet. I tried to make myself very small in the darkness, not an easy feat at five-foot-ten, but I could try.

I heard a bump and then, "Oww—shit."

Candy. I turned on my light. "In the bedroom, Candy," I hollered and waved the flashlight in her direction. When she came in, I held the light on her like a spot and she was the star of the stage. "What the hell are you doing? You're not supposed to be here."

"I know, Mavis, but like I thought I'd help by watching outside. You didn't even know I was there, huh? Pretty good, huh?"

"I'll 'pretty good, huh' you, when we get out of here. If you're watching outside, why aren't you out there?"

"It was getting, you know, really creepy. You've been in

here an hour." She rubbed her forehead where a lump was forming.

I shined the flashlight on my wristwatch. "Have not. It's barely been fifteen minutes," I said. "And stop whining."

"Like it seemed like an hour. Besides, I thought I could help."

"You can help by going home."

"C'mon, let me stay, please?"

I shook my head. "I don't have time for your foolishness. Don't you realize that what we're doing is illegal? You could get into serious trouble. You could be sent to jail and your mother would have to come get you out and then you'd probably have to quit working for me—which might not be a bad idea."

Not listening, Candy flipped on a small flashlight and went over to the chest of drawers. "Have you searched these drawers yet?"

"I don't believe you. I ought to fire you, young lady. Do you know this is breaking and entering? Burglary, my dear. A first-degree felony—burglary of a habitation."

"Only if we're attempting to do another crime, Mavis. Like I called and asked Gillian this afternoon. Have you searched here?"

"You what?"

She shined her light on my face. "Well, I wanted to know like what kind of trouble we could get into. I called her for your own good."

"I'm going nuts here, Candy. I could swear that I heard you say that you told someone outside the office that we were coming over to break into this house."

"Don't worry. I invoked the attorney-client privilege. I told her, you know, to send you a bill for her advice."

"Jesus Christ. Just wait until we get out of here. You'll be lucky to see tomorrow." I continued my search. I had better things to do than fuss at her. I wanted to find what we were looking for and get the hell out.

"So like should I look in this chest or what?"

"Yeah, but just because I let you that doesn't mean everything's all right."

"That's cool," she said and turned her light out of my eyes and toward the chest of drawers. "Jesus it's hot in here. I don't know how you stood it this long."

I ignored her last statement. After I got my vision back, we spent the next few minutes—I don't know how many—carefully picking and pulling at Annette's things, trying to leave no evidence that we'd been there. No luck in the bedroom.

We searched in between the folded towels and sheets in the bathroom cabinet. Under the mat on the floor. Between the shower curtain and the liner. In the dirty clothes hamper. Behind the toilet. In the medicine chest.

We hit the spare bedroom, but since it was sparsely furnished, it only took a couple of minutes to discover it concealed nothing except lots of yarn and crochet hooks in a bag on the floor.

Finally, we ended up in the living room where Annette had been attacked. We pulled up the braided rug and checked under the coffee tables to see if she'd taped it underneath. I didn't really think she'd had the time, but it was worth a try. Candy stuck her hands down the sides and up the lining of the sofa and came up with spare change, lint, and debris under her fingernails. I tackled the swivel rocker. And there it was, between the seat cushion and the arm, scrunched up like she had stuffed it down there in a hurry. I realized he would have found it had I not so rudely interrupted him. Lucky for me. Too bad for him.

Chapter Twenty-Nine

I emptied the contents of the envelope onto the floor and we sat down in the middle of it. Candy held my larger, police-style flashlight while I straightened the papers, smoothing the folds. There were three separate sets of insurance claim forms from National Insurance Trust.

"I don't recognize these people's names, but Annette told me Mr. Lawson was investigating claims," I said. "He was suspicious—there were too many."

"So . . ." Candy said.

"So—the forms she was going to give me were the ones Mr. Lawson had been checking out. Look, someone's made notations in pencil, *not a real person.* God, it's stuffy in here." I flipped through the set on top. A life insurance policy for two hundred and fifty thousand dollars. Enough of those and a person could take early retirement. I smiled at Candy. "Do you realize what this is?"

"Some kind of insurance junk? Like what does that have to do with Jeanine and Tommy?" Candy whispered. Her face was as yellow as a grapefruit in the glow of the flashlight. With her green hair, she was an eerie sight.

"Nothing. It has nothing to do with Jeanine and Tommy. It's fraud. Someone was defrauding the insurance company out of hundreds of thousands, if not millions, of dollars."

"Wow. So that's why Miss Jensen got clobbered. She found out about it."

"That's why Mr. Lawson got killed. Or at least one of the reasons."

"Do you know who did it?"

"Yes, I think I know what this whole thing has been about. It's too bad Annette can't tell us what she knows. With any luck, she'll pull out of it and confirm my suspicions."

"Aren't you going to take them to the police?" Candy asked. Margaret, had she been along, would have known better than to ask that question.

I grinned. "Eventually. Meanwhile, let's get these papers back to the office where we can study them so we can prove who it is."

We picked ourselves up off the floor. I was about to stoop down for the papers so we could make our way out to the kitchen when we heard the back door ease open.

Candy clutched my forearm, her fingernails sinking into my flesh. She whispered, "Holy shit."

I snapped out my light a second time and Candy did the same.

Why hadn't I forced Candy to go home? My heart beat like a snare drum solo in my ears. The kitchen floor creaked. I pushed Candy toward the rocker, which was a dark shadow, and she backed over beside it, shrinking to fit between it and the end table.

At another creaking sound, I searched frantically for a hiding place. It was too late to run to another room. The living room was sparsely furnished and left me no choice but to get down beside the sofa, which I did as quickly and quietly as possible. The next thing I knew, a light beamed on the far wall. Oh, how I wished the police had given me back my gun.

Oh, how I wished I'd never gone snooping. A position bagging groceries seemed very attractive right about then.

In the back-flash from the light, I saw someone but couldn't tell who it was. The light moved. I sucked my stomach in and leaned back against the wall, crouching down behind the sofa wing as much as possible.

I followed the light with my eyes as it swept past me and back again. There were some rustling noises and footsteps and the room grew dark. I stayed where I was and prayed that Candy would also. The minutes crept by. Someone moved about in other parts of the house. It grew difficult to breathe. My blouse dripped with perspiration; my stomach overflowed with fear.

I risked sticking my head out and peered through the corner between the V of the arm and the sofa wing. There wasn't enough light to make out Candy. The stranger's light in the other room barely illuminated the hall.

It seemed like years later when the light came back in our direction. I reared back as it swept the room again and stopped. I had to see what was going on so I peeked out and saw a shadowy figure wearing some kind of hood. He or she crouched over the insurance papers I'd left on the floor, the flashlight stuck under his or her arm. The light hit right between the rocker and the end table, on Candy's face.

Concentrating intently on the papers on the floor, the intruder hadn't yet seen Candy. The flash illuminated an expression of stark terror: her mouth hung open, her eyes large and wide, whites shining. Candy gasped like a drowning victim coming up for air the last time. A voice I didn't stop to identify said, "You. Stand up where you are."

As Candy started to rise, her hand swept toward the lamp on the end table. I wanted to cry out to her not to do it—I had just seen him, her, it—whatever, pull a gun—but no words came out. Everything happened at breakneck speed. A crash and a gunshot both echoed off the walls of the little shut-up house. A flashlight lay on the floor pointed away from Candy so I couldn't see her.

"No!" I hollered as I leapt across the room. I hit the coffee table in front of the couch and fell against the attacker's knees, bringing him down. I lay there for a couple of seconds with my cheek against the coarse fabric of his pants before reaching over my head to feel for his arms and the gun. He must have been stunned for as long as I was because he seemed to recover just as slowly and began kicking me at the same time as I groped for the gun. In the dark, with the flashlight pointed against the far wall, I still couldn't see much. I hollered to Candy just about the same time as his foot caught me in the stomach.

"Run, Candy!"

She didn't respond. I knew then she was dead. Dumb kid. Why couldn't she have just done what I told her?

I groped my way up his body, pulling at his clothes as he continued to kick and struggle. There was a familiar smell. I got hold of his right wrist and jerked it, trying to twist it outward where it would hurt. I figured he didn't have hold of the gun or he would have shot me. About that time, the gun went off again and I could see just for an instant as it flashed. I swear I almost peed in my panties.

There was a lot of rustling and footsteps. I remembered my flashlight and while I held on to his wrist with all my might, I groped around for it. We struggled on the floor in the dark with just the glow of the light near our feet. To reach that flashlight to use as a weapon, I'd have to let go of his arm. I wasn't about to do that when the gun was at the end of it.

He belted me with his other fist, but it caught me on the

shoulder and didn't do much damage except cause me to fall onto my back. He swung himself on top of me, panting like a mad dog, his breath smelling worse than a dirty ashtray. While he clutched my left hand, with my right I shoved at his chest and found my flashlight, boosting my confidence. That's not to say I forgot who had a gun and who didn't—I didn't—but I'm a big girl and pretty strong. I clobbered whoever it was right in the kisser with my flashlight. I'm sure I busted his lip. While he was recovering, I rammed him right in the nuts with my knee.

His grunt and groan confirmed that my attacker was, in fact, a *he,* though I had little doubt by that time. Momentarily he failed to move his body, but jerked his hand down pointing the gun at my face. I pushed it away just as it went off again, echoing loudly next to my ear. I threw him off me into the wall and started pounding with all my might, my anger at Candy's death giving me strength. He dropped the gun and reached for it again, but I wouldn't let his hand near it. He started hitting at me, but it didn't do much good. I was madder than hell because he'd killed a girl who was like a daughter to me.

I battered him with my flashlight and fist until he seemed to weaken. Putting my knee on his chest to hold him down, I seized his throat, my fingernails digging in, the stench of his breath stronger than ever. His clothing smelled like a lit cigar. I groped until finding the gun and was about to switch it over to my right hand and blow his brains out when I heard Candy's voice.

"Mavis. What should I do?"

Relief flooded me. "I've got him, Candy. Grab your flashlight." I had the gun in my right hand as I started to tear the hood off his face, but I must have relaxed too much when I heard Candy's voice, because he pushed me backward and made his escape. I would have fired at him but didn't know where Candy was. I didn't want to shoot her.

A loud *bonk* sounded. A moment later, another *bonk*. I ran to the kitchen just as the light came on. Candy stood in the doorway with a flashlight in one hand and a big cast-iron cornbread pan in the other. The perpetrator lay on the floor. He wouldn't be going anywhere for a few minutes.

I grinned, never so overjoyed about anything in my life. "Why didn't you answer when I hollered at you?" My ears still rang from the earlier gunshot.

Candy grinned back. "All you said was 'run.' I was gonna, too, but like when I got to the kitchen I thought of getting this iron pan off the stove. I'd seen it when I came in. Besides, I was afraid he would have shot at me again. The next thing I knew, he came right at me so I, like, let him have it."

"Twice for good measure," I said, laughing, and put my arms around her. "I thought he'd killed you."

Candy said, "Like you would have been sorry, wouldn't you, Mavis?"

I pulled back. "Of course I would have been sorry, but let's not get mushy about it, kid."

"It's okay, Mavis, you don't have to say anything else. Are we going to see who it is?" She stepped toward the body.

"I'm pretty sure I know, but you want the honors?" I held the pistol with both hands and pointed it in his direction in case he was playing possum.

Candy leaned down and tugged at the mask. When it came off, we saw that it was exactly as I thought. The winner of the ugly man contest, Kelby McAfee, who looked a lot worse than he had the day I met him.

Candy backed toward me. "Who's that?"

"That, my dear, is the man who has been stealing tons of

bucks from the insurance company. How about running out to my car and getting my cell so I can call Captain Milton?"

"Hey, I've got my mobile right here." Candy whipped her own cell phone from her back pocket and handed it to me.

"Kid, you could have gotten us killed if this had rung while he had the gun."

"Like, give me some credit, would you, Mavis? I turned it off before I came inside."

I made a call to the police department and told dispatch I needed to speak to Captain Milton, giving Candy's number. After he called me back, I called Ben and told him where we were. And after that, Candy and I pulled out kitchen chairs and sat down to wait. I kept the gun steady on McAfee the whole ten minutes or so it took for the street in front of Annette's house to fill up with police cars.

Chapter Thirty

I would be exaggerating if I said Captain Milton congratulated me on solving Harrison Lawson's murder, but he did at least give me a little credit. When he arrived, Milton had a uniform take McAfee into custody, which came as a big relief. That gun had gotten heavy after a while so I was glad to hand it over.

He then lectured Candy about how irresponsible she had been to place herself in danger like that and sent her home after she agreed to go down to the police station the next day when school let out and make a statement.

"Can I go, too, Captain? I feel like I'm going to fall on my face if I don't get some rest."

"Not yet, Mavis," the captain said. "Let's go into the living room and sit down, shall we?"

I knew that wasn't a genuine request, so I obeyed after grabbing a paper towel from the roll in the kitchen and dabbing at my wounds.

When the captain turned on the living room lights, we found a room in great disarray and insurance documents lying helter skelter across the floor. He grunted like an old boar.

"I think you'll find the motive for murder in those insurance documents, Captain," I said, gathering them and handing them over.

The captain righted a chair and sat down. I got the rocker.

Ben looked over the captain's shoulder. "What are they?"

"Proof of insurance fraud." Something about the situation triggered a desire for a cigarette. Nothing would taste as good at that moment. Just one cigarette, inhale deeply, and exhale a long stream of smoke that in my imagination would spell out some wonderful words about me like in comic strips. But that wasn't about to happen. "Anybody got a stick of gum?"

The captain stared from the papers to me. "You want to tell me about it?" His tone spoke volumes.

"I knew it was McAfee who killed Mr. Lawson, but he wasn't in it alone, though he and Hilary had different motives. I knew she was a depraved woman, but she already had lots of money. She didn't need more."

"Mrs. Lawson?" the captain asked.

I nodded. My head had begun to pound. "How about a couple of aspirin?" Glancing around the room, I saw that no one was offering me sympathy or anything else for that matter. "Okay then. My theory is that she wanted to get out of the marriage to Harrison Lawson and into one with James Rush. Harrison was older and had heart problems—who knows why she preferred Rush—except he's richer, younger, more handsome, and probably more capable sexually."

The captain crossed his arms. I could see that he would need convincing. "I'm not clear on these motives," he said.

"It started with McAfee needing or wanting money, the usual motive, right? I think Mr. Lawson found out that McAfee was engaged in insurance fraud. He checked it out for himself. When he was convinced, he may have let something slip to Hilary, her being his little devoted wife and all. Hilary may very well have seized on that opportunity to persuade McAfee to kill Harrison. Once you question him, I bet he'll implicate Hilary if you offer him a deal."

The captain gave me a look I won't soon forget. "How did you know it was McAfee? Everyone needs money."

"Let me outline it for you, Captain. It's rather convoluted." I couldn't help it. I felt somewhat smug. My mother's voice inside my head chastised me for my cocky attitude, but I pushed it to the back of my mind. After all, I didn't get to sit in the catbird seat often.

Milton shook his head but didn't say anything.

"Okay. There was a dinner party at the Lawson's the night before the murder. Frankie told me so. That's the housekeeper, Captain."

"I know who Frankie is."

"Anyway, at first I thought that the night before the cocktail party the poison had been put in a bottle of imported schnapps, but later I realized that it couldn't have been because it was too risky. Someone else might have drunk it, too, although it has a unique, and I might add, nasty, taste and not many people like it."

"Go on."

"There were several possibilities. They could have poisoned Lawson's food the night before at the dinner party. Or he could have been poisoned at breakfast or lunch the day of the cocktail party. That definitely would have made Hilary the main suspect unless it could be proved that someone else had access to his food. Like Arthur, but I'll get to that in a minute." I yawned. "Couldn't I go home and come back in the morning after I get some sleep, Captain?"

"Just tell me the facts and you can come in to make a formal statement in the morning, all right?" He frowned. "I'd like to get some shut-eye myself."

"Okay. So whoever it was had to poison the schnapps the day of the pool party if they wanted to be sure he would die."

"And Arthur Woodridge didn't have access to his food or drink," the captain said.

"No, though I think they would have liked to figure out a way to make out like he did. It's a bit confusing that they would choose a party setting to kill someone, but I think perhaps Arthur's getting paroled had something to do with it."

"Changing their timetable so they could frame him—or at least attempt to."

"Right, and it almost worked, but we know where he was at the time."

"But how did you figure it was McAfee? We were looking at several people who were at that party." He rose and picked the lamp up off the floor.

"I thought several of them were suspicious, too. For one thing, the phone call to the police. Several people at the party were on their cells around the time that Harrison fell. McAfee was only one of them, but I bet if you check his records you'll see his call was to the police, part of implicating Arthur."

The captain nodded and glanced at Ben.

"As to some of the others, Hadley needed money. The real estate market was killing him. He had no liquidity and all his properties had lost their values. He couldn't unload them, but even without many tenants, he had to keep making the payments. He had a large insurance policy on Lawson, by the way."

"How'd you know that?" Ben asked. Mostly he'd stood staring at me like a wax figure.

I shrugged. "McAfee told me."

"So you withheld evidence again?" The captain's face grew pink.

"Well, he said it just to throw me off the track, Captain. And it did for a day or so. There are also large policies payable to Hilary and the kids." I uncrossed and recrossed my legs, trying to find a comfortable position in which to sit. No matter where I shifted my weight, it put pressure on a bruise. "There's even a very old small one payable to Annette."

"What about Smythe?" Milton asked.

"Smythe also had a motive. Lawson had been bad-mouthing him all over town. It cost him his business, but he was able to get hired by another firm and is getting back on his feet. For a while I suspected Smythe, but he just didn't seem the type, not that typecasting means anything, and then when he came to the office last night . . ." I glanced at Ben. "He scared some burglars—or someone—away from my back door. If he had been the one he could have done something to me last night. Not that I thought it was him. I already knew by then who the killer was."

"Mavis, you amaze me sometimes," Ben whispered.

That was the nicest thing he'd said to me in quite a while. I smiled and wanted to reach for him, wanted a big, warm hug from him, but stayed where I was.

"Hilary was having an affair with Rush. It apparently started years ago when he represented Arthur. Rush was young and gullible and she got him into her bed. But she married Harrison Lawson because he had money and Rush didn't back then. Also, marrying Lawson was part of her plan for after she framed Arthur."

"Jesus," the captain said.

"Yes, she did do that, but I don't believe that Rush knew it. He was just a dupe. If he suspected later, he never did anything about it. It would have ruined him. I also don't think Lawson knew. He really loved those kids, but I don't think he would have gone along with framing Arthur. He seemed like a decent man the few minutes I knew him." I glanced again at Ben. "Could we please finish this in the morning, Captain? I feel like I'm going to fall on my face."

"Just a few more questions, Mavis. Have you figured out when McAfee started defrauding the company?"

I sighed with fatigue. "I'm guessing it was when he was a sales rep."

"Because . . ."

"You have to make a lot of sales to move up in the company. A young rep told me that at the party. What McAfee did, I think, was buy insurance under another name. He'd get the name out of the obits. He'd pretend to sell the policies. I figure the plan was originally to boost his sales so he could be promoted faster."

"Wasn't he hoping to be the next president?" Milton asked.

"Yes. His sales record was astounding. His scheme evolved as time went by. He went from trying to get promoted faster to actually claiming the death benefits. He'd forge the death certificate. It's all right there in those files, Captain."

"But how did you know about it? How come we didn't find this out?" Milton asked as he glanced over the papers.

"It was something Annette said when I first went to the insurance office. After she got hurt, I thought she just wanted to show me all the insurance beneficiaries. When I went to the hospital to see her, though, she was trying to tell me something else—only I didn't figure it out right away." I still felt responsible for her assault. I hoped that somehow I could make it up to her.

"The night she was supposed to meet me, she had those papers, only I was out looking for the kids instead of meeting her. It wasn't until I knew how Lawson died that I realized who killed him and that Annette had something more to show me."

"Did Sorenson tell you how Lawson died?" the captain asked with a glance at Ben.

"No. I have other sources, you know." Smugness doesn't become me, my mother used to say, but I couldn't help myself.

"If you're so smart, Mavis Davis, you tell me. How did Lawson die? I just got the report on my desk this morning."

I wasn't doing a good job at hiding my glee. "Captain, I was there. I saw McAfee pour Lawson's drink from a strange-looking bottle under the bar. A few minutes later, he stumbled over Harrison Lawson when he pretended to slip in the water around the pool. Lawson spilled the remnants of his drink. He walked right back over to the bar and refilled it from the same bottle."

"So the poison was in the bottle?" the captain asked.

"Of a rather exotic, expensive brand of schnapps. Not a popular drink with the River Oaks set, but with Lawson's German heritage, he practically grew up on it."

"Schnapps is pretty strong stuff," he said.

"When I arrived, Mr. Lawson already appeared to be ill."

"But you didn't question them having a pool party?"

I shrugged. "Not my business at the time. Anyway, I think Hilary and McAfee tried to bring on the heart attack earlier but hadn't given him enough poison, whether in his food or drink, I'm not sure, perhaps both. They had to make sure he got more to finish him off."

"Because of Arthur."

"Right. I bet if someone did some checking they'd find that Hilary had begun a pattern of ordering very unusual flowers with which to decorate her house. Captain, also, if you think about it, many of the plants used in the landscaping around the pool are oleanders. I wish I'd remembered earlier how sickly sweet the scent of all those flowers in the backyard was when I'd first gotten there. I just failed to put it together until now. Oleanders are pretty toxic and I wouldn't be surprised if some of those other flowers are poisonous, too."

"Oleanders are very poisonous," he said. "Everyone knows that. But Lawson died of a heart attack."

"Yes, brought on by the poison. Dried oleander leaves affect the heart rhythm, among other things. If he hadn't had the heart attack, he'd have died pretty quickly anyway."

"And how do you know it was the schnapps?" the captain asked.

"Well, I saw the bottle initially and didn't recognize it as anything I'd ever seen before, not that I'm that heavy a drinker. So when I went back to see Mrs. Lawson, I sneaked a better look at it."

"We'll get a search warrant and go over to the Lawson home."

"You can," I said, "but when I was there, the bottle looked fresh. I can't believe Hilary would be dumb enough to leave the original one there." I refrained from mentioning that Lon was dumb enough to leave it on the day of the murder. Of course, he had assumed it was a heart attack.

"We'll get a warrant anyway," the captain said. He sighed as he stood, like he was bone weary.

"Look for florists' records. Maybe she charged the flowers."

"I'm not even going to get angry at you for having come here, Mavis," the captain said. "I think the abuse you took from him, by the look of it, probably taught you a lesson."

I grimaced and didn't reply. I wondered whether I looked as bad as my wounds felt. I wanted nothing more than to go home and nurse myself.

The captain's cell phone rang. After he hung up, he said, "McAfee wants to make a statement. They're taking him to the interrogation room. That's all for now, Mavis. But be in my office at ten sharp."

"Yes, sir."

Ben walked me out to my car. He didn't say much except that when everything was wrapped up, we needed to talk. I agreed and headed for home.

The next morning, I got Margaret and headed for the police station. Ben and the captain told me that McAfee made some damaging accusations against Hilary after he'd had his Miranda warning read to him the night before. They were waiting for an assistant district attorney to come over and authorize a deal. When the ADA arrived, the captain sent Ben to arrest Hilary Lawson. I read and signed my statement.

Margaret and I watched part of the interrogations before we got tired of the whole mess and went back to the office. After all, we needed to make some money and quick.

After school got out, Candy and I went back downtown for her to make her own statement and then over to the Lawson house. That was the hardest part. Tommy and Jeanine were going to need some extensive psychiatric help to recover emotionally—if they ever could.

The day after that, I met with Gillian at the courthouse where she took me to give a statement to the grand jury. A court reporter took it down. It was pretty much as I've above-stated. Later, another ADA accompanied us to a courtroom where I stood in front of the judge and listened as the DA's office dropped the charges against me. Gillian said I didn't have to, that she'd see to it, but just the same . . .

While I was there, Arthur Woodridge came in. They had released him the previous evening, but he also wanted to be present when the state dismissed their case against him.

It turned out that the special investigator located one of

the witnesses against Arthur and talked to Frankie who was now willing to testify. His investigation had convinced him that Harrison Lawson was innocent of everything except being fooled by a pretty woman. James Rush, he said, as brilliant as he was, was a dope, too. Hilary had convinced Rush in the earlier case against Arthur that his client was guilty. Rush had taken it from there.

The last I heard, the judge, the district attorney himself, and Gillian Wright had all applied to the Governor for a pardon for Arthur. Arthur was living with his kids in the Lawson house, which Harrison had left them in his will. The court appointed Arthur as guardian of the children's estates. With Gillian's help, Arthur applied to have the termination of his parental rights set aside. If that didn't work, he would adopt the kids. He was also suing Hilary for, among other things, false imprisonment.

As for James Rush, we found out later that I was correct in my assumption that he would have been Hilary's next husband. Lucky him. He changed his mind after the police arrested Hilary for murder.

The Woodridges guaranteed Frankie a job for life.

After several months, Annette Jensen recovered except for a very slight speech impediment. As a reward for her loyalty, the insurance company promoted her to a high managerial position. She has forgiven me for not meeting her that night. We've become good friends and meet often for lunch.

Kelby McAfee pled guilty and was sentenced to life with no parole in exchange for his testimony against Hilary.

Hilary Lawson is out of jail on bond. Her lawyer keeps stalling the murder trial. Where she lives is a mystery, but it's not River Oaks.

James Rush won another big lawsuit and is probably richer than King Midas. I saw him once downtown. He drove a convertible Mercedes and a buxom blonde sat beside him. The State Bar of Texas gave him a public reprimand for his part in the Woodridge case. That just shows how much money helps a person. Gillian said they would have disbarred her.

Mandy retired, and Angela Strickmeier took over her position. She's pregnant again. Her husband is working steadily now.

Lon Tyler is still with homicide, much to the captain's and Ben's chagrin.

Captain Milton didn't get promoted to deputy chief. He allegedly doesn't hold that against me.

Ben and I are still together and still halfway discussing marriage.

Candy really did graduate from high school and still works for me while she attends community college.

Margaret's relationship with what's-his-face is still hot and heavy. I wonder sometimes if I'm going to have to give her away.

And my Mustang was finally repaired with the huge bonus that Arthur, Tommy, and Jeanine forced on me against my will.

About the Author

Susan P. Baker has spent most of her adult life working in the legal system, first as a probation officer, then as an attorney, later for twelve years as a state district judge, and, currently, as a visiting judge and arbitrator. She and her husband make their home in the Texas hill country. This is her third mystery novel. Read more about the author at www.susanpbaker.com or contact her by e-mail at snana456@austin.rr.com.